CHANGE-UP

John Feinstein

CHANGE-UP

MYSTERY AT THE WORLD SERIES

ALFRED A. KNOPF

New York

This is for Jake Pleet
with warm thanks from his protégé, Danny.

CHANGE-UP

1: SUDDEN VICTORY

EVEN THOUGH HE WAS ONLY FOURTEEN YEARS OLD, Stevie Thomas considered himself a veteran of sports victory celebrations. He had been to the Final Four, the Super Bowl, the NBA Finals, and the U.S. Open—in both tennis and golf. He had seen remarkable endings, miracle shots, and improbable last-second heroics.

But he hadn't seen anything quite like this. He was standing just outside the first-base dugout inside Nationals Park, the home stadium for the Washington Nationals, and even though the game had been over for several minutes, the noise was still so loud he couldn't hear anything Susan Carol Anderson was shouting in his ear.

"Mets . . . clubhouse . . . press box . . . ," he managed to make out over the din. Since she was starting to pick her way through the celebrating Nationals and the media swarm surrounding them, he guessed that she had told him that she was going to make her way to the clubhouse of the New York Mets and then meet him back in the press box. She was taking the harder job—talking to the players on a team that had just suffered a shocking defeat. His job was easier: talking to the winners.

The ending of the game had been stunning. With the National League Championship Series tied at three games all, both teams had sent their star pitchers out to pitch game seven: Johan Santana for the Mets, John Lannan for the Nationals. Both had pitched superbly, and the game had gone to the ninth inning tied at 1–1.

Nationals manager Manny Acta brought Joel Hanrahan, his closer, in to pitch the ninth, a bold move in a tie game. And it seemed to have backfired when Carlos Beltran hit a two-out, two-run home run to give the Mets a 3–1 lead. In came the Mets' closer, Francisco (K-Rod) Rodriguez, to get the last three outs needed to give the Mets the pennant.

He got two quick outs, and it wasn't looking good for the Nats when shortstop Cristian Guzman hit a weak ground ball. But somehow Mets all-star shortstop Jose Reyes booted it, allowing Guzman to make it safely to first base. Clearly upset and distracted by the error, Rodriguez then walked Ronnie Belliard, bringing Ryan Zimmerman, the Nationals' best hitter, to the plate.

Guzman began dancing off second base, stretching his lead each time Rodriguez looked back at him. Second baseman Luis Castillo kept flashing toward the bag, as if expecting a pickoff throw from Rodriguez. Sitting in the auxiliary press box, Stevie was wearing headphones that allowed him to hear the Fox telecast.

"Rodriguez and Castillo need to forget about Guzman," he heard Tim McCarver say. "Right now K-Rod has one job, and that's to get Zimmerman out."

"But if the Nats double-steal, the tying runs would both be in scoring position," play-by-play man Joe Buck said.

"True," McCarver said. "But I'm telling you, there is *no* way Guzman is risking making the last out of the season trying to steal third. He's not that much of a base stealer to begin with."

Rodriguez finally focused on the plate and threw a 97-mph fastball that Zimmerman just watched go by for strike one. Again Guzman danced off second base. This time Rodriguez whirled and did make a pickoff throw as Castillo darted in to take it. Guzman dove back in safely.

"That tells me Guzman has gotten inside K-Rod's head," McCarver said. "You don't risk a pickoff throw in this situation. The only man in the ballpark he should care about right now is Zimmerman."

Rodriguez threw another fastball, and Zimmerman fouled it straight back to the screen.

"That one was ninety-seven too," Buck said. "He doesn't seem *too* distracted."

"Zimmerman was about two inches from crushing that ball," McCarver said. "You see a batter foul a fastball straight back like that, it means he *just* missed it."

Rodriguez came to his set position again. Guzman was

off the bag once more and Rodriguez stepped off the rubber. Everyone relaxed for a moment.

"Zimmerman has to look for a fastball here, doesn't he?" Buck said.

"Absolutely."

Rodriguez set again, checked Guzman one more time, and threw. Stevie glanced at the spot on the scoreboard that showed pitch speed, and saw 98. Rodriguez had thrown a fastball, and Zimmerman had in fact been looking fastball. This time he didn't miss it. He got it. He got *all* of it. The ball rose majestically into the air and sailed in the direction of the left-field fence. Mets left fielder Daniel Murphy never moved. The ball sailed way over the fence, deep into the night, and complete bedlam broke out in every corner of the stadium. The Nationals had won the game 4–3 and the series 4–3. Shockingly, they were going to the World Series.

The auxiliary press box was down the left-field line, and Stevie and Susan Carol had seen Zimmerman's shot go right past them heading out of the park. As 41,888 people went crazy, they had joined other members of the media who were scrambling to get down to the field and the clubhouses.

There had been no point trying to squeeze onto the elevators, so they had dashed to the ramps—which weren't too crowded, because most of the fans were still standing at their seats, celebrating. The Nationals were on the field, spraying one another with champagne—which someone had brought out from their clubhouse to allow them to celebrate in front of the fans—so the media was directed down the tunnel to the home dugout and stood just outside it watching the celebration.

"I guess when you go seventy-six years between championships, you're entitled to go a little crazy," a voice shouted behind Stevie.

He turned and saw Bobby Kelleher, his friend and mentor, standing there with a wide grin on his face. Kelleher, a columnist for the *Washington Herald,* had been sitting in the main press box and had apparently just reached the field.

"Is Walter Johnson smiling somewhere?" Stevie asked Kelleher, referring to the Hall of Fame pitcher who had been the Washington Senators' star in the 1920s and their manager when a Washington baseball team last played in the World Series—in 1933.

"My guess is someone will claim to have *spoken* to him by tomorrow morning," Kelleher said, still shouting because the noise had abated only a little bit. "It's hard for people to understand how remarkable this is. Washington's always been a town that either had no baseball or played *bad* baseball."

Not one but two teams had left Washington—the original Senators left town in 1961 to move to Minnesota; then an expansion version fled to Texas ten years later.

"Where'd Susan Carol go?" Kelleher asked.

"Mets clubhouse," Stevie said.

"Figures," Kelleher said. "She's always willing to take on the tough jobs. That's where Tamara went too. I have to write the Nats. I mean, seventy-six years without a pennant. Not to mention that this team lost a hundred and two games a year ago."

Tamara Mearns was Kelleher's wife, a columnist for the *Washington Post*. The two of them had taken Stevie and Susan Carol under their wing when the teenagers won a writing contest and were awarded press credentials to the Final Four in New Orleans.

That was a weekend that had changed Stevie and Susan Carol's lives forever. They had gotten off to a rocky start: the wise-guy kid from Philadelphia clashing with the seemingly wide-eyed Southern belle from a small town in North Carolina. But they had stumbled into a plot to blackmail a star player and had worked together to nail the bad guys, starting them on what had often been a bumpy road to media stardom.

Since then they had found trouble at the U.S. Open tennis tournament and the Super Bowl; been hired and fired by a cable TV network; and, finally, settled into part-time work as writers—Stevie working with Kelleher at the *Herald*, Susan Carol working with Mearns at the *Post*.

They had even managed to cover several major events in recent months—their second Final Four, the U.S. Open golf tournament, another U.S. Open tennis tournament—without ending up on the front page. That had been a relief—their parents had been threatening to never let them out of their sight again after the scandal at the Super Bowl—but also a little bit disappointing. Stevie didn't want to think himself jaded at the age of fourteen, but a couple of times he had found himself forgetting to tingle when he put on his press credential to cover a big-time event.

But now, standing in the sparkling new Nationals Park, surrounded by fans who were still screaming their heads off with joy, listening to what felt like the hundredth playing of "We Are the Champions," and looking at the happiness on the faces of the players, Stevie realized he was in the middle of a genuinely tingle-worthy moment. As he was soaking it all in, he heard Kelleher shouting at him again over the noise.

"Just work the clubhouse," he said. "See what you find. I've got to focus on Zimmerman. Anything else in there is yours unless Sally wants it—but I think she's writing a what-this-means-to-the-city piece."

Sally was Sally Jenkins, the *Herald*'s other sports columnist, whom the paper had stolen from the *Post* for big dollars a year ago. Jenkins was so good Stevie wasn't sure he was worthy of reading her stuff, much less working with her. He followed Kelleher and the onrushing cameras, notebooks, and tape recorders up the ramp into the Nationals clubhouse.

Not surprisingly, it was a mob scene inside. Stevie wasn't two steps inside the door before he was sprayed with champagne. He knew from experience that he didn't want to get hit in the eyes by the stuff, so he put his head down and tried to maneuver away from the mass of people in the middle of the room. The clubhouse was huge, with enough room for fifty lockers even though only twenty-five were absolutely needed. Stevie had noted earlier in the series that most players had two lockers to themselves, with ample space around each locker.

He headed toward some breathing space in the back corner of the room. From there he would be able to see who was still spraying champagne and who was moving away from the melee and making themselves available to talk.

"Pretty wild, isn't it?" Stevie heard a voice say behind him.

He turned and saw a player standing at a locker. He had a bottle of champagne in his hands but clearly wasn't involved in the celebration. After seven games Stevie thought he knew all the Nationals players, but he was drawing a blank on both the face and the number, which was 56.

Apparently, the player noticed the blank look on Stevie's face, because he stuck his hand out and said, "Norbert Doyle. You've never heard of me because I've never done anything."

Stevie laughed and shook hands with Norbert Doyle, whose name sounded only a little bit familiar.

"Steve Thomas," he said. "*Washington Herald*."

Saying the name of the newspaper always made Stevie feel very grown-up. Doyle smiled and nodded. "Of course, I should have known it was you right away. You're one of the two kid reporters who keep breaking all those big stories. My twins are big fans of yours and your friend . . ."

"Susan Carol," Stevie said. "Susan Carol Anderson."

It would be a stretch to say that Stevie had gotten used

to being recognized, but it happened often enough that it no longer surprised him. This was a little bit different, though: an athlete knowing who he was when he didn't know who the athlete was.

"How old are your twins?" Stevie asked.

"I think the same age as you," Doyle said. "David and Morra turned fourteen in July. I'm pretty sure David's got a crush on Susan Carol."

"Who doesn't?" Stevie said. "You should see the fan mail she gets. . . ."

"Come on, Steve," Doyle said, smiling. "I'm sure just as many teenage girls have crushes on you."

"Not so much," Stevie said, shaking his head. "But Susan Carol likes me, which makes me pretty lucky."

"Norbert!" someone yelled from the middle of the room. "Get over here. You're part of this too, you know!"

Doyle smiled and waved his hand. "Be right there," he said. Turning to Stevie, he said, "That's a stretch to say I'm part of this."

"But . . . you're on the team," Stevie said.

"Well, yes and no," Doyle said. "They brought me in at the tail end of the regular season. Started three games, relieved in three others. Didn't get a win. I'm not on the postseason roster, but they let me hang around."

That was why Stevie knew the name. He remembered seeing Doyle's name in the postseason media guide he had paged through on the train down from Philadelphia. If he remembered right, Doyle was kind of an interesting story: the Nationals had traded for him at the end of August because two of their pitchers had been hurt and they needed someone to come up from the minors and make a spot start. What made the story interesting was that Doyle was in his late thirties and had never pitched in a major-league game prior to the trade. Then, suddenly, he'd been thrust into the middle of a pennant race.

"You didn't win a game, but you pitched really well, didn't you?" Stevie said, hoping he was right.

"I pitched okay," Doyle said. "I was thrilled to be here. I just wasn't quite good enough to make the postseason roster."

"Hey, Norbert, come on over here!" someone was shouting.

"Sounds like a lot of guys think you *are* part of this," Stevie said.

Doyle smiled. "They're good guys," he said. "I'll tell you one thing. I'll never forget a minute of this experience."

He shook Stevie's hand again. "Good luck with your story tonight," he said. "My kids will be thrilled to know I met you."

With that he was gone, and Stevie stood alone, still in search of a story. Too late, as Doyle was doused in champagne, it occurred to him that he had just let a terrific story walk away.

2: THE WORLD SERIES

STEVIE WAS SOUND ASLEEP on the train back to Philadelphia the next morning when his cell phone rang. He stared blearily at the number for a moment, then realized it was Susan Carol and answered.

"Are you still sulking?" she asked.

"Can you sulk when you're asleep?"

She laughed. "Lazy bum," she said. "I'm about to go to school."

Stevie grunted. He knew she had more reason to be tired than he did. It had been after 1 a.m. before they left the ballpark, and she had caught a 7 a.m. plane back to North Carolina, which meant she'd had to be up at four. He'd been able to sleep until seven before catching a train home.

"I don't know how you do it," he said to Susan Carol. "Don't you have swimming practice today too?"

"Adrenaline," she answered. "Actually, swimming will feel good."

Sometimes he wondered if Susan Carol was really a mortal or if she was from another planet. She was tall, gorgeous, smart, tough, and full of energy—sleep or no sleep. It was no wonder Norbert Doyle's son had a crush on her. What was really amazing was that Susan Carol, with her pick of any boy she wanted, liked *him*. Even though he had grown steadily from five four when they first met to almost five eight now, she still had about three inches on him and still looked about eighteen to his, well, fourteen. But she told people that he was her boyfriend, and he liked that . . . a lot.

"So," she repeated, "are you still sulking?"

"A little bit."

After Norbert Doyle had disappeared to join the other revelers the night before, Stevie had been left to piece together a sidebar story from predictable quotes: "Greatest moment of my life . . . Guys really stepped up when they had to. . . . We're a family. . . . Everyone in here gave a hundred and ten percent."

He had been angry with himself for not asking Norbert Doyle how it felt to be part of the team but not part of the team.

"Don't feel bad," Kelleher had said when Stevie lamented his inability to think or act faster. "No one else saw it as a story either. He'll probably be around for the

World Series. You can do a sidebar on him from there if you still think it's worth doing."

The World Series was scheduled to begin in Boston the following Tuesday. *If* Stevie got two papers done for English and did all right on his Spanish test on Monday, he would fly up there on Tuesday morning. His parents weren't thrilled with the idea that he would miss yet another week of school, but he knew his dad would stand by him as long as he wasn't falling too far behind.

"Look, this is what Stevie wants to do someday," his dad had said to his mom when the chance to go to the play-offs had come up. "He's already proven he's good at it, so this is as much a learning experience as school is for him right now."

"Bill, you're rationalizing," his mom had said. "He doesn't need to cover *every* event."

"I know," his dad had answered. "But let's be honest. How many kids have this kind of opportunity? He loves it and I think we should support him."

His mother had finally bought in—at least enough to agree to let him go. Stevie knew his mom didn't exactly understand his fascination with sports and sportswriting, and she hadn't been thrilled at all by the various scrapes he and Susan Carol had gotten into, but he also knew that deep down she was proud of him. His father, on the other hand, loved every second of it.

"If you can't be a great athlete, the next-best thing is getting to tell their stories," Bill Thomas said. "Sometimes I wish I'd tried sportswriting instead of going to law school."

Stevie wasn't worried about a career path right now, just ninth-grade English and Spanish.

Susan Carol was talking, and he realized he'd been daydreaming, looking out the window. "Just make sure you get your work done this weekend," he heard her say. "I don't want to go to the World Series without you."

"Don't worry," he said, snapping back to attention. "I'll be there for sure."

"And don't sulk," she said. "You'll get another shot at Doyle."

Stevie wondered if Doyle would travel with the team to Boston. If not, he could try to talk to him when the series moved to Washington for game three.

"Yeah, you're right," he said finally. "I'll be fine."

"We're pulling into school, gotta go," she said, slipping into the Southern accent she tried to lose north of the Mason-Dixon Line.

"Talk to you later, Scarlett," he said, unable to resist using the nickname he'd put on her when they first met.

She clicked off. Stevie closed his eyes again, smiling. But all he could see was Doyle being sprayed by champagne. Oh yeah, Steve Thomas, sportswriting genius . . . A moment later he was asleep.

The next few days crawled by for Stevie. After the excitement of the playoffs, being back at school was a complete bore.

The weekend was spent writing an English paper, which

wasn't nearly as much fun as writing a sidebar on game seven—even a *bad* sidebar—Stevie thought. His spirits picked up on Sunday morning when he spotted a headline in the *Inquirer*'s "World Series Notes and Quotes" column. It read: "Doyle to Be Activated."

Stevie read the three-paragraph item raptly:

> Norbert Doyle, the 38-year-old rookie acquired by the Nationals in late August, will be on the team's roster for the World Series, manager Manny Acta said today. Acta said he decided to put Doyle on the roster instead of fifth starter Tom O'Toole because Doyle is more comfortable coming out of the bullpen than O'Toole.
>
> "You really don't need a fifth starter in postseason unless there's an injury," Acta said. "Tom only got into one game in the LCS [giving up two runs in $1\frac{1}{3}$ innings of relief work in game three] and relieving really hasn't been his role. Norbert's been comfortable in any role we've put him in."
>
> Doyle, who had never made a major-league appearance prior to being traded to the Nationals in late August, pitched six times in September—three times in relief and three times as a starter. He was 0-0 with an ERA of 3.23.

That was it. Stevie was elated—for Doyle, who would now get to be part of a World Series as an active player, and for himself because he knew Doyle would be in Boston. Then it occurred to him that with Doyle on the active roster, he would be a natural story for anyone looking for a column or a sidebar. No one could resist the underdog-makes-good story line.

Still, he did have a little bit of an in with Doyle, if only because the pitcher had twins his age—one of whom had a crush on Susan Carol. All of that might help him once in Boston. He wouldn't miss the story twice, that much he knew for sure.

When he wasn't working on English or Spanish over the weekend, Stevie read everything he could get his hands on about the impending World Series. Once, the Red Sox had been baseball's perennial hard-luck story: frequent contenders, never champions. Some years they simply collapsed in September. In others they made it to October only to break their fans' hearts: they had lost the seventh game of a World Series four times—in 1946, 1967, 1975, and 1986.

The loss in '86, especially, was a crusher. The Sox had had a three-games-to-two lead going into game six against the Mets and took a 5–3 lead in the tenth inning. When the first two Mets' hitters in the bottom of the tenth were retired, the scoreboard operator at Shea Stadium, apparently forgetting there was still one out to go, flashed

"Congratulations Boston Red Sox, 1986 World Champions" on the board.

The third out never happened. The Mets got three straight singles, Bill Buckner made an infamous error, and the Mets won the game 6–5. Two nights later, with the Red Sox leading 3–0, the Mets came back to win game seven and crush Boston's hopes once again.

It all changed in Boston in the fall of 2004. That October the Red Sox came back from three games down to beat the lordly New York Yankees in the American League Championship Series and went on to finally win the World Series for the first time in eighty-six years.

It was the end of the much-talked-about Curse of the Bambino. A year after winning the 1918 World Series, the Red Sox had traded the great Babe Ruth to the Yankees. Acquiring Ruth had turned the Yankees from a struggling franchise into a dominant one. Yankee Stadium was built in 1923, and it became known as the House That Ruth Built. From 1919 until 2004 the Yankees won twenty-six World Series; the Red Sox, none. The Sox's long drought had begun with the trade of Ruth—and rumors of a curse were born.

But now the Red Sox were four victories away from winning their third World Series title in six years. In a sense, they had *become* the Yankees: the team with lots of money, lots of stars, and the swagger of past championships. The Nationals, on the other hand, were the quintessential underdog. They had been awful for years—first while playing in Montreal, then after moving to Washington in 2005.

They had been picked to finish last in the National League East before the season began and had shocked people by winning the division title.

They had won fourteen of their last sixteen games to sail past the Mets—who ended up making the playoffs as the wild card team—and the Phillies. The Nats' young pitchers all seemed to come into their own at once, and they pulled out one improbable win after another, including a late-September victory in which Johan Santana pitched the first no-hitter in Mets club history, only to lose the game 1–0 when the Nationals scored in the ninth inning on an error, a stolen base, a sacrifice bunt, and a sacrifice fly.

In the playoffs they had trailed the Chicago Cubs two games to none in the best-of-five Division Series before rallying to win, and then had pulled off their miraculous seventh-game victory in the League Championship Series.

Now, amazingly, they were in the World Series. And Kelleher was interviewing Walter Johnson's ghost for his Sunday column. Stevie wasn't sure which story was more unbelievable.

He was engrossed in his research when he noticed an IM coming in on his computer.

"Did U C they activated Doyle?" Susan Carol was asking.

"Yeah," Stevie replied. "Now everyone will write it. But I'm thinking maybe talking to his kids will give me an angle no one else has."

"Great idea," she answered. "Have U contacted Dever

to set something up?" she asked, meaning John Dever, the Nats' PR director.

Stevie stared at the screen for a moment. As usual, she was a half step ahead of him.

"Not yet. U still have his e-mail?"

"Of course."

"Y R U always smarter than me?" he asked.

"Because I'm a girl. Talk later. Bye."

Stevie sighed. He sent Dever an e-mail asking if he could set him up with Doyle and the twins, then decided to take a break. He pushed back from his desk and went to join his dad watching the Eagles and Redskins— which reminded him it was late October. The sports seasons just got longer and longer.

3: FIRST NIGHT AT FENWAY

BY THE TIME STEVIE'S DAD DROPPED HIM at the airport Tuesday morning, Stevie had a breakfast scheduled for Wednesday with Norbert, David, and Morra Doyle. There had been one condition in Dever's return e-mail: "He wants to know if Susan Carol can come too."

Stevie laughed when he read that; David Doyle's crush on Susan Carol was clearly pretty strong. "I think I can arrange that," he wrote back. He then wrote to Susan Carol to make sure she was okay with it.

"Don't say I've never done anything for you," she had written back.

Stevie took a cab to the Marriott Long Wharf as soon as his plane landed. The cab ride was brief—Logan Airport was only a couple of miles from downtown, and at one o'clock there wasn't much traffic. About sixty seconds after emerging from the Sumner Tunnel, Stevie found himself in front of the hotel.

"Welcome to the Marriott, Mr. Thomas," the doorman said as Stevie climbed out of the cab. Seeing the stunned look on Stevie's face, he smiled. "This is Boston," he said. "We're all big sports fans. I'm Mike. Anything I can do to help, let me know."

Stevie took an escalator up to the lobby level and found Kelleher waiting.

"Come on," Kelleher said. "Tamara and Susan Carol are in the restaurant. We'll get a bite to eat before we go to the ballpark so you don't have to eat the box lunch."

"They serve a box lunch at the World Series?"

"Yup. You can have the oh-so-appetizing dried-out apple for dessert."

The restaurant overlooked Boston Harbor. Stevie could see planes taking off directly across the water. Susan Carol got up to give him a hug. Stevie could never completely get over just how pretty she was, even with her hair tied back in a ponytail. Her hair, he noticed, was wet.

"Did you just shower?" he asked.

"After I swam," she said. "Bobby got me into the pool at Harvard."

Stevie was baffled. Harvard, he knew, was in Cambridge.

"Isn't Cambridge a ways from here?" he asked.

"Actually, it's not," Kelleher said. "Only about ten minutes. Nothing in Boston is very far. But the Harvard athletic facilities are all on this side of the river, in Boston."

Stevie admired Susan Carol's dedication to her sport—she always managed to find places to swim away from home. But if he was being honest with himself, he'd admit that it also bugged him just a little that Susan Carol was a much more accomplished athlete than he was. He was hoping to make the JV basketball team, and he knew that even if he did make it, he wouldn't be a starter. Susan Carol, on the other hand, was a nationally ranked swimmer. Her 100-meter butterfly time ranked fourth in the country in the fourteen-and-under age group. If he didn't love her, he might be inclined to hate her . . . just a little.

They ate quickly and took a cab to Fenway Park to get settled in for game one. Stevie spotted the famous Citgo sign that loomed over the stadium. And they got out of the cab on Yawkey Way—a street named for Tom Yawkey, the former Red Sox owner.

It was four hours before game time, but people were everywhere. There were all sorts of souvenir shops and bars and restaurants lining both sides of the street. Kelleher led them through the crowds—including the inevitable ticket scalpers, all screaming, "Anyone selling tickets?" which Stevie now knew was code for the fact that they were selling tickets but didn't want to get nailed by a plainclothes cop—to a small door with a sign that said Media. None of the stadium's gates were open yet.

Stevie had come prepared with two different kinds of photo ID: his student ID from school and a passport. The first time he'd covered a major event, the guy handing out credentials had insisted on seeing a driver's license, until more sensible heads prevailed.

Stevie was about to pull out his various forms of ID when he heard Kelleher let out a shout: "Phyllis!" he said. "About time you showed up someplace."

He was giving a hug to a woman with dark hair who had walked up to the credentials pickup area just as they arrived.

"I was at the American League playoffs, you know that," she said, hugging Kelleher in return. "I can't help it if you work in a National League city."

"You're still an American Leaguer at heart, aren't you?" Kelleher said.

"Please don't tell on me," she said, flashing a wide smile.

Spotting Stevie and Susan Carol, she gave a little gasp. "Now, these are the people I really want to meet."

"Stevie, Susan Carol, this is Phyllis Merhige," Kelleher said. "I know there's a general perception that Bud Selig runs Major League Baseball, but it's not true. Phyllis does."

"Stop it, Bobby," Phyllis said.

She shook hands warmly with Stevie and Susan Carol and gave Tamara a hug. "I've followed you two since the Final Four in New Orleans," she said. "The only reason I'd ask you for ID is because I can't believe you're both only fourteen."

"It is a *pleasure* to meet you," Susan Carol said, her Southern accent popping up as it often did when she wanted to charm someone. "Every time I see your name, it's always something about 'the great Phyllis Merhige' or 'the wonderful Phyllis Merhige.'"

"That's because she *is* great," Tamara said.

"Enough, enough!" Phyllis said.

She turned to the three staffers sitting at the credentials desk. "Have we got the passes for these guys?" she asked.

"Right here," said one.

"I need to make sure the kids have locker room badges," Kelleher said. "That's where they'll do most of their work after the game."

"They're not down for the locker room," one of the women said.

"Don't worry," Phyllis said. "They are now."

She reached into her pocket and produced two badges that said Postgame Locker Room and handed them to Stevie and Susan Carol. "If you have any trouble when you get to Washington, find me and I'll take care of you. Anyone asks where you got 'em, say you don't remember." She winked.

"I owe you one," Bobby said.

"You owe me a lot more than one," she said. "Have fun tonight."

Stevie's first impression of Fenway Park was simple: it was old. Walking through the dank hallways underneath the stands, Stevie found it hard to believe that this was the legendary place he had heard and read so much about.

"This is it?" he said. "This is Fenway Park?"

"Just wait," Kelleher said.

"Patience has always been Stevie's strength," Susan Carol said, smiling.

They rounded a corner in the empty hallway, and Kelleher led them up a short ramp. As soon as they emerged, Stevie gasped.

"Wow," he said, even though he knew the word was completely uncool.

"Worth the wait?" Mearns said, standing right behind him.

The ballpark was completely empty except for some maintenance guys and a few security people who were just beginning to fan into position. The grounds crew was just setting up the batting cage so the Red Sox could start batting practice. Standing ten rows behind home plate, Stevie felt as if he could reach out and touch it because the stands were so close to the field. The place was *tiny*. A lot smaller than Nationals Park in Washington. But he could see instantly why it carried the aura that it did.

The first row of seats were so close to the field they seemed to almost be in fair territory. The seats around home plate were all red and glowing in the late-afternoon sunlight. The famous Green Monster loomed in left field, looking even bigger than it did on television.

"Everything is so close," Susan Carol said, echoing Stevie's thoughts. "What an incredible place to watch a game."

"There are two places left in baseball that are really special," Kelleher said. "This place—"

"And Wrigley Field," Susan Carol said, finishing the sentence for him.

"Exactly," Kelleher said. "Some of the new parks—Oriole Park, Safeco Field in Seattle, the place in San Francisco—can be charming. But not like Fenway and Wrigley."

"What *do* they call the park in San Francisco now?" Tamara asked.

"Not sure," Kelleher said. "They keep changing corporate names on it every few weeks."

"This place will never have a corporate name on it, will it?" Stevie asked.

"God, I hope not," Kelleher said. "But most owners will do anything to make a buck these days. Come on, let's go up to the press box and drop our stuff off. We can't go on the field until BP starts anyway."

They walked back under the stands to an elevator that whisked them to the top of the ballpark. The press box was glass-enclosed and seemed to be about nine miles up from the field.

They made their way to the seats assigned to Kelleher and Mearns. "In the old days this was a one-tier ballpark, and the press box was on the roof," Kelleher explained. "Then they built all these corporate boxes on top of it and put the press box on top of *them*. We went from the best view in baseball here to one of the worst."

"We don't get a lot of sympathy about it, though, do we, Bobby?" a voice said behind them.

Kelleher turned and smiled at the sight of a middle-aged

man with thinning brown hair and a big grin. Stevie wasn't sure why, but he looked familiar.

"No, Richard, we don't, do we?" he said, shaking hands with the man.

Richard laughed. "I tell my friends back home that October's a tough month for me because I'm away from my kids covering the playoffs and the World Series. They just look at me and say, 'Yeah, tough life you lead, pal.'"

"Ever call one of them at about two o'clock in the morning when you're trying to get a cab outside a ballpark?" Kelleher said.

"Thought about it," Richard said. "But I still don't think I'd have a lot of people crying for me. So, are you going to introduce me to these two guys or not? That's the only reason I came over here—to meet them."

"Figures," Kelleher said. "Richard Justice of the *Houston Chronicle* and *PTI*, meet Susan Carol Anderson of the *Washington Post* and Steve Thomas of the *Washington Herald*."

As soon as Kelleher mentioned *PTI*—the one ESPN show Stevie watched regularly—Stevie knew why Justice had looked familiar.

"I'm a big fan," Justice said, shaking their hands.

Susan Carol gave Justice the Smile, the one guaranteed to charm anyone and everyone who came into its range. "Why, thank you. As much as I enjoy you on *PTI*, I *really* love your writin' in the *Chronicle*," she said. "I read you online all the time."

Once, hearing Susan Carol rhyme "laan" with "taam"

would have made Stevie shake his head. Now he got a kick out of it.

"Speaking of *PTI*," Tamara said. "Rumor has it that Mr. Tony may actually show up at a game when the series moves to Washington."

Justice laughed. Mearns was referring to Tony Kornheiser, the *PTI* co-host whom Stevie had met at the Final Four in New Orleans. "*If* they send a car to his house and *if* they give him four extra credentials so he can be carried in by litter, he may show up," he said.

"What about Wilbon?" Mearns asked, referring to Kornheiser's co-host.

"Michael's checking his schedule," Justice said. "He's got golf with Chuck one day, and something with Mike another day, and I think he's supposed to give the keynote address at the NBA owners meetings, but he'll try to make it if he can."

Mearns looked at Stevie and Susan Carol. "If you're scoring at home, Chuck is Charles Barkley, and Mike is Michael Jordan."

"You're kidding, right?" Stevie said to Justice.

"Yeah," Justice laughed. "But when Wilbon tells you his schedule, it usually comes out something like that."

Mearns nodded. "It's true," she said. "Every time I talk to him on the phone, he says something like, 'Gotta go, I promised Mike I'd call him right back,' or, 'The commissioner's on the other line, he's been bugging me for days.'"

Stevie loved this kind of talk about famous sports people, whether it was true or not. He knew Kornheiser wouldn't be borne into the World Series by litter, but he suspected he would insist on having a car sent for him.

"Hey," Kelleher said, nodding toward the field, where the Red Sox had started batting practice. "We probably ought to get down there. Did we miss anything at the press conferences yesterday, Richard?"

Justice shook his head. "You'll be stunned to know that both teams have great respect for one another," he said. "They're both happy to be here."

"Let me guess," Susan Carol said. "Everyone plans on giving a hundred and ten percent, and they hope that they can step up under pressure."

"Congratulations," Justice said. "You not only have the cliché handbook down, but you already have the best quotes from *today's* press conferences."

"Did anyone talk to Norbert Doyle yesterday?" Stevie asked.

Justice shook his head. "Don't think so. The clubhouses were closed to us, and the only ones who came to the press conference for the Nationals were Manny Acta, Ryan Zimmerman, and John Lannan, since he's pitching tonight."

Stevie was glad to hear that. It seemed likely he'd be the first to talk to Doyle at any length at their interview the next day. And since Doyle was now on the World Series roster, the story was actually better than it would have been a week earlier. Maybe, he thought, he'd gotten lucky.

"Come on," Kelleher said, pulling Stevie out of his reverie. "Let's get downstairs."

"Yeah," Mearns said. "The sooner we get down there,

the sooner we can stand around and talk to each other there rather than here."

Stevie knew from his experience at the playoffs what Mearns meant. Other than a short press conference with each team's manager and the next day's starting pitcher, there was just about no access to players pregame. During the regular season the media could go into the clubhouses almost any time and talk to players. Stevie had done that in Philadelphia during the summer on several occasions. But the postseason was different: the players were given a lot more privacy in October. So most of the pregame time on the field was spent talking to other writers. Still, for Stevie, that was fun too.

After all, he *was* really glad to be here. And he did plan on giving 110 percent and stepping up his game. This was the World Series—his first World Series. He was ready.

4: DAVID AND MORRA

THEY STAYED ON THE FIELD until they were required to leave, an hour before the game was to begin. Stevie spent most of the time taking in what was going on around him: when the gates opened to the public, people came streaming into the stands, most in red or in red and white, many wearing uniform tops with players' names on the back. Stevie was surprised to see a number of Ramirez shirts, since Manny Ramirez, the oft-troubled Red Sox slugger, had been exiled to Los Angeles. Some Red Sox fans apparently remained loyal to him.

Stevie watched with amusement while fans lined up next to the dugouts, pleading with players to stop on their way off the field to sign autographs. During the regular season Stevie would occasionally see players stop to sign. But not in October. They were all business now.

"Did you see who's singing the national anthem?" Susan Carol said, wandering over near the Red Sox dugout while a number of fans pleaded with Jason Bay to "sign one, just one!"

"Kate Smith?" Stevie asked, referring to the late singer who had become a legend in Philadelphia as a good-luck charm for the hockey team in the 1970s.

"No," Susan Carol said. "It's the twenty-first century, Stevie. Try Beyoncé."

That did impress Stevie. Beyoncé was quite beautiful *and* she could sing. He remembered watching her sing "At Last" during the inaugural ball earlier in the year.

The pregame introductions were every bit as impressive. The crowd even gave the Nationals a nice round of applause when the PA announcer said this was the first World Series in the forty-year history of the franchise and the first for Washington since 1933.

Every player from both teams was introduced, and the cheers seemed to grow louder for each Red Sox, with the loudest cheers saved for David Ortiz—"Big Papi" to Red Sox Nation—the postseason hero of their past world championships. By the time Beyoncé was introduced, the entire building was shaking with noise, and even sitting way down the right-field line in the auxiliary press box, Stevie couldn't help but tingle.

The ceremonial first pitches were thrown out by Bob Ryan and Peter Gammons, which certainly got the attention of everyone in the press box. Ryan and Gammons were both Boston legends, having worked for the *Boston Globe* since the 1960s.

"I guess the Red Sox have been in the series so much lately they finally had to recognize someone in the media," Kelleher had said when he heard that his two friends were being honored.

"Can't think of two better guys," Mearns said. "It's a nice gesture."

There was very little nice about the game itself—except for the roaring fans of Fenway. The Red Sox scored five runs off Nationals starting pitcher John Lannan in the first inning, and Josh Beckett, the Red Sox ace, was unhittable as usual in postseason, not allowing the Nats a single base runner until the fifth. The Red Sox added three more runs in the sixth, then another in the eighth, and won 9–0 in a completely one-sided game.

The game took under three hours—warp speed, Stevie knew, for a postseason baseball game. But there were no mound conferences, no pauses to bring pitchers in from the bullpen, and not a lot of pitches taken in the late innings with the outcome no longer in doubt. Stevie noticed the stands starting to empty in the ninth. Even a fast game ended close to midnight in the World Series.

"Well, here we go again," Richard Justice said as they all made their way down to the clubhouses. "We haven't had a decent World Series now since '02."

"It's just one game," Susan Carol said. "Beckett can't pitch every night."

"Dice-K tomorrow," Kelleher said, referring to Daisuke Matsuzaka, the Red Sox number two pitcher. "Anyone care to wager on a sweep?"

"You're just saying that because the Red Sox swept in '04 and '07," Mearns said.

"Well, yeah," Kelleher said.

The Nationals clubhouse was a lot quieter than it had been after game seven of the NLCS. Stevie was now accustomed to how crowded postseason clubhouses were, but the visitors clubhouse in Fenway was so tiny he could barely move from locker to locker. He managed to scrounge a couple of quotes from several players about Beckett—Kelleher had suggested he write his sidebar on how good Beckett was in postseason—but couldn't get close to Ryan Zimmerman, who was surrounded by at least ten cameras, not to mention all the notebooks and tape recorders.

It was already midnight, and Stevie had to file his story by 12:45. There was no time to hang around until the crowd around Zimmerman began to disperse. Stevie was heading for the door when he saw Norbert Doyle. He was standing at a locker near the door with one reporter talking to him. Seeing Stevie, he waved.

"Eleven o'clock tomorrow?" he said.

"Absolutely," Stevie said. "We'll be there."

"Great. My kids are really looking forward to it."

Stevie was tempted to say, "You mean David is looking forward to meeting Susan Carol," but he resisted.

"Us too," he said, and raced back upstairs to try to write. Once again he knew what he was writing wasn't particularly inspired. The quotes were hardly brilliant. "The guy's got great stuff and great control," left fielder Adam Dunn had said.

Great, Stevie thought, like anyone watching couldn't figure that out. Kelleher often reminded him that some nights you just do the best you can and make deadline. Stevie knew that was true, and he knew everyone else was dealing with the same banal quotes. Still, it didn't make him happy to file such a nonstory.

He was even less happy when he found Susan Carol writing away with a big smile on her face. "What are you so happy about?" he asked.

"Me? Oh, nothing," she said, still smiling. "I'll tell you later."

"Give me one sentence," he said.

She shrugged. "I got lucky," she said. "Bill Buckner was in the Sox clubhouse, and he recognized me, I guess from when we were doing *Kidsports*. They had told everyone he was off-limits until the off-day press conference, but he talked to me."

Stevie stared at her. In the middle of a packed World Series clubhouse, she had gotten an exclusive story. Buckner was famous for the error he had made in the 1986 World Series when Mookie Wilson's ground ball darted between his legs, allowing the New York Mets to score the winning run.

For years Buckner had been the symbol of Boston's postseason futility. Stevie remembered being at lunch one time with Kelleher and Esther Newberg, his literary agent. Newberg was one of those crazed Red Sox Nation fans.

"Watch this," Kelleher had said quietly to Stevie while Newberg was going on about how much she hated Buckner.

"So, Esther, do you remember what the score was when Buckner muffed the ball?" Kelleher said.

"I don't know," she said. "Was it six to five, five to four? I know we were ahead by a run."

"No, you weren't," Kelleher said. "The score was tied. All you Red Sox fans act like Buckner lost the World Series for you, when even if he makes the play, the game just goes to the eleventh inning."

"I don't care," Newberg had answered. "I hate him. I don't want to hear this."

Stevie remembered wondering what it was like to be Buckner, with so many people hating him so passionately. Buckner had been "rehabilitated" after the Red Sox finally won the World Series in 2004 and then again in 2007. That was why he was in Boston—as an invited guest of the team. And Susan Carol had gotten to talk to him—alone.

"I should have known," Stevie said. "Everyone else has zilch, and you've got Bill Buckner."

"Stop it, Stevie," she said. "I got lucky. Now go write."

He did, but he wasn't happy. Susan Carol had once called him the most competitive person she had ever met, and he knew she wasn't far wrong. He wasn't a good enough athlete to shine that way, so journalism was the way he competed. And his girlfriend had just whipped him.

On the media shuttle back to the hotel, Kelleher asked Susan Carol how it had gone with Buckner.

"You'll have to read about it in the *Post*," Mearns said with a smile. "She wrote a great story."

"I don't doubt it," Kelleher said. "Did your genius editors find some extra space?"

"Uh-huh," Mearns answered. "They put her on the front. They actually put a Redskins feature inside."

"Whoa," Kelleher said, turning again to Susan Carol. "You must have had great stuff to knock a Redskins story off the front."

"I think it was a story about the backup quarterback," Susan Carol said, stealing a glance at Stevie, who was pretending to look out the window. "It wasn't *that* big a deal."

"A hangnail is a big deal in Washington when it comes to the Redskins, you know that," Kelleher said. "So what'd he say?"

"He said it was really nice of the Red Sox to invite him back, but he still didn't feel completely comfortable in Boston," she said. "It still bothers him when people ask him what it felt like to cost the Red Sox the '86 series. And get this, he said he kind of hopes the Nationals win, because Boston has been winning so much recently. The Nationals are the underdogs now. Washington could use a championship, and Boston's had two World Series, three Super Bowls, and an NBA title the last few years."

"You'll make a few headlines in Boston with that story," Kelleher said.

Stevie stared out the window. Susan Carol had written a story that everyone would be talking about the next day. He had written a story that his parents would read.

Maybe.

The World Series hadn't started a whole lot better for him than it had for the Nationals.

Stevie and Susan Carol had agreed to meet at 9:30 for a prebreakfast before they met with the Doyles, but Stevie woke up early and went downstairs by himself. He needed a little time alone to pout. He sat at a window table, staring at the harbor and wolfing down some French toast and coffee.

He was halfway through Bob Ryan's column in the *Globe* when Susan Carol walked in, looking around the room until she found him.

"Couldn't wait for me?" she said, glancing at his empty plate.

"Sorry," he said. "I woke up early and I was hungry."

She slid into the chair across from him, took the pot of coffee that was on the table, and poured a cup for herself. He kept reading.

"Are you mad at me or something?" she said after several seconds of silence.

"Me? Angry? Why would I be angry?"

She raised an eyebrow. "Steven Richman Thomas, other than your parents—*maybe*—is there anyone who knows you better than I do?" she said.

He didn't answer for a moment, trying to think of something clever to say.

"No," he said finally.

"Okay then, let me take a stab at what's going on here," she said, taking a long sip of her coffee. A waitress came up and Susan Carol ordered fried eggs, orange juice, bacon, and toast.

"Is that part of your swimmer's diet?" he asked.

"Don't change the subject," she said. "I can eat pretty much what I want as long as I'm working out."

"And you're always working out," he said.

She flashed him the smile he had seen charm so many people. "True. Now, as I was saying . . ."

He put up a hand. "Do we really have to start the day with you psychoanalyzing me?"

"Yes, we do," she said. "Because that's the only way to clear the air."

He sighed, knowing that nothing could deter her.

"Okay, okay, go ahead," he said.

She leaned forward. "You're upset because you feel like you blew it with Norbert Doyle after the seventh game of the playoff series," she said.

He started to respond but she put up a hand. "Wait till I finish," she said. "So, you beat yourself up about that, and then he makes the series roster. You get an interview with him and his kids, *but* the boy asks that I come along, so that upsets you even though it's no big deal and you know it. Then, last night, I catch a lucky break—one that you might very well have caught if you'd been sent to the Red Sox clubhouse—and so you're angry at me even though I haven't done anything to make you angry. Nothing at all."

He knew she was right. As much as he liked her, *really*

liked her, it still bothered him that she was a little bit taller than he was, a little bit more athletic, a little bit smarter, and, clearly, a little bit more rational.

"Stevie?" she said, bringing him back from his musings.

"Sorry," he said. "Look, you're right. I know you're right. But sometimes it's hard to be your friend, even your boyfriend."

"Why?" she said.

He shrugged. "You know why," he said. "Sometimes it's just hard trying to keep up with you."

"Do I ever act like I'm better than you?" she asked.

"No," he said. "But you don't have to. You just are."

Her food arrived, and she waited until the waitress had left before answering.

"Sometimes it's hard to be *your* friend," she said. "You're *so* smart, and such a good writer, and you're good-looking, and you're funny, and you're brave. And you *still* don't think you're good enough."

"Well," he said. "I may be good enough, but I'm not as good as you."

She sighed. "Now you're just being difficult, and you know it," she said. "Today I had the big story. But you're about to do an interview for a story no one else will have tomorrow. So get over yourself already."

She picked up her fork and began to eat. Stevie poured himself another cup of coffee and went back to Bob Ryan's column.

• • •

They started talking again on the twenty-minute walk to the Ritz-Carlton Hotel, which was where the Nationals were staying.

"This is your story, so I'm going to stay quiet while you ask the questions," Susan Carol said.

"You have to at least be nice to David."

"Of course," she said. "I'll be nice to David. And Morra. I'm just here to help. Where are we meeting them?"

"There's a restaurant in the lobby. We're having breakfast again."

They rounded the corner onto Essex Street, following the directions the concierge at the Marriott had given them. As they turned onto Avery Street and approached the front door of the Ritz, they could see a coterie of security people and police stopping people from going inside.

"I didn't think about this," Susan Carol said. "Of course there's security. Otherwise the place would be overrun with fans and autograph seekers."

"What do we do?" Stevie asked.

"You follow me," a voice behind them said.

Stevie and Susan Carol turned at the sound of the voice and saw a tall young man with light brown hair, blue eyes, and a big smile on his face. He looked at Susan Carol, still smiling.

"I'm David Doyle," he said. "It's great to meet you, Susan Carol."

Stevie could see that Susan Carol was startled by David Doyle's appearance. He was a good three inches taller than she was—which made him about six foot two, Stevie guessed. Since Norbert Doyle had said his twins were four-teen, Stevie had expected someone more like himself and less like a J.Crew model. Susan Carol had no doubt expected the same thing.

"Why, it's very nice to meet you too," she said, putting her hand out. Stevie noticed instantly that the Southern accent was turned up all the way: "Whaa, it's verra naace to meet you toooooo," the last word strung out as if she couldn't cut herself off.

"Steve," he said, stepping in between them to break up the handshake. "Steve Thomas."

"Oh, right," David said. "Yes, very nice to meet you."

He wasn't looking at Stevie as they shook hands. Stevie felt as if he was standing in a hole looking up at David Doyle, not to mention Susan Carol, even though she was wearing running shoes.

"Come on," he said. "My dad and sister are waiting for us inside. Just follow me."

Stevie was feeling a little queasy as he followed David Doyle and Susan Carol. At the Super Bowl the previous winter, Susan Carol had worked with Jamie Whitsitt, the lead singer of a famous boy band. Stevie had been quite jealous until she had assured him that she had absolutely no interest in him. But David Doyle seemed different.

She'd slipped into full Scarlett O'Hara mode the instant she'd laid eyes on him. She'd never done that with Jamie Whitsitt.

David showed a key card to one of the guards as they approached the hotel entrance and said, "They're with me," hooking a thumb at Stevie and Susan Carol, which was good enough to get them past the guards and through the front door.

Even with all the security, the lobby was crowded. "The restaurant's in back," David said. "Dad was hungry, so he's already eaten. Morra and I waited for you. We're starving."

"Me too," Susan Carol said, almost causing Stevie to gag. He started to say something, then thought better of it.

They walked through the restaurant to a booth in the back. Norbert Doyle stood up when he saw them coming. "Good to see you again, Steve," he said, shaking hands. "Obviously, this is Susan Carol. Nice to finally meet you. I'm glad David found you." He turned to the girl sitting on the inside of the booth. "This is my daughter, Morra. Morra—Steve and Susan Carol."

Stevie could tell right away she was David's twin. She had long light brown hair, bright blue eyes, and the same friendly smile.

"Nice to meet you both," she said.

Stevie was determined not to let her pretty face affect him as obviously as a handsome one had affected Susan Carol. He was here to do an interview—not flirt.

"You both must be very proud of your dad," he said.

"Let's all sit down," Norbert Doyle said, sliding in next to his daughter.

True to her word, Susan Carol ordered a second breakfast when David and Morra ordered. Norbert asked for coffee, as did Stevie.

"So, where do we begin?" Norbert Doyle asked after the

orders had been taken. He turned to Susan Carol. "I sincerely doubt we can say anything that will match your Buckner story. It was all anyone was talking about on local TV and radio this morning."

"What an amazing story," David said to her. "I read your stuff all the time."

"Why, thank you, David," Susan Carol drawled. "That is *so* nice of you to say."

Stevie smiled what he hoped was a professional smile. He had a feeling this was going to be a long day.

5: SURPRISE STARTER

THINGS ACTUALLY WENT A LOT BETTER once Stevie took his tape recorder out and started asking questions. Even putting aside how long it had taken him to make it to the big leagues, Norbert Doyle was not your typical professional athlete in many ways—most of them good fodder for a story.

He had grown up in Springfield, Massachusetts—a Red Sox fan—and had signed a contract with the hated New York Yankees right out of high school when they picked him in the thirty-fifth round of the draft. "Most kids who get drafted that low don't sign, they go to college," he said. "But at that point in my life, I thought school was boring. All I really wanted was to play baseball—even if it meant playing for the Yankees."

He had bounced all around the minor leagues over the years. On six different occasions he had been released, and he had pitched for teams belonging to the Yankees, the Blue Jays, the Angels, the Rockies, the Mets, the Marlins, the Red Sox, the White Sox, the Devil Rays, the Padres, and the Reds before the fateful trade to the Nationals that had finally gotten him to the majors.

"I was close on a few occasions," he said. "Or at least I thought I was. In '01 I thought I was going to make the Mets roster out of spring training. I pitched fourteen innings that spring and gave up one run. I thought I had the team made until they told me there was a kid they had acquired in the Rule Five draft who they had to keep, so I ended up back in Triple-A, at Tidewater."

"What's the Rule Five draft?" Stevie asked.

"It's a draft they hold in the winter for minor-league players," Norbert explained. "If a team takes a player, they have to keep him on their major-league roster that season or return him. A lot of times teams will take a chance on a younger player they know isn't ready and keep him around a season, so when he *is* ready, they'll still have his rights. I guess the most famous Rule Five draft pick was when the Pirates took Roberto Clemente from the Giants."

"Sounds like you should have gotten someone to take *you* in that draft," Susan Carol said, causing David Doyle to laugh—at least Stevie thought—a little too hard.

"Yeah, you're right," Norbert said. "But once you hit about twenty-seven or twenty-eight, no one even looks at you during that draft."

That was pretty much when he knew, he said, that he was probably destined to be what was known as an organization player, signed by teams to fill out minor-league rosters and not really considered a major-league prospect.

"I had to take a hard look at my life about then," he said. "I had two kids, and I knew I could play awhile longer, but I wasn't going to get rich, and I wasn't going to be one of those guys who retires and does TV or doesn't need to work. So I went to college."

He enrolled during the off-seasons at Springfield College and found that he loved it then as much as he had hated it as a kid. It took him eight winters to get his degree, but by then he was hooked, and so he went on for a master's degree in English literature at Boston University. "My specialty," he said, "is English and Irish poets. Which means I've read a lot of great stuff, but I'm still not sure how I'm going to make a living when I'm done with baseball. I need to finish my dissertation this winter to get the degree."

"Teaching?" Stevie suggested, amazed that someone would *want* to read poetry, but impressed nonetheless.

"I hope so," Norbert said. "I'd enjoy that."

Stevie asked about Norbert's wife. Was she here in Boston too?

As soon as he saw the look on all three Doyles' faces, he knew he'd made a mistake. It suddenly occurred to him that when he'd read the postseason media guide handed out by the Nationals, there had been a mention of David and Morra but no mention of Norbert's wife.

"My wife passed away," Norbert said softly.

"Oh, I'm *so* sorry," Stevie said, feeling sick to his stomach. "I didn't know. . . ."

"It's okay," Norbert said, waving his hand. "It was twelve years this August, but it still feels like yesterday. It's not something we like to talk about often, but it's part of our lives."

"Was she ill?" Susan Carol said, much to Stevie's relief, because he wasn't sure he had the guts to ask any more questions on the topic.

Norbert shook his head. "No. It was an accident. A drunk driver. I was playing Class A ball in Lynchburg, Virginia, at the time and was just beginning to wonder if it was time to give up the dream. We were on our way home from dinner when it happened. . . ."

His voice trailed off. Stevie could see that both David and Morra had tears in their eyes. He didn't blame them. This wasn't the way he had envisioned the interview either.

"You were in the car too?" he asked.

"Yes," Norbert said very softly. "I got off with a broken collarbone and cuts and bruises. And she was killed. It wasn't fair."

"Dad, stop," Morra said. "Do we have to talk about this?"

Norbert looked at his daughter and forced a smile. Stevie knew he should probably have a follow-up question, but he couldn't think of anything to ask that wouldn't sound morbid or prying. He looked at Susan Carol, but she was looking away, as if something on the other side of the room had caught her attention.

"Of course not," he said to Morra. "I really apologize. . . ."

Norbert shook his head. "Don't apologize. It's a logical question to ask. The worst part, to be honest, is that the kids were so young they don't really remember her."

"I remember her giving us baths," Morra said quietly. "At least, I think I do."

"She used to sing me to sleep," David added.

"We've done a pretty good job of sticking together and getting through things," Norbert added. "I know that's what Analise would have wanted. That's why the kids travel with me whenever they can. When they're in school and I'm on the road, my brother and his wife take care of them for me. But I miss them a lot when I'm away."

The story, Stevie realized, had taken a turn he hadn't expected. Time to switch gears.

"So, Morra, David, sounds like you travel with the team a lot," he said. "Tell me what that's like."

Morra thought for a moment and then laughed. "It's a whole lot different up here in the majors than the minors," she said.

"Charter planes instead of charter buses," David said. "Dad's been given more stuff—gloves, bats, caps, even socks—in the last two months than the whole time he was in the minors."

"Pretty close to true," Norbert said, nodding.

"They even put your number on your socks," David added.

"Why do you think they do that?" Susan Carol asked, suddenly curious.

"I asked that myself," Norbert said. "It's so they can tell whose socks belong to whom when they do laundry."

"So they do your laundry for you?" Stevie said.

"They do *everything* for you," Norbert said. "When we go on a road trip like this one, there's a clubhouse kid assigned to me—just to me—to make sure all my uniforms and equipment and anything I need gets into a trunk and gets on the plane. When I drive to the airport to meet the team, there's no security check and I just hand my bags to someone, and the next time I see them is in my hotel room."

"On this trip they had a charter for the families," David said. "It was amazing."

"A little different than Sumter or Boise or Greensboro, that's for sure," Norbert said. He laughed. "It was in Sumter that my battery blew in hundred-and-five-degree heat, and I didn't have enough money to buy a new one. I had to go around the clubhouse and . . ."

He stopped in midsentence. Nationals manager Manny Acta was approaching the table.

For a second Stevie wondered if maybe they'd lingered too long and Acta didn't like the idea of one of his players spending so much time with a couple of reporters on the morning of game two of the World Series. But he had a smile on his face as he approached. "Talking to my favorite kid reporters, huh, Norby?" he said as he walked up. Both Stevie and Susan Carol had spent some time with Acta during the playoffs, and he'd always been accommodating and accessible.

"Telling them about every city I ever played in," Norbert said. "That takes a while."

Acta laughed. "We play at eight-thirty tonight," he said. "I'm not sure there's enough time."

He shook hands with Stevie and Susan Carol and said hello to the Doyle kids, whom he clearly knew. He looked at Norbert and said, "Can I talk to you for a minute?"

The implication—that he didn't want to talk to Norbert in front of everyone—was obvious. "Sure, Manny," Norbert said, clearly a bit baffled.

He and Acta walked across the restaurant and out the door.

"What do you think that's about?" Susan Carol asked. "I mean, it's okay for your dad to be interviewed now, isn't it?"

"Sure, it's okay," David said. "I have no idea what this is about."

They sat quietly for a moment. Stevie wanted to say again how sorry he was about their mother but decided it wasn't a good idea. Susan Carol broke the silence by asking what sports David and Morra played. Not surprisingly, David said he played basketball and baseball. Morra, as it turned out, was a swimmer. She and Susan Carol launched into a discussion of times and splits and sets that left David and Stevie rolling their eyes at one another. Stevie was extremely relieved when he saw Norbert Doyle walking back toward the table.

"What was that about, Dad?" David said, asking the question for all four of them.

Norbert Doyle sat down, looking a little stunned. "You aren't going to believe it," he said. "I don't believe it."

They waited. "Ross Detwiler got out of bed this morning and felt something click inside his knee. They think it's his MCL, but it could be worse. Either way, he can't possibly start tonight. None of the other starters are close to rested enough, since the LCS went seven games and all the other long guys in the bullpen worked last night."

Stevie could see that Morra and David's eyes were popping out. "Dad," Morra said. "Are you saying . . . ?"

"I'm starting tonight," Norbert Doyle said. "I'm starting game two of the World Series."

Stevie and Susan Carol left soon after that. Acta wanted Norbert Doyle to meet with pitching coach Randy St. Claire and catcher Wil Nieves as soon as possible to go over the Red Sox lineup, since he had never faced it. "The good news is, they've never faced me either," he said. "They probably don't have much of a scouting report, since I wasn't supposed to be on the postseason roster."

"You nervous?" Stevie asked.

"Absolutely not," Norbert said. "What's about five steps up from nervous? Scared to death? I'd say that's about right."

They broke up in the lobby, Norbert heading off for his meeting. Stevie and Susan Carol thanked the Doyle kids, and they all exchanged cell phone numbers. "What a day this is turning out to be for you guys," Susan Carol said.

"No kidding," David answered. "To be honest, just seeing Dad introduced on the field last night was pretty huge. I don't think any of us thought he'd get into a game unless it was ten to nothing one way or the other."

Susan Carol was beaming. "What a wonderful story."

Morra shook her head. "It's wonderful that he's pitching. But let's see *how* he pitches."

"That's my sister," David said. "She can find the black cloud in every silver lining."

"Maybe she's really *Stevie's* twin," Susan Carol said. She was smiling when she said it, but he knew she meant it.

Susan Carol was practically skipping on the way back to the hotel. "I don't know who I'm happier for right now, Norbert or you," she said.

"Or David Doyle maybe?" he said.

"Huh?"

"Come on, Susan Carol, you had the full Scarlett O'Hara bit going on back there."

Susan Carol reddened a little, something he had never really seen her do before. "Well, that was my role here, right? Be nice to David?"

"Yeah, but there's nice and there's 'naaace'—or let's put it this way, I didn't think you would enjoy it quite so much."

Stevie was hoping she would say something like, "Come on, Stevie, you know you've got nothing to be jealous about."

She didn't say that, though. She didn't say anything. He decided to drop it. He was sorry he had brought it up. Instead he took out his cell phone and called Kelleher.

"How'd it go with the old man?" Kelleher said. "He fill your notebook with stories about Amarillo, Texas?"

"He did," Stevie said. "He also filled my notebook with a story about the fact that he's starting tonight."

There was silence on the other end of the phone. "He's *what?*" Kelleher said. "What in the world are you talking about?"

"Ross Detwiler did something to his knee getting out of bed—" Stevie said.

"Getting out of bed?"

"Yeah, apparently. Anyway, none of the other starters are on schedule to pitch tonight, and they used the other two long guys in the bullpen last night—"

"So he's it," Kelleher broke in. "Wow. You better get back here and write this right away so we can get it up on the Web before anyone else finds out."

The Internet had changed the newspaper business. There was no such thing as a first-edition deadline for the next day's newspaper anymore. The writers were on twenty-four-hour call. If something happened that was newsworthy, they were expected to write it instantly to get it up on the Web. This was a perfect example.

"We'll be back in a few minutes and I'll start writing," Stevie said.

"Good. Why don't you come to my room with your computer? You can tell me about the Doyle kid gawking at Susan Carol while you write."

Stevie almost gagged when he heard that. He looked at Susan Carol, who he knew would pick up on anything he said in response. "Sounds good," he said, keeping his voice as even in tone as he could. "I'll see you in a few minutes."

He snapped the phone shut. He and Susan Carol walked the rest of the way to the hotel in silence.

6: MYSTERY MEETING

IT DIDN'T TAKE STEVIE VERY LONG TO WRITE the story about Norbert Doyle replacing Ross Detwiler on the mound for game two of the World Series. Kelleher was delighted with the details of Acta walking up during breakfast to give Doyle the news while he was sitting with his kids.

"You two really have a knack for walking into stories," Kelleher said. "And this one doesn't even involve getting yourselves into trouble, the way you guys usually do. You can write the profile on Doyle later and plug in details on how he pitches tonight for the late editions. Good job breaking this, though—no one else will have it, that's for sure."

Stevie laughed weakly. "Better to be lucky than good," he said.

"Best to be both," Kelleher said. "Tell me about the Doyle kids. Were they nice? Was David completely tongue-tied meeting Susan Carol?"

Stevie shook his head. "Not exactly," he said. "If anything, it was the other way around."

Kelleher looked up in surprise. "What? Susan Carol? I've never seen *her* tongue-tied."

"Me neither," Stevie said. "David is really tall and really good-looking."

Kelleher waved a hand. "She's been around good-looking guys before. I wouldn't worry about it. You were jealous of Jamie Whitsitt, and there wasn't anything to that, was there?"

"No, there wasn't," Stevie said. "But Jamie was four years older than she was and not too bright. David is our age and smart. She went all Southern belle as soon as she laid eyes on him."

Kelleher shrugged. "Be honest, Stevie. Are there girls at school you think are good-looking? Of course there are. It doesn't change the way you feel about Susan Carol. She was probably caught a little by surprise. It's human nature, nothing more."

Stevie knew he was probably right. Still, he couldn't shake the queasy feeling in his stomach.

Once Stevie had filed his story, Kelleher suggested they take a walk through Faneuil Hall. "Where's Tamara?" Stevie asked.

"She went to tape something for TV," he said. "ESPN keeps asking her to come on because they want to hire her.

She knows it's a really bad idea, but they're throwing a lot of money around, and it doesn't hurt to let the newspaper know they're interested in her. And given what's going on in the newspaper business, she has to give it some thought."

"I'm surprised they didn't blackball her just for being married to you," Stevie said.

"Maybe they think I'd be less critical of them," Kelleher answered, laughing.

"I doubt that."

"Me too," Kelleher replied. "Come on, let's go."

Stevie tried to call Susan Carol, first in her room and then on her cell, to see if she wanted to go with them. There was no answer, which surprised him a little.

"Maybe she turned her cell off to take a nap," Kelleher said. "We'll find her when we get back."

Given the coolness between them on the walk back, Stevie thought some time apart might not be a bad idea. So they headed out the door of the hotel for what Kelleher said was a short walk to Faneuil Hall.

"That's the great thing about Boston," he said. "When the weather's good, you can walk just about anyplace. It's a major city but a small town—at least geographically."

While they walked, Kelleher explained some of the history of the place. The original Faneuil Hall had existed during the Revolutionary War. It was a thriving marketplace for years, which led the city to build the even bigger Quincy Market next door. It had all fallen into disrepair, but then the city came up with the idea to turn the area into a place with shops and restaurants, and now it was thriving again.

"We'll go to Regina's for pizza," Kelleher said. "It's as good as any in the country. But first I want to show you Red."

"Red?"

"You'll see," Kelleher said.

They walked under an archway into what looked like a small town. There were cobblestone walkways and, on either side, long brick buildings that housed stores and restaurants. The smell of food drew Stevie toward an open doorway, but Kelleher headed straight down the cobblestones until he came to a bench.

"Red," he said.

He was pointing at a statue of a man sitting on the bench with a cigar in his hands. The statue was life-size and looked almost real.

"Red Auerbach," Stevie said.

"Very good, Stevie," Kelleher said. "You pass today's history test."

Stevie was reading the plaque next to the statue. It said that Arnold "Red" Auerbach had led the Boston Celtics to fifteen NBA titles as coach and general manager of the team.

"Fifteen titles, that's amazing," Stevie said.

"Actually, it was sixteen," Kelleher said. "Look at the date on the plaque—1985. The Celtics won another one in 1986. Just before Red died, I was in town, and I called him from right here to tell him I was sitting next to his statue.

"First thing he said to me was, 'Did they fix that damn plaque yet to make it sixteen championships?'"

"How did you know him?" Stevie asked.

"Believe it or not, he lived in Washington," Kelleher said. "He had a group of buddies that went to lunch every Tuesday, and I used to go. There were some basketball people, but there were also a couple of lawyers, a couple of Secret Service agents, some of Red's doctors—a very eclectic group. Red knew everyone. Might have been the most fun I ever had."

"I guess the group broke up after he died," Stevie said.

"Actually, no," Kelleher said. "We still get together every Tuesday. It's not the same without Red, it can't be. But we all know Red would have wanted it that way. At the end of lunch we open a fortune cookie for Red and read it to him."

"Sounds like you really miss him," Stevie said.

"Oh yeah," Kelleher said. "You don't get to meet too many guys who are truly larger than life. Red was one of them. He had this incredible feel for people—no matter what they did. He was always asking questions, trying to learn, to be smarter, even though he was *really* smart. And he was the most competitive person I ever met. He wanted to win at everything all the time."

He put his hand on top of Red's head and held it there for a moment. "Come on, let's go get some pizza," he said.

Stevie followed Kelleher down the cobblestoned walkway and into the most delicious-smelling building he had ever been in. There were places to get lobster and shrimp, crab cakes and chowder, hamburgers and hot dogs, Chinese food, ice cream, apple pie, fried dough, Italian sausages—just about any food Stevie could think of or imagine. Kelleher stopped in front of a place that said Pizzeria Regina. It didn't look like anything special to Stevie, but he had learned to trust Kelleher on the subject of food.

"Couple slices?" Kelleher asked. "Or should we just split a pie?"

"I think a couple of slices will be plenty for me," Stevie said.

"We'll see about that," Kelleher said.

He ordered four slices and a couple of Cokes. Balancing the pizza on paper plates, drinks in their other hands, they continued down the hallway.

"There's tables and chairs in the middle of the building," Kelleher said. "If we're lucky, we'll find a place to sit."

The dining area had a vaulted ceiling and was gigantic, with tables and chairs in the middle, and tall tables around the edges where people could stand and eat.

"Over there to the right," Kelleher said, pointing. They began walking in that direction. Stevie was a step behind Kelleher when, out of the corner of his eye, he saw a familiar figure seated at a small table.

It was Susan Carol. He'd know that ponytail anywhere.

And sitting across from her was David Doyle. He was leaning forward in his chair and appeared to be talking with great feeling. Stevie stopped dead in his tracks, staring. Fortunately, David Doyle was so intent on his conversation with Susan Carol that he didn't see Stevie. Stevie was pretty convinced that he could burst into flames and

David wouldn't notice because his eyes were so completely locked in on Susan Carol.

Kelleher had apparently reached the table, put his food down, and then noticed that Stevie wasn't behind him. He walked back to where Stevie was standing.

"Stevie," he said. "What's up? Something wrong?"

Unable to find his voice, Stevie simply gestured with his Coke hand in the direction of the table where Susan Carol and David were sitting.

Kelleher looked. "Oh, it's Susan Carol," he said. "Who's that she's with?"

"David Doyle," Stevie said through clenched teeth.

For a split second Kelleher didn't respond. Then, apparently, he got it. "Okay," he said calmly. "Come with me and let's sit down before he notices you shooting daggers at him."

Stevie went. He wanted to do two things: find out what the hell was going on at that table and eat his pizza. For the moment, he would have to settle for the pizza.

Stevie sat so he could see Susan Carol and managed to eat his pizza without ever taking his eyes off the two of them. They were both leaning forward as they talked, and although Stevie couldn't be sure, he was convinced they were holding hands.

"Let's not overreact here," Kelleher counseled. "There may be a perfectly simple explanation."

"Really?" Stevie said. "They just met this morning and

last saw each other all of two hours ago. What could possibly have happened to get them together here now, looking as if someone's life was at stake."

Kelleher semi-laughed. "Given your history, isn't it at least a possibility that someone's life *is* at stake?" he said.

Stevie had to concede Kelleher had a point. But he didn't think it was likely. He had seen the way the two of them had looked at one another back at the Ritz.

"I'm going over there," he said, starting to stand up.

"Oh, no you're not," Kelleher said, pulling him back down. "You're going to sit here and eat your pizza and wait until later to see if Susan Carol tells you what happened on her own. If she doesn't, then—and *only* then—do you consider asking her about it."

"But look at her!" Stevie said, exasperated.

Kelleher glanced over his shoulder. Stevie might have told him not to look, except that there was no way either one of them was going to notice.

"I will grant you," Kelleher said, "that it doesn't look great. But you have to admit that there have been many times when things were not what they appeared to be."

"Yeah, but . . . look at how he's looking at her."

Kelleher smiled. "I know how you feel," he said. "But you don't know how *she's* looking at him. Or why. So you've got to be patient."

He pointed at Stevie's empty plate. Stevie had completely devoured the two slices of pizza without even noticing.

"You want more?" Kelleher said.

"Absolutely," Stevie said, starved, hurt, and angry all at once.

"Come on," Kelleher said. "We'll get some more and then go eat outside."

Stevie started to argue, then stopped. This wasn't the time for a confrontation. And as much as he wanted to know what was going on, he was fairly convinced that he wouldn't like the answer.

7: UNANSWERED QUESTIONS

KELLEHER WAS SMART ENOUGH not to try to engage Stevie in further conversation. They walked outside with their fresh pizza slices, while happy throngs of Bostonians enjoyed the brisk October sunshine all around them.

"Just try not to jump to any conclusions until Susan Carol has a chance to explain what was going on," Kelleher said as they rode the escalator back up to the hotel lobby. "I know that's hard, but there's no sense making yourself crazy over something that may turn out to be nothing."

Stevie nodded. "I know you're right," he said. "But I've already jumped to about a million conclusions—none of them very appealing—and it's pretty hard to unjump."

Kelleher put his arm around Stevie. "Let's just wait and see what we see," he said.

Stevie went back to his room and turned on the TV. He sat watching some talking heads analyzing game one for the fiftieth time and then noticed a crawl on the bottom of the screen that said, "A published report claims that Norbert Doyle will start game two of the World Series tonight in place of Ross Detwiler. ESPN's Peter Gammons reports that Nationals manager Manny Acta is refusing comment."

Stevie couldn't help but laugh. ESPN couldn't confirm the story, so they had found a way to report it and make it sound shaky all at once.

His phone rang.

"You watching ESPN?" It was Kelleher.

"Yeah."

"Typical of them. I love it."

He hung up. Stevie tried to focus on what was being said on the screen but couldn't. His mind kept flashing back to Faneuil Hall and the sight of David Doyle and Susan Carol talking. There *had* to be an explanation, right? But what in the world could it be? Several times he reached for the phone to call her but stopped himself. He would play it Kelleher's way and see if she mentioned it without his asking.

The droning voices made him drowsy. He figured he would rest his eyes for five minutes. The next thing he knew, the phone was ringing. He looked at the clock and saw it was 3:30. Uh-oh, he was late.

"Stevie, where are you?" a voice said when he picked up. It was Susan Carol.

For a moment he forgot everything. "Sorry," he said. "Fell asleep. Give me a couple minutes."

"Hurry. Bobby and Tamara are here, and they're ready to go."

Stevie splashed some water on his face to wake up. Then he grabbed his jacket and his computer bag and raced to the door. He was in the jam-packed lobby five minutes after Susan Carol's call.

"Catching up on your beauty rest?" Susan Carol said, giving him the Smile when he walked up to them.

"I guess I don't have the energy some people have," Stevie said, causing Kelleher to give him a look.

Stevie saw Tim McCarver, the longtime Fox TV analyst, crossing the lobby and heading in their direction. Stevie liked McCarver's work, and he had a soft spot for him, since he had finished his playing career with the Phillies.

Every time he saw him, Stevie was reminded of a story his dad had told him. Near the end of McCarver's playing days, his main job had been to catch Steve Carlton, the temperamental Hall of Fame pitcher. Carlton was so adamant about McCarver catching him that McCarver once said, "I think when Steve and I die, we're going to be buried sixty feet, six inches apart"—that being the distance between the mound and home plate.

McCarver shook hands with Kelleher and Tamara and said, "Don't think me rude, but I'm actually hoping you'll introduce me to young Mr. Thomas here."

Kelleher laughed. "Gee, I wonder why you want to talk to him, Tim. Steve Thomas, this is Tim McCarver."

McCarver shook hands with Stevie, then introduced himself to Susan Carol, impressing Stevie when he said, "I'm Tim McCarver, nice to meet you." Stevie had noticed that a lot of celebrities either didn't even speak to people they didn't "need" at that moment or blew through any introduction that was made.

McCarver turned to Stevie. "Bobby's right, of course. I need your help," he said. "We like to tape our opening when we get to the ballpark. We've been trying to get the Nationals to confirm your story about Doyle pitching, but they're playing it very close to the vest. Can you just give me an idea of how well-sourced you are on this?"

Stevie looked to Kelleher. He didn't think there was any reason not to tell McCarver why the story was fail-safe, but he wasn't certain.

"Put it this way, Tim," Kelleher said. "He didn't get the story secondhand."

McCarver smiled. "Excellent. That's all I need." He put his hand out to Stevie again. "Congratulations on breaking the story."

A voice behind them said, "Tim, the car's downstairs."

Stevie saw Ken Rosenthal, Fox's sideline reporter, standing behind McCarver.

When Kelleher saw Rosenthal, he grinned and said, "Hey, Kenny, we never see you anymore now that you've gone TV."

Rosenthal was short and had brown hair and a quick

smile. Stevie always liked watching him on TV because he clearly knew what he was talking about but never pontificated.

"Yeah, I've come a long way, Bobby," Rosenthal said, laughing. "I used to be your caddy, now I'm McCarver's caddy. But I *do* get better seats now."

"Too true, Junior," Kelleher said.

McCarver thanked Stevie again, and he and Rosenthal waved goodbye as they headed for the escalator.

"Please tell me you think they're good guys," Susan Carol said. "I really do like their telecasts."

"They're good guys," Kelleher said. "Junior still thinks like a reporter and is *not* in love with himself."

"Junior?" Stevie and Susan Carol said together.

Kelleher and Mearns both laughed. "Believe it or not," Mearns said, "when Kenny was a young reporter with the *Baltimore Sun,* Jose Canseco thought he looked like Cal Ripken, so he started calling him by Cal's nickname."

"There are probably only about five of us who still remember that," Kelleher added. "Come on, let's go."

They took a cab to the ballpark, and since they already had their credentials, they were inside and on the field just as the Red Sox started batting practice. Since the managers' pregame press conferences didn't begin until 5:30, everyone stood around in groups chatting while David Ortiz, Jason Bay, and J.D. Drew crushed long home runs into the seats and over the Green Monster. Stevie had half expected people to come up and ask him about the story, but no one did.

"The lineup is posted in the dugout," Mearns reported. "Doyle's the starting pitcher. I guess ESPN can confirm the story now."

"I wonder if they can call the lineup card a source?" Stevie asked.

Mearns went off to do an interview with one of the local Boston TV stations. Kelleher was called away by a couple of writers Stevie didn't recognize. That left him standing alone with Susan Carol a few feet from the Nationals dugout.

"So what'd you do this afternoon?" Stevie asked, trying to sound casual. "Bobby and I tried to call you for lunch, but you didn't answer."

"Oh, I just went for a walk," she said. "I didn't swim this morning, so I wanted to get some exercise."

"What happened to your cell?"

She forced a smile. "Left it in the room. I decided I could live without it for an hour. Where did you guys go to eat?"

Stevie paused for a second. He really hadn't thought out what to say if Susan Carol didn't volunteer the fact that she had been with David Doyle.

He decided to tread softly and see where that led. "Faneuil Hall," he said. "A place called Regina's. Really good pizza."

She looked at him as if trying to learn something from the look on his face. At least, that's what Stevie thought she was doing. "Nice," she said.

Stevie waited for her to say something else, but she didn't. It was as if they were playing a game of chess, each trying to anticipate what the other's next move might be.

"So where did you walk?" he said after another long silence.

"Oh, all over," she said. "I walked through Faneuil Hall, actually. Isn't it cool? Then I went over to City Hall, which is right across the street, and walked through the North End for a while to see some of the sights."

"Sights?"

"Come on, Stevie, this is Boston. Our hotel is really close to Paul Revere's house and the Old North Church, just for starters. Then there's the Freedom Trail, which you can follow and see all these historic places."

Stevie liked the fact that she was talking to him in her "Stevie, you're an idiot" tone. That felt normal at least.

"'One if by land, and two if by sea'? 'The British are coming'? That Paul Revere?"

"No, the other one," she said, and laughed, making Stevie forget for a moment that she wasn't telling him the whole truth about her afternoon. She might very well have spent the afternoon exploring the Freedom Trail. But she was leaving out a crucial part of the story.

He decided to quit the chess game and just be honest. He took a deep breath and said, "So, did David Doyle join you on the Freedom Trail?"

As soon as the words came out of his mouth, Stevie

wished he could reach into the air and grab them back. Susan Carol looked stunned—and angry.

"Excuse me?" she said, her tone having gone from teasing to biting in an instant.

"Nothing," he said.

"No, it's not nothing," she said.

She was staring at him, waiting for an answer. Stevie felt stuck. If he told her what he had seen, she might blow up at him completely—which hardly seemed fair, since he wasn't the one who had been withholding information. But she was already angry anyway, and if he didn't plow ahead, he certainly wasn't going to get any answers.

"I'm sorry if you're upset," he said, trying to choose his words carefully. "But I saw you . . . with him . . . in Faneuil Hall, and—"

"Were you spying on me?" she said, raising her voice, so that several people standing near them turned their heads.

"*No!*" he said, whispering and shouting at once, wanting to be emphatic without drawing any more attention to the argument. "I told you, Bobby and I went over there for lunch. We were looking for a place to sit—"

"And you saw me talking to David," she said. "So now you've gone and drawn about twenty different conclusions—all of them wrong."

"You're probably right," he said, hoping against hope that she was about to give him a logical explanation that had never crossed his mind. "I'll admit I was baffled when I saw you—"

"So why didn't you just come over?" she said, cutting him off.

She had a point. That might have resolved things quickly. But the shock of seeing them there, along with the intense way they were talking, had thrown him.

"I don't know," he said. "It just looked, you know, from a distance, like you were talking about something really serious. I guess I thought you didn't want to be interrupted."

She didn't say anything for a moment, so Stevie pressed back. "Why didn't you mention that you'd seen him?"

She shook her head. "It's complicated."

"So, explain," he said. "I've got time."

"I can't," she said.

"What do you mean you can't?" he said, getting angry again. "You say I'm reaching the wrong conclusions, but you can't explain the right ones?"

"That's right," she said. "I can't. I promised."

"*Promised?*" He was screaming now, drawing more looks. He dropped his voice. "Promised? You made a promise to someone you just met to keep some kind of secret from *me*? What is that about?"

She shook her head. "I'm sorry, Stevie," she said. "I just can't tell you. I'll tell you this much: there will come a time when you'll understand. But please, don't ask me about it again."

She turned and walked away. Stevie watched her walk

behind the batting cage in the direction of the Red Sox dugout. At that moment all he wanted to do was go home. He didn't even care what Susan Carol's secret was.

All he knew was that she and David Doyle had a secret and that he felt sick to his stomach. And it had nothing to do with the four slices of Regina's pizza he had eaten that afternoon.

8: SUDDEN STAR

STEVIE WASN'T SURE HOW LONG he spent staring at the players in the batting cage without actually seeing them before someone put a hand on his shoulder. He turned to see Peter Gammons standing there.

"Steve, I'm Peter Gammons, have you got a minute?" he said.

"Sure," Stevie said, wondering why in the world Gammons would want to talk to him. No one needed to confirm the Doyle story anymore, so what could he possibly want?

"I was just talking to Bobby," he said. "He was teasing me about the crawl this afternoon, saying I couldn't confirm your story. I just wanted you to know I feel badly about the way it was worded and the fact that my network didn't even give the *Herald* credit for the story."

Stevie was surprised. He had always been a fan of Gammons's, but Kelleher had convinced him that just about everyone in TV was evil. Gammons was a print guy who had become a TV guy. Maybe that was different?

"Don't worry, Mr. Gammons—"

"Peter," Gammons interrupted.

"Peter," Stevie continued. "I never thought you wrote the crawl."

"I didn't, but I still feel badly." He put out his hand. "No hard feelings, I hope."

"Of course not," Stevie said. "I know how these things work."

Gammons clapped him on the back. "You know a lot of things, apparently," he said. He walked in the direction of the batting cage, where Terry Francona, the Red Sox manager, was standing, calling his name. Being Peter Gammons, Stevie decided, was a pretty cool thing.

Alone again, he tried to act as if he was intently watching Dustin Pedroia, who had stepped into the cage. But his mind was still on his conversation with Susan Carol. What secret could David Doyle have told her that she couldn't share with him? Why had David told *her*? Actually, that wasn't too hard to guess. If Stevie were a fourteen-year-old boy with a secret to share, he'd certainly want to share it with Susan Carol. Well, he *was* a fourteen-year-old boy. He just didn't have a secret.

Mearns walked back over to him, her TV interview concluded. "You look like you just got terrible news," she said. "Are you okay?"

"Fine," he said. "No bad news. I'm just a little bit tired."

The truth was he had *no* news at all. And in this case, no news felt like bad news.

The night was about as perfect as one could hope for in late October in Boston. Even though the game didn't start until 8:35, it was still sixty-two degrees when Daisuke Matsuzaka threw the first pitch. As he had done during game one, Stevie sat in the auxiliary press box, which was located way out in right field, with Susan Carol on his left and George Solomon, the Sunday columnist emeritus for the *Washington Post*, on his right.

Solomon was short and had thick glasses. Tamara had explained to Stevie that he had been the *Post*'s sports editor for twenty-eight years and had retired to write a Sunday column. Now he had been brought back from complete retirement for the World Series. He had been friendly on the first night but kept making football references throughout the game.

"Fourth and ten for the Nats," he had said when the Red Sox opened up their early lead. He had suggested late in the game that the Nats "drop back ten and punt" and, when the Nats put a couple of men on base in the eighth inning, had commented that they were "trying to score a consolation touchdown."

"I guess you're more of a football guy," Stevie had said after the last football reference.

"Love baseball," Solomon said. Even so, he had spent

chunks of the game asking Barry Svrluga, another *Post* reporter who normally covered the Redskins, what he thought about that Sunday's game in Green Bay.

"Congratulations," Solomon said as Stevie sat down for the start of game two. "Good story on Doyle this afternoon. There was some good spadework there."

Stevie had now been around reporters enough to know that *spadework* was a term that meant someone had done a lot of digging to get a story. The truth was the story had landed in his lap while he was eating breakfast. But he just said, "Thanks. Sometimes you get lucky."

"Based on past history," Solomon said, "you and the young lady are more than lucky."

Susan Carol was, at that moment, engaged in conversation with Mark Maske, another *Post* football writer who had been assigned to the World Series. Mearns had mentioned earlier that the *Post* had a total of twenty-two people in Boston—fifteen sportswriters, two editors, three photographers, a writer from the Style section, and a writer from the Metro section who was assigned to write one of those awful stories on fans. The *Herald* "only" had sixteen people in town—including its own Metro reporter, who was doing what Stevie assumed would be an equally awful story on fans.

He was extremely grateful that he didn't have to wander the streets or the ballpark looking for people who had painted their faces Nats red and blue. Look at the glass as half full, he told himself, even though it felt quite empty at that moment.

The Nats managed to score a run in the top of the first off Matsuzaka when leadoff hitter Austin Kearns singled, took second on a wild pitch, moved to third on a ground-out, and then scored on another groundout by Ryan Zimmerman.

"Guess the Red Sox figure they're going to score off Doyle, so they can play the infield back," Stevie said to Susan Carol, figuring he'd be safe keeping the conversation on baseball.

"You never play the infield in this early in the game, no matter who's pitching," she snapped. "You should know that."

So much, Stevie thought, for casual baseball talk.

Doyle trotted to the mound to some applause—Stevie guessed it was from the Nats fans scattered throughout the crowd—and a low murmur. Most of the Red Sox fans had apparently not been paying attention when the line-ups were announced, and when they saw an unfamiliar number—56—trot to the mound, they wondered who in the world it was.

Doyle was clearly nervous at the start. He walked Kevin Youkilis on four pitches to start the game and then hit Dustin Pedroia with a pitch. Whatever Stevie's thoughts were on David Doyle and Susan Carol, he didn't want to see Norbert Doyle humiliated in front of millions of people. As David Ortiz stepped into the batter's box and Jason Bay stood on deck, Stevie did a little math: two men on, no one out, postseason baseball's best clutch hitter up, with another one-hundred-plus RBI man to follow. Stevie wondered if Doyle would survive the first inning.

Everyone in the ballpark was on their feet as Ortiz stared in at Doyle. He was now thirty-four, and starting to slow a little bit: he had "only" hit twenty-nine home runs during the regular season. In postseason—Big Papi time, as it was called in Boston—he already had five home runs and fifteen RBIs.

"This could get ugly in a hurry," Stevie said.

Susan Carol said nothing. Stevie was having about as good a night so far as Norbert Doyle.

Doyle threw three straight pitches that were way out of the strike zone. They almost reminded Stevie of the scene in *Major League* when Charlie Sheen's character, Wild Thing, comes into his first game and immediately throws a pitch that goes straight to the backstop, causing Bob Uecker, playing the radio announcer, to say, "*Just* a bit outside."

These pitches were nearly as far outside.

Ortiz dug in, knowing that Doyle had to try to throw a strike rather than face loading the bases for Bay.

"I'll bet he's got the hit sign," George Solomon said. "Might as well go for the long pass right here."

Stevie figured that was a lock. On 3-0, Doyle was likely to groove a fastball, and Ortiz might hit it nine miles.

Sure enough, Ortiz was swinging on 3-0. Doyle's fastball looked right down the middle to Stevie, but instead of hitting it nine miles, Ortiz hit a wicked grounder right down the third-base line. For a moment Stevie thought it was going into the corner for a double. But Zimmerman, who hadn't overshifted because of the runner on second, somehow stabbed it on his backhand side and in one motion stepped on third base and flicked a throw to second. Ronnie Belliard, the Nats' second baseman, grabbed the throw and then turned and fired to first. The stunned—not to mention painfully slow—Ortiz was still two steps from the bag when the throw hit the first baseman's glove.

For a second Stevie didn't even realize what had happened. Then, all at once, he noticed how quiet the ballpark had suddenly become, and he heard Susan Carol's voice very clearly saying, "A triple play, oh my God, a triple play!"

It was, in fact, the rarest play in baseball—three outs on one play. This one had been amazingly simple because Ortiz had hit the ball so hard. It got to Zimmerman so quickly it was actually an easy around-the-horn play from third to second to first.

Stevie had never seen a triple play in his life. The Nationals high-fived one another as they jogged off the field. Doyle just put his head down and walked off as if it had been routine.

"Unless my memory fails me, that's the first triple play in the World Series since Bill Wambsganss," George Solomon said. "Of course, I'm more a football guy than a baseball guy."

"No, you've got it right," Svrluga said. "It was 1920. Unassisted."

"Unassisted?" Stevie said. "You mean he got all three outs by himself? How's that possible?"

"Easy," Svrluga said. "He was playing second base. Men on first and second, no one out—just like this play. Except he caught a line drive hit right at him. He ran over, touched second base to force out the runner who'd been on second. The runner at first hadn't realized he'd caught the ball and ran right into his tag. It was almost easy, it happened so fast."

"How do you know?" asked Maske.

"Saw the replay on *SportsCenter*," Svrluga answered with a straight face.

"Pretty good break for your new friend's dad," Stevie whispered to Susan Carol while the discussion of Wambsganss and triple plays continued.

"Stop it, Stevie," she said quietly. "Don't be a jerk."

"*I'm* a jerk?" he said, looking around to make sure no one was paying attention. "I'm not the one who sneaked off today, lied about it, and is now acting as if she's protecting national security with some big secret."

"Stop it," she said. "Stop saying things you'll be sorry you said later."

Stevie started to say something else but realized she might be right.

"Fine," he said. "But it better be damn good, whatever it is."

"Don't threaten me, Stevie," she said. "You're not my father."

"I know that," Stevie said. "I thought I was your boyfriend."

"You are," she said. "For now."

A chill went through Stevie. She wasn't smiling when she said it. She was staring down at the field, where Adam Dunn was stepping to the plate to lead off the second inning for the Nats.

Stevie was at a loss for a response. She was threatening *him* now, and—as with everything else—she was very good at it.

Both pitchers settled down after the first inning, and the game became an old-fashioned pitcher's duel. Matsuzaka was good, allowing only three hits over seven innings. Remarkably, Doyle was better. He walked Jason Bay leading off the second and through seven innings had walked five batters in all, in addition to the hit batsman in the first.

But he hadn't given up a hit. The Red Sox appeared baffled by his pitches, best described by Svrluga: "Slow, slower, slowest."

He didn't throw a fastball that was clocked at more than 82 mph. Every ballpark now had a radar gun behind home plate and a place on the scoreboard that showed the speed of each pitch. Matsuzaka was hitting 95 mph regularly, even occasionally getting to 96. Doyle was usually in the high seventies and low eighties, except when he threw his breaking pitches, which sometimes didn't even crack 70.

"Reminds me of Tom Glavine and Jamie Moyer,"

Maske said at one point, talking about two superb left-handers known for keeping batters off balance even though they couldn't throw very hard.

"Except that they've won about five hundred fifty-five more games than he has," Svrluga said.

"When was the last no-hitter in a World Series?" Stevie asked.

For the first time in six innings Susan Carol said something to him. "There's only been one," she said. "Don Larsen's perfect game in 1956."

Stevie remembered reading about when Larsen had pitched for the Yankees. He hadn't been a star, but he'd had one great day. Doyle's story was even more amazing. Not only was he pitching in his first postseason game ever, he had never won a game in the major leagues.

"Here's the question," Svrluga said. "The guy has thrown a hundred twelve pitches. Normally, you'd go to the bullpen here."

"You'd take him out when he's pitching a no-hitter?" Stevie said, almost gasping at the thought.

"The manager's job is to win the game," Svrluga said. "This is the World Series, not some game in mid-July. If it was five–nothing, it might be different, but at one–nothing I think he has to take him out."

"With a no-hitter?" Stevie repeated, still stunned at the thought that a pitcher who hadn't given up a hit might come out of a game.

"Yup," Svrluga said. "With a no-hitter."

Stevie couldn't believe it. Hideki Okajima came on in

relief of Matsuzaka in the top of the eighth and retired the Nats in order. During the inning Stevie noticed two pitchers warming up in the Washington bullpen. But when the inning was over, Doyle popped out of the dugout and jogged to the mound. The small cadre of Nationals fans cheered when they saw him come back out. Apparently, they felt like Stevie: you don't pull a pitcher who has a no-hitter going, even if it is the World Series.

The stadium was buzzing with anticipation as Doyle threw his eight warm-up pitches. Under normal circumstances, Stevie and Susan Carol would have been trading comments and questions about what they were about to see. Stevie looked at Susan Carol. She was staring down at her scorecard as if it contained all of life's secrets.

Pedroia led off in the bottom of the eighth for the Red Sox. He took the first two pitches, one for a ball, the other a strike. "They're trying to work the count on him," Susan Carol said to no one and everyone. "They want to tire him out."

"He's already tired," Maske said.

Pedroia didn't take the next pitch. He hit a fly ball to right-center field, by far the deepest part of the ballpark. Elijah Dukes ranged almost to the warning track to make the catch.

"He hits that anyplace else and it's out," Solomon said. "This guy needs to take a knee and run out the clock."

"That's the beauty of baseball," Svrluga said, rolling his eyes at another football reference. "There's no clock."

David Ortiz walked to the plate. Stevie now understood

why Acta might think about going to the bullpen. He didn't think Doyle had much chance of getting Ortiz and Bay out one more time.

The Red Sox fans were on their feet as Ortiz stepped in. It was pretty clear they had no interest in seeing a no-hitter. "Don't fans sometimes get behind a pitcher on the other team going for a no-hitter?" Stevie asked.

"Not in the World Series," Svrluga said.

Doyle's first two pitches were nowhere near the plate. He had now thrown 117 pitches. Most starting pitchers came out after about 100 pitches, and the absolute maximum was usually 120. Stevie had checked the Nats' post-season media guide and found that the most pitches Doyle had thrown in his three starts in September was 87.

On 2-0, Doyle tried to trick Ortiz, who was no doubt expecting a fastball, with a curve. But the pitch never broke down and away, as it should have. Instead it stayed up and went right at Ortiz. At the last second Ortiz realized the breaking pitch had no break, and he tried to duck out of the way. But the ball somehow hit his bat and trickled straight back to the mound. Ortiz was still lying on his back when Doyle picked the ball up and threw it to first.

"Oh my God," Solomon said. "Talk about a Hail Mary!"

"Talk about dumb luck," Svrluga said. "That may be it for Doyle."

Acta was walking to the mound. Even though Doyle

had gotten two outs in the inning, it was clear he was exhausted. The breaking ball that didn't break had to be the last straw.

The entire Nats infield surrounded the mound while Acta talked to Doyle. "No signal to the bullpen yet," Susan Carol said.

"Good point," Maske said. "I would have thought he'd be waving someone in when he left the dugout."

And then Acta patted Doyle on the shoulder and trotted back to the dugout.

"Oh ma God," Susan Carol said, lapsing into a Southern drawl. "He's stayin' in."

"Acta's either going down as the gutsiest manager in series history or the dumbest," Svrluga said. "There is no way this guy can get four more outs."

Bay dug in to the batter's box. He had joined the team in 2008 to replace Manny Ramirez, the enigmatic slugger who had thrilled and mystified Boston fans—not to mention teammates—with his bat and his antics for almost eight years. It was a hard act to follow, but Bay had become an instant fan favorite and had played well from the first day he arrived in Boston.

Doyle threw a fastball that was outside. Then he threw three more just like it.

"That was an intentional walk," Svrluga said. "No way was he giving him any kind of pitch to hit."

Mike Lowell, the third baseman, was up next. He had been the MVP of the World Series in '07. Doyle's first pitch was an 80-mph fastball right down the middle. Lowell never moved.

"He surprised him by throwing a strike," Maske commented.

The next pitch was also a strike, and Lowell hit a bullet toward the left-field wall—the Green Monster. It was hit so hard it looked like it might go *through* the wall. But it never rose above shoulder level. Dunn, the Nats' left fielder, had been playing almost on the warning track, so he took one step to his left and put up his glove, and the ball slammed into it. The groan from the fans was audible.

"That may have been the luckiest inning I've ever seen a pitcher have," Stevie said.

"You need luck to pitch a no-hitter," Susan Carol answered.

"He's going to need a miracle to get three more outs," Maske said.

No one argued. Terry Francona brought his closer, Jonathan Papelbon, in to pitch the ninth—he wanted to be sure the margin stayed at 1–0 so they'd have a final shot at winning in the bottom of the inning.

Papelbon rolled through the Nationals, throwing only nine pitches to set them down one-two-three.

Acta was really letting Doyle try to finish the no-hitter. Doyle walked slowly to the mound for the bottom of the ninth. Stevie noticed his warm-up pitches weren't much more than lobs to the plate. He was clearly saving his strength. He had now thrown 124 pitches. The temperature had dropped since game time, and Stevie felt chilled as he watched Jason Varitek, the Red Sox's catcher, walk to the plate.

Doyle rocked and threw his first pitch to Varitek. It was, Stevie noticed on the scoreboard a moment later, a 79-mph fastball. Varitek jumped on it, and it was clear the moment it left the bat that Doyle's luck had finally run out. The ball screamed toward the gap in right-center field. As soon as it landed between Dukes and right fielder Austin Kearns, the crowd roared. By the time Dukes ran the ball down and got it back to the infield, Varitek was standing on third and Stevie could feel the park literally rocking underneath his feet.

"He threw into coverage once too often," Solomon said.

Acta was walking slowly to the mound. The no-hitter now gone, he instantly waved to the bullpen for his closer, Joel Hanrahan.

"Probably too late," Svrluga said as Hanrahan began to jog in. "Best-case scenario, they hold them to one run here and get the game to extra innings."

Doyle had opted to wait on the mound until Hanrahan arrived, instead of leaving right away the way most pitchers did when coming out of a game. When Hanrahan walked onto the mound, he handed him the ball, said something, and began walking off the mound. As he did, the entire stadium stood and cheered.

"At least the Red Sox fans appreciate the effort," Susan Carol said.

"Now they do," Stevie said, feeling very sad for Doyle

and the Nats. "Now it's okay because they're about to tie the game."

Doyle received handshakes and hugs all around in the Nationals dugout. Hanrahan finished his warm-up pitches and looked in at J.D. Drew, the Red Sox right fielder.

Drew had power, although it was more the line-drive-double type of power than home-run power. The Nationals moved the infield in, positioning all four of them on the grass so that they could throw home to try to get Varitek out on a ground ball and keep the Red Sox from tying the game.

"No pinch runner for Varitek?" Susan Carol asked. "Wouldn't they want more speed at third base?"

"They're thinking if they tie it, they don't want their starting catcher on the bench in extra innings," Svrluga said.

"Team that wins the toss usually wins in overtime," Solomon said, causing everyone to look at him as if he were from Mars.

Hanrahan looked in for a sign and threw a strike, Drew taking all the way. The next pitch produced a ground ball right at third baseman Ryan Zimmerman. He scooped it on a short hop, glared at Varitek for a second, as if daring him to leave third base, then threw across the diamond to get Drew out at first by a step.

"Still alive," Susan Carol said softly.

Stevie realized that he was also relieved to see the lead still intact. He had been so caught up throughout the game thinking about what was going on with Susan Carol that he had almost lost track of the fact that he might be witnessing history. Now, with the no-hitter gone, he wanted very much to see Doyle at least get the win and to see the Nationals even the series at one game apiece.

Red Sox manager Terry Francona had decided to go to his bench, bringing up Julio Lugo to pinch-hit for short-stop Nick Green.

The whole stadium was standing now, wanting Lugo to at least get the tying run in with less than two outs. Hanrahan, knowing that Lugo had home-run power, worked carefully, falling behind 2-1 before Lugo fouled a pitch off with a vicious swing.

"He just missed hitting that pitch a long way," Maske said.

Hanrahan was like most relief pitchers in that he never used a windup, just pitching out of the stretch because he often came in with runners on base. Now he stretched and threw again.

Lugo reached out for the pitch and hit a fly ball to right field. It wasn't deep, but it wasn't shallow. Austin Kearns took a step back and then came in to make the catch, clearly trying to get himself in position to make a throw to home plate. Varitek tagged up, Kearns made the catch, and Varitek took off for home.

"This is going to be close," Stevie heard Susan Carol say, even over the din of the crowd.

Kearns's throw was strong but just a little bit off-line on

the first-base side of the plate. Varitek started to slide as the ball was arriving, and Nationals catcher Wil Nieves grabbed the ball out of the air and dove back in, trying to get the ball on Varitek before Varitek got to the plate.

Varitek, Nieves, and the ball—in Nieves's glove—appeared to arrive all at the same moment. Nieves landed almost on top of Varitek's legs, applying a tag as Varitek slid into home. Plate umpire John Hirschbeck stared at the two men for a moment, then pointed at Nieves's glove, which he was holding in the air to show that he still had the ball. Hirschbeck's arm came up in the air, and Stevie thought he heard him say, "You're out!" even though he couldn't possibly have heard him from so far away in the cauldron of noise. Nevertheless, the arm raised in the air was enough. It was a double play. Varitek was out. The game was over. Somehow the Nationals had won, 1–0.

As soon as Hirschbeck gave the out call, Susan Carol jumped from her seat, yelling, "They did it, they did it!"

Stevie had also jumped from his seat and, instinctively, he turned to hug Susan Carol. She did the same thing. Then, almost in midhug, they both stopped, awkwardly pushing back from one another.

The reaction of the other writers around them was considerably more subdued: they were clearly surprised by the sudden ending but not emotional. Stevie had covered enough sporting events to know that journalists taught themselves to try not to show emotion even if they felt it.

Seeing that she and Stevie were the only ones who

appeared excited, Susan Carol calmed down quickly. "That *was* an amazing game," she said, as if defending herself.

"Yes, it was," Stevie said, trying to sound cool and restrained—even though he didn't feel the least bit cool.

Then they gathered up their notebooks and followed everyone else in the direction of the clubhouses.

9: SILENT TREATMENT

IT TOOK SEVERAL MINUTES to make their way through the crowds to the locker room area, which, unlike in the newer ballparks, was not on a separate level where there was no public access. The media had to stand against a wall so that fans could pass by on their way out of the ballpark.

As planned, Stevie went first to the interview room to meet Bobby Kelleher and the other *Herald* staffers at the game. They would discuss their postgame plans—who would write which stories. There wasn't much doubt what the story of the game was: Norbert Doyle.

Kelleher, who had taken the elevator from the main press box along with Nationals beat writer Doug Doughty, was waiting in the back of the room when Stevie walked in. Susan Carol had gone to wait outside the Nationals clubhouse, having already talked to Tamara Mearns by cell phone.

"Nice of Doyle to turn what was a decent news story into a made-for-TV movie, wasn't it?" Kelleher said when he spotted Stevie.

"What happens with my story now?" Stevie asked, then realized he was being selfish thinking about that first.

"Good question, actually," Kelleher said. "I already talked to the desk. They're going to insert a couple of paragraphs up high about how Doyle pitched tonight, but leave most of the game description for the game story and my column." He smiled. "There is one other change."

"What's that?"

"The story was inside the Sports section for the early edition. Next edition it's on the front page."

"Of the Sports section, right?"

"Of the newspaper," Kelleher said. "You did it again, kid."

Stevie felt good about that, although he knew he'd backed into the A1 story. Still, like Doyle in the eighth inning, he didn't mind catching a break or two.

"So what's my sidebar now?" he said, hearing a microphone being tested in the background. Deadline was closing in.

"Wil Nieves," Kelleher said. "He's a good story in himself—journeyman catcher, up and down from the minors his whole life. He was Mike Mussina's personal catcher for a while in '07. Doyle pitches kind of like Mussina—changes speeds, good control, doesn't throw hard. Plus, Wil's a good guy. You may have to wait him out a little bit, though, because a lot of people are going to want to talk to him about the last play at the plate."

"And you'll do Doyle?"

Kelleher grunted. "Everybody will be doing Doyle," he said. "He'll come in here first, which will be okay. It will be a mob scene when he goes back to that tiny clubhouse and all the columnists want to talk to him some more."

"Columnists like you?"

"Yup. This guy is now officially *the* story of this World Series—maybe even if he never throws another pitch."

"He'll pitch again after tonight, won't he?"

"Oh, he'll pitch game six or game seven," Kelleher said. "But there's no guarantee there will be a game six or a game seven. Who knows? Maybe the Nats will win in five."

Now *that*, Stevie thought, would be a storybook ending.

Assignment in hand, Stevie made his way back down the hallway in the direction of the Nationals clubhouse. He couldn't help but notice how quiet the walkway under the third-base stands was—especially when compared with the night before, when the Red Sox fans had been celebrating winning game one.

He wasn't the only one who noticed. "The silence is deafening, isn't it?" said Jeff Arnold, another writer for the *Herald*. His assignment was to talk to Austin Kearns about his throw on the last play.

"I guess they're surprised," Stevie said as they fell into the back of the media line waiting to get into the clubhouse.

"Not surprised, stunned," Arnold said. "It's funny how things change. Once, Red Sox fans expected disaster in October. But they've gotten used to winning now. This is the first time they've lost a World Series game since 1986."

Stevie hadn't thought about it that way. The Red Sox had swept the World Series in both 2004 and 2007 and had won the opener in this one. There had been years when they weren't in the Series, but lately, when they got there, they were unbeatable.

The line was barely moving in the direction of the door. "Why is it so slow?" Stevie said. "It only took a few minutes to get into the Sox clubhouse last night."

"The security guy on the visiting clubhouse here is a real pain in the neck," Arnold said. "He looks at every pass as if it *must* be fake, does everything but ask your blood type. I guarantee he'll give *you* a hard time."

Stevie shrugged. Security guards never seemed to believe someone his age could actually be accredited to cover events like the Final Four and the U.S. Open tennis tournament. He steeled himself as he followed Arnold to the clubhouse door, which was blocked by a burly man who was—as Arnold had predicted—checking every pass as if the secret to happiness were written there in code.

Arnold survived inspection and stopped just inside the door. "What are you waiting for?" the guard snarled, looking over his shoulder while Stevie waited for his inspection.

"The young man there and I are partners," Arnold said. "I'm waiting on him."

The guard turned back toward Stevie, grabbed his pass—which was around his neck—looked at it, and then looked back at Stevie.

"How old are you?" he asked in an accusatory tone. Stevie wanted to ask if he questioned the age of everyone who walked through the door, but he took the easy way out instead and just said, "I'm fourteen."

"Fourteen and you have a press pass? How'd that happen?"

That probably warranted a wise-guy answer, but he heard a voice behind him saying, "He's got a press pass because he's a first-rate reporter, Bill. And if you paid *any* attention to anything except proving you're in charge here for fifteen minutes a night, you'd *know* who he is."

Stevie looked behind him and saw Bob Ryan, the *Boston Globe*'s star columnist. Given the guard's bullying attitude, Stevie thought Ryan was taking a major chance standing up for him. Then again, this was Boston, and he was Bob Ryan.

"I really don't need you giving me a hard time here, Bob," Bill said, but the snarl was gone from his voice.

"And we really don't need you holding up the line when we're all on deadline," Ryan answered. "Arnold and I have both told you the kid's legit, he's got a pass, let's go!"

Bill hesitated. Clearly, he didn't want to concede that

he was wrong and Ryan was right. Just as clearly, he had to know that picking a fight with Bob Ryan wasn't a great idea.

"All right, Bob, on your word I'll let it go for now. But I'm going to check this out."

"Yeah, you should do that," Ryan said. "And then you can apologize to the kid for doubting him."

Bill reluctantly stepped aside to let Stevie and Ryan pass.

"Thanks, Mr. Ryan," Stevie said. "I really appreciate your help."

Ryan shook his head. "The Red Sox should have fired the guy years ago."

He headed off, and Stevie began making his way into the tiny locker area of the clubhouse. He stood for a moment getting his bearings, looking for Wil Nieves's locker.

"Who you looking for, Steve?"

It was John Dever, the Nationals' PR guy.

"Nieves," he said.

"Right there, somewhere in the middle of all those people," Dever said, pointing to a locker in the corner of the room.

Stevie nodded his thanks and moved to the outside of the circle. At that moment he couldn't see or hear Nieves. He would have to be patient. The TV crews would push their way forward first, cameramen using the sheer bulk of their equipment to forge a path. They would get their sound bites and move away, and the circle would grow smaller. It was late at night, so almost everyone was on deadline. Stevie knew he would get close to Nieves eventually if he just waited the others out.

He looked at his watch. He was in pretty good shape. Because it had been a low-scoring game, it had taken only two and a half hours to play, lightning fast for a postseason baseball game, given the length of the commercials between half innings. It was now 11:20, and he didn't have to file until the *Herald*'s 12:45 a.m. deadline. Stevie knew he could write eight hundred words in forty-five minutes, so as long as he was upstairs in the media workroom at his computer by midnight, he would be okay.

A couple of TV crews came out of the circle, and everyone else moved closer. Now Stevie could hear a little of what Nieves was saying.

"Every pitch was where we wanted it to be," he said with a slight, though noticeable, Spanish accent. "The first six innings I could have put my glove down and closed my eyes because the ball was going to be right where I put it."

That was a good line, and Stevie turned his body so he could scratch some notes down while still leaning in to try to hear. What he really wanted was to get Nieves to talk about Doyle off the field, since they had played together in the minors and he probably knew him as well as anyone on the team. Doyle had mentioned that to Stevie over breakfast, which felt like it had taken place about a month ago.

More people moved out of the circle. Now Stevie could actually see Nieves, who was sitting on a chair, still in uniform, streaks of sweat and dirt running across his shirt.

There was still an ESPN crew that hadn't finished up. The guy holding the mike, whom Stevie didn't recognize, asked Nieves if he felt vindicated playing in the World Series after the Yankees had released him. Typical TV question, Stevie thought. It had nothing to do with the game, and if you looked at Nieves's statistics, it was easy to understand why he'd been released. Before 2008 he'd never come close to hitting .200 in a season.

Nieves apparently felt the same way. "I don't blame them for releasing me," he said. "They traded for a guy who was better than I was. But I've improved my hitting the last two years, and that's why I was able to stick with this team."

Stevie already liked Nieves. He sounded like he was smart and honest. He didn't give cliché answers. The ESPN crew finally moved away, and Stevie was behind only a handful of guys with notebooks. It was 11:35. Still in good shape.

There were more questions about Doyle's control and his stamina near the end of the game. Nieves had clearly been through this already, but he understood that the media came in waves, often with repeat questions. He patiently answered the questions again. More guys moved away. Now it was only Stevie and three other guys. One, whose credential identified him as Tom Stinson from the *Atlanta Journal-Constitution*, asked the question Stevie had wanted to ask: "You and Doyle were in Triple-A ball together early this season and a few years ago when you were both in the Padres organization. Do you know him pretty well?"

Nieves smiled, then shook his head. "I probably know him as well as anybody. But that's not saying much."

That got Stevie's attention. The four reporters all stayed quiet, waiting for Nieves to continue. Stevie was thankful there were no TV people around, because undoubtedly one of them would have plowed through the brief silence and asked something lame.

Seeing that no one was saying anything, Nieves shrugged. "Look, I'm not saying Norbert's not a good guy. He's a *really* good guy. Just quiet, very quiet."

Stinson followed up: "Is he shy?" he asked.

Nieves thought for a moment. "I wouldn't say shy," he said. "He always seems to have a lot on his mind. He's friendly, I'm sure you guys have talked to him. But for the most part, he keeps to himself. I just always thought he was, well, kind of sad, to be honest.

"Maybe it's raising two kids by himself, that can't be easy. Tonight when we got in here, before they let you guys in, everyone was pounding him on the back because he pitched such an amazing game, and he just kind of smiled, said thank you, and asked John Dever when he had to go to the interview room. That's the way he's been as long as I've known him. Joy doesn't seem to be his thing."

Stevie had been right about Nieves. He was clearly very perceptive and very honest—surprisingly honest, especially in a locker room situation. Stinson started to ask another question, but all of a sudden Stevie saw a microphone pop up in Nieves's face and noticed a cameraman sticking his lens right over his shoulder.

"Wil, you guys have to be thrilled to go back to Washington tied at one game all," the guy with the microphone said, asking an answer, something Stevie had gotten used to seeing TV people do a lot.

Nieves looked startled by the interruption, but he politely answered the question. The guy started to ask another question. Apparently, that was enough for Stinson.

"Hold it," he said. "Wil was talking to the four of us, and you just barge in here and interrupt. You need to wait until we're done, which will be about another minute."

He didn't shout, but his tone was firm.

"Hey, pal, I'm on deadline here," the TV guy said.

"Just like everyone else," Stinson said.

The TV guy turned from Stinson and asked another question. This time Nieves didn't have a chance to answer because Stinson put his hand right over the microphone and stepped in front of Nieves.

"Your choice," he said to the TV guy. "Wait sixty seconds, or we can stand here and both blow deadline."

The TV guy started screaming profanities at Stinson and tried to grab the microphone back from him. Stevie saw the cameraman start to reach toward Stinson with his free hand. Without thinking, Stevie blocked the guy's arm, throwing him off balance.

"Hey, what the hell do you think you're doing?" the camera guy said, stumbling backward and almost dropping his camera.

Before Stevie could answer, Stan Kasten, the president of the Nationals, whom Stevie had noticed walking around the clubhouse when he came in, materialized, stepping between Stevie and the camera guy.

"Hey, fellas, you aren't supposed to fight each other, you're supposed to fight guys like me," Kasten said, smiling. "Let's all get along here."

The TV guy was yelling at Kasten about Stinson's not letting him do his job. Kasten had been the president of the Braves for almost twenty years and apparently knew Stinson. "Tell me in ten seconds or less what happened, Tommy," he said.

"Sure," Stinson said. "The four of us were talking to Wil, and this guy barged in, stuck the microphone in Wil's face, and went off on a tangent that had nothing to do with what we were talking about."

"Free country," the TV guy said.

"He's right, Stan," Nieves said, much to Stevie's surprise. He had watched the scuffle with a bemused smile on his face. "These guys were almost done when he interrupted."

"Norman," Kasten said to the TV guy, "when these guys are done, I will personally escort you back over here to talk to Wil."

Stevie noticed that everything in the clubhouse had stopped so people could watch what was going on. In fact, he noticed several TV cameras rolling on the scene.

"But—"

"It's that or nothing," Kasten said. "Your call."

The TV guy slunk away. As he turned to follow, the cameraman said to Stevie, "I'll find you later."

"Oh please," Stevie said, even though a chill went through him. "What're you going to do, hit me with your camera?"

He turned back to Nieves only to find that the circle had now grown, with others wanting to hear Nieves's version of what had just happened. Stinson was standing next to him. "Well, I guess that takes care of getting anything more from him tonight," he said. "You can't win. You don't say anything, you lose the flow of the interview completely. You do say something, you lose the interview anyway." He put out his hand: "We haven't met. Tom Stinson from Atlanta. Thanks for helping me out there."

"Steve Thomas," Stevie answered. "I'm sorry the guy interrupted. That was pretty good stuff."

"Yeah," Stinson said. "Worth following up on. Well, gotta run. I've got about twelve minutes to write before deadline. See ya later."

Stevie looked at his watch. It was almost midnight. He had more than twelve minutes, but he needed to get going too.

He ran into Arnold leaving the clubhouse. "How'd you do with Nieves before the scuffle?" Arnold asked.

"Pretty good. I'd like to talk to him again without being interrupted."

Arnold laughed. "Good luck with that," he said. "Come on, we need to get moving."

Stevie followed him to the elevator, wondering about Nieves's final comment: "Joy doesn't seem to be his thing." The Norbert Doyle he'd had breakfast with had certainly seemed cheerful to him—except when the subject of his wife's death came up. But there was the whole Susan Carol–David secret, whatever that was. There was a story here, Stevie knew that for sure. Unfortunately, he had no idea what the story was.

10: THE MYSTERY DEEPENS

STEVIE WANTED TO SHARE what Wil Nieves had said with Bobby Kelleher, but there was no time. Everyone was fighting deadline when he got back upstairs. Then in the cab back to the hotel, he didn't want to say anything with Susan Carol sitting there.

He left the personal quotes about Doyle out of his story because they didn't really fit with what his sidebar was about: Nieves's view of how Doyle had managed to baffle the Red Sox so completely. He knew that Tom Stinson and the other two writers who had been standing there might well use the quotes, but he was thinking long-term: he wanted to consult with Kelleher when he got the chance and then follow up.

Normally, the person he would have talked to first in this sort of situation was Susan Carol. That, however, was not an option, in part because they were working for different newspapers, but more because they weren't speaking to each other very much.

The next morning the four of them took the short cab ride back to Logan Airport. The series, and everyone in it or covering it, was on its way to Washington. Stevie spent most of the flight trying to catch up on some reading for his English class and trying briefly to work on some algebra, but the math might as well have been written in Chinese, so he gave up fairly quickly. It was a beautiful day, and the plane flew straight down the Potomac River, past all the monuments as it landed.

"Pretty spectacular," he said to Tamara, who was sitting next to him.

"On a day like this, landing here is actually fun," she said. "In bad weather, though, it's not fun at all because the runways are so short."

They took another cab to Potomac, Maryland, where Bobby and Tamara lived. They had two extra bedrooms, so Stevie and Susan Carol would be staying there for the weekend. Games three, four, and five would be played at Nationals Park on Friday, Saturday, and Sunday—all night games, of course, so that TV could get the largest audience possible.

They were talking over lunch about whether there was any need to attend the off-day workouts and press conferences. Bobby and Tamara, who were writing every day with their local team in the World Series, had plenty for their columns, and Susan Carol and Stevie had been given the day off.

But Stevie still wanted to go to the ballpark. The clubhouses would be open while the managers and starting pitchers for the next day were in the interview room, and he thought he might be able to get some time alone with Nieves. Or even Doyle, although he suspected Doyle would be the target of a lot of writers on the off day. With no game until the next night, he was still the big story.

"I'd like to go to the park," he said. "You never know what you'll stumble into when there aren't a million people in the clubhouse."

"Spoken like a real reporter," Kelleher said. "Tell you what, I'll drive down there with you. I'd actually like to talk to some of the Red Sox if I can. I can write from down there if necessary."

That was perfect as far as Stevie was concerned. The tension between him and Susan Carol was almost unbearable, and the car ride would give him a chance to talk to Kelleher alone.

They left the house with Tamara sitting at her computer and Susan Carol reading a history book.

"So I take it things aren't any better with Susan Carol?" Kelleher said as they drove down the George Washington Parkway. It was a perfect fall day in Washington, and Stevie was struck by how pretty the area was with the leaves in full color.

"Worse," he said. "She lied to me at first about meeting

with David yesterday, then when I told her we'd seen her, she got mad and told me she couldn't tell me what they were talking about."

Kelleher was silent for a moment—rare for him—as if deciding what to say next. "She flat out lied?" he asked.

"Pretty much," Stevie said. "She said she'd gone over to Faneuil Hall and walked around the Freedom Trail but never mentioned spending time with David."

"A lie of omission," Kelleher said. "But a lie nonetheless." He turned and went up the ramp onto the Fourteenth Street Bridge, and Stevie noticed they were back near Washington National Airport again.

"It wasn't just that," Stevie said. "She totally clammed up when I tried to ask her what they were talking about. Said it was a secret and then practically ran away from me."

"Huh," Kelleher said. "That doesn't sound like her at all. But I'm sure she'll open up sooner or later."

Stevie hoped that was true. "I suppose. Different subject: listen to this." He took out his notebook and read Kelleher the quotes from Nieves.

"Those weren't in your story," Kelleher said.

"They didn't fit with what I was writing, especially with only eight hundred words," Stevie said, feeling a bit defensive. "That's why I want to go down there today. So I can follow up and see if there's more to it."

Kelleher nodded. "Okay, good. It seems like there's something about Doyle that we don't know—but I haven't a clue what it is. I mean, right now the guy is a true

Cinderella story—all the years bouncing around the minors, single father, two great-looking kids. . . ."

He paused to look over at Stevie. "Sorry," he said.

"No big deal," Stevie said. "You're right. They are great-looking."

"Anyway," Kelleher continued. "Something's missing here. We just need to figure out what it is."

"Could be nothing to it," Stevie said. "Or it could be something not even worth a story. Who knows?"

"You might be right," Kelleher answered. "But you need to ask the questions to find the answers—or the non-answers."

He eased the car off the highway at the South Capitol Street exit and headed for the new ballpark. The best description of Nationals Park, Stevie had decided, was efficient. Everything was sparkling and new, it had all the new ballpark amenities: huge scoreboard that could do everything but make a plane reservation for you; several fancy clubs; a lot of luxury boxes; all sorts of different foods; interactive video games on the concourses. But it wasn't nearly as nice (in Stevie's perhaps biased view) as the ballpark in Philadelphia. For one thing, Stevie's home park had a spectacular view of the city's skyline from almost anywhere. Nationals Park had no views at all from the lower deck, and from the press box—which was so high up it was almost scary—you could see the Capitol dome but little else worth seeing.

The ballpark was right on the Anacostia River. Almost

no one was around as they made their way inside the media entrance and took the elevator downstairs.

"Should be perfect timing," Kelleher said. "It's five minutes before the Nats' press conference at two."

"You going to listen to that?" Stevie asked.

"Nah," Kelleher said. "If someone says something interesting, it will be on the transcript afterward. I don't need to hear how much respect Manny Acta has for the Red Sox."

He and Kelleher rode the elevator to field level and walked down the hall to the Nationals clubhouse, which was on the first-base side of the building. A knot of about ten reporters was standing outside the door, waiting for the media to be allowed inside. One of those waiting was Tom Stinson.

"Hey, Bobby, did your protégé tell you how heroic he was last night?" Stinson said, shaking hands with both Stevie and Kelleher as they walked up.

"I heard about the scuffle," said Kelleher, who hadn't been in the clubhouse when the Nieves near-fight had broken out. "But heroics? Stevie, you holding out on me?"

Stevie hadn't been holding out, but he hadn't mentioned his blocking the cameraman as he reached toward Stinson. "It was no big deal," he said.

"No big deal?" Stinson said. "The cameraman was ready to crack me in the head with his camera."

"Come on," Kelleher said. "I doubt if he'd risk a ten-thousand-dollar camera on your skull."

"Good point," Stinson said with a smile. "But still, Steve was great."

"Clubhouse is open," Stevie heard a voice say. "You guys have forty-five minutes."

The security guard here was just a little bit different than Big-Time Bill in Boston. As Stevie walked by, he said, "Nice stuff this morning." Stevie smiled and thanked him.

Stevie had been inside the Nationals clubhouse during the playoffs, but seeing it again after two nights in Fenway reminded him how huge it was—at least four times bigger than the Red Sox clubhouse. He and Kelleher scanned the room. There were perhaps a dozen players inside, some at their lockers, others sitting on couches in the middle of the room watching TV.

Kelleher pointed at Doyle's locker. "He's not here," he said.

"How do you know?"

"No clothes," Kelleher said. "If he was still here, his street clothes would be hanging in his locker."

The lockers—which were gigantic, like everything else in the room—were the open kind, so it was easy to see clothes and uniforms that were hung in each one. Kelleher was right. Doyle's locker was untouched. Two uniforms hung neatly, and there were several gloves piled up along with some of those socks with numbers they had talked about the day before. But no street clothes.

Aaron Boone, the veteran utility player, was sitting on one of the couches reading a newspaper. Boone was another remarkable story. He'd had open-heart surgery in the spring and had then come back in August to play for the Houston Astros. Just prior to the trading deadline on

August 31, he'd been traded back to Washington—where he'd played the year before. He'd provided both maturity and leadership on a young team in the heat of its first pennant race.

Stevie had noticed during the playoffs that Boone was one of those rare players who actually knew the names of media people. Boone looked up, overhearing the conversation.

"He wasn't here today at all, Bobby," he said to Kelleher.

"Gave him the day off, huh?" Kelleher said.

"I think he's holed up with his agent," Boone said. "Let the bidding begin, eh?"

"That stuff can't wait until after the series?" Kelleher said.

"You gotta strike while the iron is hot, man," Boone said. "Unless he wins game six or seven for us, he'll never be hotter. I mean, my God, if *The Rookie* was a movie, what's this?"

Stevie remembered watching *The Rookie* with his dad. It was based on a true story about a pitcher who hurt his arm in his twenties, became a high school baseball coach in Texas, and then, in his midthirties, signed after an open tryout by the Tampa Bay Devil Rays. He made it to the major leagues briefly as a relief pitcher. Stevie had liked the movie; his dad had *loved* it.

"Good point," Kelleher said.

"Started the season in the minors, never won a big-league game, and he pitches a one-hitter in the World Series!" Boone said. "Not to mention being a good guy and a single dad. Heck, *I'd* love to be his agent right now."

Stevie and Kelleher looked at one another, both thinking the same thing: what was there about Norbert Doyle that all the people who wanted to tell his story *didn't* know?

Stevie noticed Wil Nieves walking through the room to his locker. "I'm going to talk to Nieves," he said, hoping there wouldn't be a mad dash to talk to him. Most of the writers were talking to Ryan Zimmerman at that moment.

"Go for it," Kelleher said.

Stevie walked over to Nieves and was relieved to see no one else walking in the same direction.

"Wil, hi, my name is Steve Thomas, I work for the *Washington Herald*," Stevie said, putting his hand out when Nieves, having tossed his catcher's glove into his locker, turned to face him.

Nieves took his hand and gave him a friendly smile. "I know you," he said. "You were there last night when those two guys almost got into a fight."

"Right," Stevie said.

Nieves knew more. "You and that girl, Susan, right? You're the two kid reporters who are so famous."

"I don't know about famous . . . ," Stevie said.

"Don't be modest," Nieves said. "I read about you in our playoff program."

The Nationals had done a story on the fact that Stevie and Susan Carol were covering them for the *Herald* and the *Post* in their postseason program, which was sold at the ballpark for the startling price of $10. Stevie's dad had bought one but said, "When I was a kid going to the old ballpark in Philadelphia, you paid twenty-five cents to buy a scorecard and a program—*and* they gave you a pencil to keep score with."

"What was it like watching Babe Ruth?" Stevie had said in response to his father's moaning.

"Well, thanks," Stevie said to Nieves. "Since I'm so famous, can I talk to you for a minute?"

"Fire away," Nieves said. He sat down on the chair in front of his locker and pulled a chair over from the one next to his and offered it to Stevie.

Stevie didn't try to pick up where they had left off in Boston the night before. He asked Nieves first about his own background, which was actually interesting. He was from Puerto Rico and had signed with the San Diego Padres as an eighteen-year-old. He had spent most of the thirteen years since then in the minors, making it briefly to the majors with the Padres in 2002 and then with the Yankees for parts of 2005, 2006, and 2007.

After the Yankees had released him, he had signed with the Nationals as a minor-league free agent and had stuck with the team for most of two seasons because he had finally been able to hit a little. He had hit his first-*ever* major-league home run early in 2008.

As Nieves talked, Stevie worried that someone might interrupt them. A couple of times he saw writers approaching, but they veered away. There seemed to be an unwritten rule that if someone was seated, talking to a player, you didn't interrupt.

"So, would you say last night was the biggest thrill

you've had in baseball?" Stevie said, steering the conversation back to the present.

Nieves thought for a minute. "That and the home run," he said. "The home run was a walk-off in the ninth inning, so that was pretty cool too."

Stevie asked Nieves again about Doyle's performance and then, slowly, returned to what he had said the night before. "Before we were interrupted last night, you were starting to talk about knowing Norbert in the minors. . . ."

"Or not really knowing him," Nieves said, smiling.

That was a relief. Stevie had been afraid a night's sleep might have made him more cautious about discussing his team's sudden star.

"Right," Stevie said. "Nice guy, just shy . . ."

"Not exactly shy," Nieves said. "Always friendly. I'm not sure I've ever seen him laugh, though, really have fun. Even when we were celebrating winning the pennant last week, we had to practically beg him to get involved."

Stevie remembered that. He had been standing with Doyle while his teammates kept trying to get him to join them in the celebration. Then again, he hadn't been on the roster for the playoffs.

"You said something about joy not being part of his life. . . ."

"I can't say it isn't part of his life, I've just never seen it. I asked him about it once—"

"You did?" Stevie said, realizing instantly he had made a mistake by stopping him in midsentence and perhaps appearing a bit too eager. For the first time since they had started talking, he saw Nieves hesitate.

"Well, yeah, it was no big deal or anything. . . ."

This time Stevie said nothing. Thankfully, Nieves filled the silence.

"It was a few years ago. We were both in Columbus, which was a Yankee team back then. He'd been traded over in midseason and I was the only guy on the club he knew, so we hung out a little on the road. One night at dinner I asked about his kids. I knew his wife had died years earlier in the accident. . . ."

He paused again. "You know about that, right?"

"Yes," Stevie answered honestly. "He told me about it the other day."

Nieves nodded. "He started talking about how proud he was of them, what great kids they were, and how much he wished his wife could be around to see them."

"Uh-huh," Stevie said, not wanting to interrupt, just encouraging him to go on.

"Perfectly understandable, right?" Nieves said. "But then he said something I didn't understand."

Stevie waited, afraid to say anything.

"He said that sometimes when he looked at them, he believed in God because they were so wonderful. But then, when he thought about it, he decided God was pretty cruel, because every time he looked at his kids, he was reminded that he had taken their mother away from them."

Nieves stopped suddenly. Stevie was scribbling madly in his notebook. "Oh wait, hang on, I shouldn't have said that. Please don't write that. I don't even know what Norbert meant by that."

"I promise I won't unless I talk to him about it," Stevie said.

Nieves sagged a little. "Okay," he said finally, "that's fair."

"But one more question," Stevie asked. "What *do* you think he meant? They were hit by a drunk driver. How could that be his fault? Or was he saying, you think, that it was God's fault?"

"That's what I asked him."

"What did he say?"

"Nothing," Nieves said. "He just asked the waitress for some more iced tea."

11: NORBERT DOYLE, SUPERSTAR

STEVIE STOOD UP A MOMENT LATER and thanked Nieves. Someone was walking around the room saying it would close to the media in five minutes. When they shook hands, Nieves said, "I probably said too much. I hope you handle that gently with Norbert. I know it has to be upsetting for him to even think about it."

"We talked about it a little yesterday, and he did get choked up," Stevie said, telling the truth. "It's probably nothing. He probably feels guilty because they were in the wrong place at the wrong time that night."

Nieves nodded. "I guess so. Or he somehow thinks he should have been able to avoid the accident. He never brought it up again and neither did I. I'm so happy for the guy right now. I wouldn't want to see anything take away from this."

"Me neither," Stevie said. "Don't worry about it."

Stevie felt a little guilty. Nieves had been remarkably honest, and now he clearly felt as if he had violated the confidence of a teammate. But Stevie knew he had to follow up on what Nieves had told him—even if he wasn't sure what it was he was following up on. He knew it was personal—extremely personal. So, was it really news?

He walked back across the room looking for Kelleher but didn't see him. He remembered Kelleher saying he wanted to talk to the Red Sox, so maybe he was in their clubhouse.

"How'd you do with Wil?" Aaron Boone said when he passed him on his way out.

"Great," Stevie said.

Boone nodded. "If I was a reporter, I'd love this clubhouse," he said. "Most of our guys haven't been around long enough to become jaded about all this."

"You've been around a long time," Stevie said.

"Oh yeah—I'm old," Boone said, laughing. "But I'm not good enough to be jaded."

Stevie knew that wasn't true. Boone was famous for his home run in the eleventh inning of game seven of the ALCS in 2003 that had allowed the Yankees to beat the Red Sox and advance to the World Series. He was still known in Boston as "Aaron Bleepin' Boone" because of it, and many of the pre-Series stories had been about his return to Boston six Octobers later.

"You're being modest," Stevie said.

"Yeah, you're right," Boone said, laughing again.

Stevie was tempted to ask Boone what his read of Norbert Doyle was. Clearly, he was a smart guy with a good sense of humor. But time was up in the clubhouse, and this wasn't the right time anyway. So he waved goodbye and headed down the hallway to see if Kelleher was in the Red Sox clubhouse. He found him among a group of reporters around David Ortiz. When Stevie walked up, Ortiz was talking about the triple play.

"Someone called me this morning to tell me I'd made history," he said, smiling. "First triple play in the World Series in eighty-nine years. I can tell my grandkids about it someday. It's what I'll be known for."

Everyone laughed. Someone asked Ortiz if he'd ever heard of Bill Wambsganss. "Not until last night," he said. "Now I even know how to spell his name."

"I'm glad we came," Kelleher said, walking away while Ortiz continued to talk. "I picked up some stuff that will help my column a lot. How'd you do with Nieves?"

"So well I'm not even sure what I've got," Stevie said.

Kelleher gave him a look. "I should have known," he said. "Only you can take a story that appears to be *The Rookie* on steroids and find something hiding underneath. Let's go outside and you can tell me about it."

They walked back into the hallway, and Kelleher leaned against the wall while Stevie read back to him what Nieves had said.

"Whoo boy," Kelleher said.

"Isn't it possible he just feels guilty because he lived and she didn't?" Stevie asked.

"Of course—likely, even," Kelleher said. "But it feels like more than that, doesn't it?" He paused. "It may be time for us to ask Susan Carol about her talk with David yesterday in Boston. Before we go running around on what might be a wild-goose chase, let's find out what she knows about the goose."

"I don't think she'll tell us," Stevie said.

"Maybe not," Kelleher said. "But we'll ask anyway."

"And if that doesn't work?"

"One of us may be going on a road trip," Kelleher said.

"Road trip?" Stevie said. "Where to?"

"To Lynchburg, Virginia," Kelleher said. "And into Doyle's past."

On the car ride home Stevie asked Kelleher what the purpose of going to Lynchburg would be.

"You know Bob Woodward, right? *The* Bob Woodward, as in Watergate and Richard Nixon?"

Stevie nodded.

"He was my editor when I was starting out on the Metro staff at the *Post*. He was the best reporter I've ever met. He had a saying about stories that don't seem to add up: 'Get the documents.'"

"What does that mean?" Stevie asked.

"It means that somewhere, someplace, there is paperwork on almost everything that happens in the world. The story that really got Watergate going came when he and Carl Bernstein ran down some obscure bank records. They found a check that linked the burglary at the Watergate to Nixon's reelection committee. And, at the end, the final documents were the tapes from the White House that proved Nixon had discussed covering up the break-in right after it happened. Any time we were stalled on a story, Bob would say, 'There have to be documents, there always are.'"

"So, what kind of documents would there be on this story?"

"Court records," Kelleher said. "Or police records. Somewhere in Lynchburg there has to be paperwork on what happened the night Analise Doyle was killed."

"But what can it possibly tell us that we don't already know?" Stevie said. "She was killed by a drunk driver. What more can there be to that?"

"I have no idea," Kelleher said. "But *if* we think there's more to Doyle's story, the night she died is the place to start. And if Woodward's theory is correct—and it always is—the documents should at least give us a direction to look next."

"So you're going to go to Lynchburg, Virginia, in the middle of the World Series?"

"First we're going to talk to Susan Carol," Kelleher said. "But if that's a nonstarter, I'm not going to Lynchburg, *you* are."

"Me?" Stevie said.

"Yes, you," Kelleher said. "If Susan Carol can't or won't

tell us what this is all about, you're going to take a train down there tomorrow."

"What about the game?" Stevie asked, dismayed.

"This is potentially a lot more important than writing a sidebar off game three. You can be there in only about four hours or so on the train."

"And what am I going to do when I get there?" Stevie asked.

"You're going to take a cab to the courthouse, and you're going to ask for the police records from the accident. When was it—1997? It shouldn't take them that long to find it."

"It was in August of that year," Stevie said, remembering what Doyle had said back in Boston.

"I doubt if there will be too many police reports under the name Analise Doyle," Kelleher said. "You'll be able to find it."

"And they'll give it to me?" Stevie asked.

"Public records," Kelleher said. "You would be amazed how many things are in the public record. All police reports are unless they're sealed by a court for some reason."

Stevie was less than thrilled by the idea of a four-hour train ride and a trip to a courthouse in a strange town. He had a feeling his parents wouldn't be thrilled at the idea either. But if Kelleher thought it was important, he wasn't going to say no.

"Why can't you go too?"

Kelleher shook his head. "I can't miss the first World

Series game in Washington since 1933 to go off chasing a story that may or may not even be a story," he said. "If it were today, no game, I'd go with you. But not tomorrow."

Seeing the look on Stevie's face, he patted him on the shoulder. "Cheer up," he said. "The best stories are usually the ones that are the hardest to do. This may be one of them."

They pulled into the driveway. Tamara's car was there. "They're home," Kelleher said. "Let's go find out if you're going to become an investigative reporter beginning tomorrow."

Stevie sighed. He was pretty sure he liked sportswriting a lot more.

Both Tamara and Susan Carol were sitting at their computers writing when Stevie and Kelleher walked in.

"How'd it go?" Tamara asked cheerfully.

"Fine," Kelleher said. "Ortiz was actually funny on the subject of the triple play."

Susan Carol had barely looked up when they came in. Stevie was fairly certain if she opened her mouth, he would see her breath, given the ice-cold vibes she was putting out.

"Can the four of us talk for a minute?" Kelleher said.

Tamara shrugged and looked at Susan Carol.

"I've only got about a minute," Susan Carol said. "I have to e-mail this paper to my English teacher tonight."

"Won't take long," Kelleher said. "Let's go into the kitchen."

They walked into the kitchen and sat down, except for Tamara, who headed for the empty coffeepot. "Should I make some more?" she said. "I assume you haven't written yet."

"I haven't," Kelleher said. "But hang on a minute. Let's all talk first."

Mearns sat down next to her husband. "So what's up? You boys want to take us girls out for a big night on the town?"

"We'd love to," Kelleher said. "But there's something else first. Stevie, I want you to get out your notebook and read everything Wil Nieves said last night and then today to Susan Carol."

"He can just tell me, that'd be faster," Susan Carol said. "And why is whatever Wil Nieves said so important?"

Kelleher held up a hand. "Just hang on for a second and you'll understand," he said. "I want Stevie to read it to you exactly because I want to hear Tamara's reaction too."

"What in the world is goin' on here?" Susan Carol said, lapsing into her Southern accent. Stevie knew that meant she was upset.

Stevie had taken his notebook out of his computer bag. He flipped to the page where his Nieves notes began. When Kelleher gave him a nod, he began reading. It didn't take long. Stevie couldn't read Susan Carol's face because he was reading the notes, but when he got to what Nieves had said earlier in the afternoon, he heard her let out what sounded to him like a disgusted sigh.

"'That's what I asked him,'" Stevie quoted Nieves as

he wrapped up. "'He just asked the waitress for some more iced tea.'"

Stevie looked up and closed the notebook. Now he could see Susan Carol's face quite clearly. She was wiping tears from her eyes, trying to look composed when she wasn't.

"Tamara?" Kelleher asked, saying nothing about Susan Carol's tears.

Tamara looked at Susan Carol for a moment, then at Stevie. She took a deep breath. "I hate to say it, but it certainly sounds as if there was more to that accident than Doyle has said so far. It may not even be that big a deal, but it's clearly something that's bothering him. But short of him telling us, I'm not sure how we find out what it is."

Kelleher looked at Susan Carol. Very softly he said, "Susan Carol, if I'm wrong, just tell me, but I think you know what it is that's bothering him, don't you?"

Susan Carol shot Stevie a look. "Please, Bobby, don't ask me this," she said. "It's not fair."

"Why isn't it fair?" Stevie said, jumping in, then wishing he hadn't.

"Because I was told in confidence. It was all off the record. Have you ever heard of off the record, Mr. Can't Let Anything Go?" she said. "If someone tells you something off the record, that means you can't talk about it to anybody. Isn't that right, Tamara?"

"Sort of," Tamara said. "You aren't supposed to tell anyone specifically what you know. But the point of letting someone tell you something that's off the record is that knowing that fact can lead you to other facts that aren't off the record."

"I'm assuming we're talking about your conversation yesterday with David Doyle?" Kelleher said.

For a moment Susan Carol said nothing. Finally she just nodded.

"You aren't violating anything if you tell us whether your conversation with him had anything to do with what Nieves told Stevie," Kelleher said.

Susan Carol looked at Tamara. "He's right," Tamara said. "That's fair for off-the-record info."

Susan Carol looked at Kelleher again and nodded once more.

"Let me ask you one more question," Kelleher said. "If we were to go to Lynchburg and pull the police records from the night Analise Doyle was killed, will they tell us anything about what David told you?"

Susan Carol grimaced and rubbed her forehead for a moment, thinking. "I don't know," she said. "And that's the truth."

Stevie was pretty sure he should keep his mouth shut but couldn't resist. Trying to sound gentle, the way Kelleher had sounded, he said, "Why did David confide in you, Susan Carol?"

The soft voice didn't fool Susan Carol for even a second. "That, Mr. Steven Richman Thomas, is none of your business," she said. Then she stood up and fled the room.

Stevie looked at Bobby and Tamara. "I'll go talk to her," Tamara said, and headed after her.

Stevie looked at Bobby. "That went well," he said.

Bobby laughed. "It'll be okay," he said. "I'm going to go online and find you a train tomorrow morning."

"Oh joy," Stevie said as Kelleher got up and left him sitting alone at the kitchen table. He looked around the empty room and said, "Lynchburg, here I come."

12: INVESTIGATIVE REPORTER

STEVIE WAS STILL SITTING at the kitchen table when Kelleher returned a few minutes later.

"Well, I've got good news and bad news," he said. "The good news is it only takes about three and a half hours to get from Union Station to Lynchburg."

"So what's the bad news?"

"The train leaves at seven in the morning."

Stevie groaned.

"It won't be so bad," Kelleher said. "You fall out of bed into a shower, I'll drive you to the station, and then you can sleep again once you're on the train."

Yeah sure, Stevie thought, sleeping will be easy when I'm having a panic attack about what's going to happen once I get there. "What time do we have to wake up?" he asked.

"I'd say five-thirty," Kelleher said. "If we leave here by six, we'll miss serious rush-hour traffic and you'll be at the station by six-thirty."

Stevie sighed. He didn't have the heart or the guts to try to talk Bobby out of the trip, but he really didn't want to go. He also wondered what his parents would say about it.

"One more thing, I talked to your dad," Kelleher said, as if reading his mind. "I told him I needed you to go to Lynchburg to do some reporting for me and that you'd be back tomorrow night."

"What'd he say?" Stevie asked.

Kelleher laughed. "His first reaction was, 'Oh God, Bobby, what are they into now?' I told him we were trying to dig up some important background on Norbert Doyle but there were no bad guys involved in this one. He said your mom wouldn't be thrilled."

"I'll say," Stevie said.

"But he said it was all right as long as you took some homework with you on the train."

That reminded Stevie that he was supposed to write a report on *The Great Gatsby*, and he had barely started the book.

Tamara walked back into the room.

"What's going on upstairs?" Kelleher said.

"Nothing good," she said, sitting down. "Susan Carol feels that you two have put her in an impossible position: either she gives away something she was told in absolute confidence or she's betraying you guys by not helping with the story."

"You agree with her?" Kelleher asked.

"Honestly? Yes, I do."

"Does that mean you don't think I should go to Lynchburg?" Stevie asked—hopeful.

"No, it doesn't," she said. "The story needs to be pursued and it's clearly your story. I just don't think any of us should ask Susan Carol about it again."

They agreed to split up for dinner to give them all some time apart. Tamara would cook for Susan Carol, and Stevie and Bobby would go out. They went to a place called Rio Grande, a Tex-Mex spot one town over in Bethesda. The place was huge and packed, but they only had to wait about five minutes to get a table. Stevie had just ordered steak fajitas when he saw someone approaching the table. Kelleher saw him too, and the look on his face made it apparent he wasn't thrilled.

"Bobby, how's it going?" the man said, extending a hand as he walked up. He was, Stevie guessed, in his mid-forties and he was overdressed for a place like Rio Grande in a jacket and tie.

"David, what brings you here?" Kelleher said, shaking hands.

"I live fairly close by and I like the food," David answered. He turned to Stevie. "I'm guessing you must be Steve Thomas. I'm David Felkoff."

Stevie accepted the proffered hand and said, "Nice to meet you."

"David's an agent," Kelleher said, which instantly told Stevie why he had looked so unhappy when Felkoff walked up. Kelleher liked agents about as much as most people liked the dentist.

"Player representative, Bobby, you know that," Felkoff corrected.

"Right, of course," Kelleher said, sarcasm in his voice.

"Well anyway, just thought I'd say hello," Felkoff continued, apparently unbothered by Kelleher's cool reception. "Been on the phone all day talking to book and movie people about my new client. Made me kind of hungry."

"New client?" Kelleher said.

"Norbert Doyle," Felkoff said. "If there's ever a guy who deserves to make a few extra dollars . . ."

"It's you," Kelleher said, which made Stevie laugh.

Felkoff glanced at Stevie for a second and kept going. "Always the funny guy, aren't you, Bobby?"

"Didn't Norbert already have an agent?" Stevie asked.

"Not one who could get him meetings with Disney, DreamWorks, Paramount, and Universal," Felkoff said. "Not to mention Random House; Little, Brown; and Simon and Schuster."

"Come on, David," Kelleher said. "*Stevie* could have gotten him those meetings after last night."

"Bobby, why do you always have to be so negative?" Felkoff said. "I saw you in here and it occurred to me you might be the perfect guy to write the book—which will be optioned for a screenplay even before you're finished writing."

"Well, thanks but no thanks," Kelleher said. "I don't write other people's books, and I certainly don't get involved in projects with agents like you."

Felkoff shrugged. "Okay, fine then. I'll get Mitch Albom. He's a lot more talented than you anyway."

"No doubt," Kelleher said.

Felkoff looked at Stevie again. "Well, it was nice meeting you, young man," he said. "Don't believe everything Kelleher tells you about agents."

"No worries," Stevie said. "I can form my own opinions."

Felkoff turned and walked away just as their food arrived.

"Sorry about that," Kelleher said, "but in a business filled with bad guys, he's one of the worst. Typical of him to jump on a guy like Doyle—trying to get him a fast movie deal and then act as if he's the only one who could have gotten it done."

"There's just one thing," Stevie said. "He may not know the movie's ending."

Stevie made no attempt to say more than hello to Susan Carol when they got home. He didn't have to pack, since the plan was for him to come home as soon as he was finished at the courthouse. Kelleher seemed to think he might even make it back in time for the game.

"It's no more than a ten-minute cab ride from Union Station to the park," he said. "You catch the four-forty-five train, you can be in the park for first pitch."

Stevie was in bed by ten-thirty, but as always happened when he knew he had to be up early—especially to do something he didn't want to do, like cram before a test—he tossed and turned. He wondered if he and Susan Carol would ever be friends again, much less boyfriend and girlfriend, and he wondered if there really was anything he could find out in Lynchburg that would shed light on the story. And what did any of this have to do with baseball? He finally drifted off to sleep and woke up to find Kelleher standing over him.

"You didn't hear the alarm," he whispered. "It's five-thirty-five. Rise and shine."

He felt better after a shower and the scrambled eggs and bacon Kelleher made for both of them. But the sun wasn't even coming up when they got in the car.

"Isn't this the way to the ballpark?" Stevie said when Kelleher swung the car onto the Fourteenth Street Bridge.

"Good memory," Kelleher said, pointing at a sign ahead that said Nationals Park, with an arrow pointing to the right. "We're going to get off two exits before the ball-park exit."

Kelleher parked in the Union Station garage, and they went down two escalators to get into the station. A few minutes later, after they had gotten Stevie's tickets and Kelleher had bought him a latte at Starbucks, Kelleher pointed him to his gate.

"I'll have my cell on all day," he said. "Anything happens, and most important, if you have any trouble at all at the courthouse, call me right away."

"Okay," Stevie said, feeling his stomach twist a little because he was about to go off into the unknown all alone.

Kelleher put his hand on Stevie's shoulder. "You're going to be fine," he said. "You'll get the records on the accident, and we'll see where that leads us. Worst-case scenario? You'll be bored. So relax."

"Right," Stevie said, forcing a smile.

He squared his shoulders, pulled out his ticket, and headed for the gate.

The trip passed fairly quickly. Stevie read both the *Post* and the *Herald* as a stall and then finally turned to *The Great Gatsby*. He got through about forty pages before his eyes got heavy and he pushed the seat back to sleep. The train was half empty, so he had lots of room.

He awoke to the sound of the conductor announcing, "Lynchburg, Virginia, in five minutes. Next stop is Lynchburg."

He looked out the window and saw that they were passing through rolling hills with the leaves still green on the trees. Fall came later in southern Virginia than in Boston, Philadelphia, or even Washington.

He looked at his watch as the train pulled in to the station: it was 10:25—five minutes early. He hoped that was a sign that things would go quickly and he would be back on the train headed for Washington soon. He might even make the end of batting practice.

The Lynchburg station was very small, especially compared with massive Union Station, and he only had to walk a short way to get outside to a tiny cab stand. There were three taxis sitting there and no one was ahead of Stevie in line.

"You need a taxi, young man?" said a man leaning against the first cab in line.

"Yes, I do," Stevie said. "Can you take me to the courthouse? The address is—"

The cabbie waved him off. "Son, there's only one courthouse in Lynchburg. You don't need to tell me the address. Hop in."

Stevie took his backpack off and shoved it into the backseat ahead of him. He had brought *The Great Gatsby*, a reporter's notebook, his phone, and his computer, which he thought he might need to do some writing on *Gatsby*, or perhaps something more interesting, on the way home.

"So why in the world do you need to go to the courthouse?" the cabbie wondered aloud as he pulled away from the station.

"Doing some research on my family," Stevie said as Kelleher had suggested he say in case anyone asked. "It's for a paper at school."

"Interesting," the cabbie said. "Where are you from?"

"Washington," Stevie said, just in case the cabbie knew his train had come in from there.

"And you came down here today with the World Series going on up there?"

"Um, it got me out of school for the day," Stevie said.

The cabbie laughed. "Good point," he answered.

The trip to the courthouse took under ten minutes. When Stevie paid the fare, the cabbie handed him the receipt with a card. "When you're ready to go back to the station, give me a call," he said. "That's my cell number at the bottom. If I can't come get you, I'll send someone for you."

"Thanks," Stevie said, noting the cabbie's name on his card. "Thanks, Miles, I'm Steve. I'll give you a call later."

They shook hands, and Stevie got out and found himself at the bottom of the steps leading to the Lynchburg courthouse. It was quite big, Stevie thought, for a small town and looked to be quite old. As he made his way up the steps, he saw that he wasn't wrong: "Opened Sept. 15th, 1932," a small plaque read just outside the door.

He pulled open a heavy door and was relieved that the first person he saw was a smiling middle-aged woman behind a desk labeled Information.

He explained to her that he was looking for a police report from an automobile accident that had taken place twelve years earlier. If the request sounded strange to her, she didn't show it. "Do you know if there were any charges filed?" she asked.

"I don't honestly know," Stevie said. That was a question

he certainly wouldn't have felt comfortable asking Doyle at breakfast.

"Start with Automobile Records, on the second floor," she said, pointing up a long staircase behind her. "If they haven't got it, that means it will be in the Criminal Records section."

Stevie thanked her and made his way up the steps. The third door he came to said Automobile Records on it. He walked in and found an older man and a young woman ahead of him on line. There was only one clerk working. He quickly learned that automobile records didn't just mean records of accidents. This was also the place where people came to get license plates and vehicle registration. That's what the two people in front of him were doing.

Stevie waited while the clerk walked them through what forms they needed to fill out and answered their various questions. He decided this would be a good time to let Kelleher know he'd made it to Lynchburg and to the courthouse. He had punched two numbers when he heard the clerk's voice. "Excuse me, sir?" she said, and pointed to a sign next to the desk that said No Cell Phone Usage in the Courthouse.

"Sorry," Stevie said, snapping the phone shut, hoping his phone faux pas wouldn't turn the clerk against him.

It took about fifteen minutes for the people in front of him to clear up their various problems, but it felt like an hour to Stevie. When he got to the desk, the clerk was giving him a funny look. Stevie figured she spent most of her time dealing with people who had issues with their cars, and Stevie clearly didn't look like he had a driver's license. He wished Susan Carol were with him, because she was so good at finessing situations like this.

"What can I help you with?" the clerk asked.

"Oh yes, thanks," Stevie said, suddenly tongue-tied after rehearsing what he was going to say about a hundred times. "I'm looking for a police report on an accident. . . ."

"Were *you* involved in an accident?" the clerk asked.

"No, no, not me," Stevie said. "It's an accident that happened in August of 1997, but I don't know the exact date."

"Can you give me any more information?" the clerk said.

Remembering what Kelleher had told him to ask for, Stevie nodded. "Yes. It was a fatal accident, two cars. The victim's name was Analise Doyle."

The clerk nodded. "Well, that shouldn't be too hard to find. Fortunately, we don't have that many fatals around here. Why don't you have a seat? I'll have to go back into the archives, so it will take me a few minutes," she said.

"Thanks," Stevie said.

Five minutes went by, then ten, then fifteen. A man came in and looked at Stevie inquisitively. "Where's Mabel?" he asked. Stevie guessed Mabel was the clerk. "Um, she's in the back looking for something," Stevie said, wondering if Mabel's search was going to be interrupted.

"Okay, I'll come back in a while," he said, and left, much to Stevie's relief.

Mabel finally returned a few minutes later, carrying a file. "Sorry," she said as Stevie stood up and walked back to the counter. "Took me a while for a couple reasons. To begin with, this wasn't a two-car accident, it was a one-car. Second, someone had the file out already this morning, and it wasn't put back in the right place."

Stevie stared at her for a second, trying to digest the information she had just casually passed on to him. One-car accident? That made no sense. And who'd had the file out already today? Was another reporter onto the story?

"Do you still want the file?" Mabel said after Stevie said nothing in response to her explanation.

"Oh yes, sorry," Stevie said.

She pushed it across the desk in his direction. "You need to sign the sheet on the inside of the folder," she said. "You can look at it in the room right next door for as long as you want. When you're done, just bring it back to me."

"Can I make a copy of it?"

She shook her head. "No. It's a legal document. Unless you have a court order or can show that you represent someone involved in the case, you can't copy it."

"Even though it was twelve years ago?"

"Even if it was a hundred years ago. There's not much to it, as you'll see. You can take notes on any information you need."

She opened the file to the sheet she had been talking

about. "Sign your name there, and I'll keep the sheet until you return the file. And I'll need to see some ID. I don't imagine you have a driver's license, do you?"

"No, I don't," Stevie said. "But I've got my high school ID and a passport."

"Either one will do."

He reached into his wallet and handed her his ID. She took it and printed his name, the date, and the time on the sheet right below the only other name on the sheet—the person who had been there just this morning! She turned the sheet over to Stevie. "Just sign next to where I printed your name and it's all yours," she said.

Stevie nodded. He wrote his name slowly so he could study the name above it. The signature was scrawled and unreadable, but the printed name was clear: Donald Walsh.

"Ma'am, do you remember what Mr. Walsh looked like?" Stevie asked.

She shook her head. "There's two of us that work in here. Janice must have pulled this for him. That's why I didn't know where it was."

"Is Janice around?"

She shook her head again. "She has the early lunch today." She looked at the wall clock. "She should be back in a while. You can ask her then."

"Thanks."

If Mabel had any interest in why two men would show up on the same morning looking for the file on a twelve-year-old fatal-accident case, she didn't show it. She pointed Stevie to the door that led to the adjoining room.

"If you want coffee or a soda, there's machines down the hall," she said.

He thanked her again. He felt the urge to drink some coffee, but he was already amped up enough. Clearly, there was something here—and someone else was a couple of hours ahead of him on the trail. He had work to do. And he needed to do it fast.

13: BACK IN TROUBLE . . . AGAIN

MABEL HAD BEEN RIGHT about the fact that there wasn't much to the file. Stevie read quickly through the basics: The accident had taken place on August 13, 1997, shortly after midnight. The first officer to respond to the scene had been James T. Hatley and, Stevie gathered, he had written the report. He wrote down Hatley's name and badge number.

According to the report, the car had been traveling east on state road 260 when the driver "apparently lost control," Hatley had written, "and swerved into a tree on the right side of the road." From what Stevie could glean, the car had slammed pretty much head-on into the tree.

Hatley's description of what the car looked like when he arrived was pretty gruesome. Stevie skipped quickly over those details until he got to the part where Hatley reported on the condition of the two people in the accident: "Both parties were out of the car when I arrived. A. Doyle was clearly DOS"—Stevie knew from TV that meant *dead on the scene*—"and a call was put out for EMS. N. Doyle had been thrown out of car and was conscious and reported pain in his rib cage and shoulder and had cuts and bruises on his face and arms. He was interviewed briefly at the scene before EMS arrived. He reported swerving to avoid an animal and losing control of the car. He said he did not know how fast the car was going when he skidded. The posted speed limit is 35 mph."

Hatley went on to describe the arrival of the EMS unit and their confirmation that Analise Doyle was dead. Based on what Hatley had written about the damage to the car, it was amazing that Norbert had survived at all, let alone with such minor injuries. Later in the report Hatley detailed his conversation at the hospital with Norbert Doyle:

> Mr. Doyle had been sedated after his wife's death at the scene. He suffered two broken ribs and a separated collarbone, but his other injuries were minor. He repeated his story from the scene about avoiding an animal and skidding. He asked after his children, twins, two years old, who were home with a babysitter.
>
> An officer was dispatched to the

home, and a Ms. Erin James reported
that both children were asleep in bed
and said her parents had come to the
house to help her and that they would
look after the children until N. Doyle's
release from the hospital.

Hatley didn't say how Erin James's parents knew that
she needed help, but Stevie guessed news of a fatal car accident traveled pretty fast in Lynchburg. Later in the report
Hatley noted that Norbert Doyle was a "summer resident"
who pitched for the Lynchburg Hillcats. There were, according to Hatley, no witnesses to the accident.

Stevie read and reread the report three times. There
was, as Mabel had already explained to him, no second car,
and also no mention of a drunk driver. He looked at his
notes. There really wasn't much to go on. Maybe, he
thought, he could find James Hatley and ask him if he had
any other memories of that night. There were, it seemed to
Stevie, holes in the report, most notably Hatley's accept-
ance of Doyle's story that he had swerved to miss an animal. Stevie had watched enough TV to know that in a
one-car accident the police would at least consider the possibility that the driver had been drinking. And yet there
was no mention of a sobriety test of any kind.

He looked at the clock. It was already past noon. He
needed to call Kelleher. He closed the file and walked back
into the Automobile Records office. Mabel was nowhere in

sight. Another woman was there talking to the man who had walked in while Stevie was waiting for Mabel to hunt down the file.

When he saw Stevie, he waved a hand at the woman and said, "Okay, Janice, see you later." He nodded at Stevie and walked out the door.

"All done?" Janice asked.

"Yes," Stevie said, handing her back the file. "I understand someone was in before me today looking at this."

Janice nodded. "Uh-huh."

If she was any more curious than Mabel, she didn't show it.

"Do you remember what he looked like?"

Janice shrugged. "Dressed in a suit, I remember that. Probably in his thirties. He seemed to think he needed to explain to me why he wanted the file—which he didn't. Public document, you know. Ask for it, you get it."

"What did he say about why he wanted it?"

"He said he had a relative who was involved. We get that a fair bit."

Stevie thanked her and turned to leave. Then he remembered something. "Any chance you know if I might find officer James Hatley over at the police station?"

"No," Janice answered, which stymied Stevie a little. Then she added, "He retired about two years ago."

Stevie's heart sank. Finding Hatley would probably be impossible if he was retired. He probably didn't even live in Lynchburg anymore.

"If you really need to find him, he's usually home

around now. He tends to fish in the mornings, then go home around lunchtime."

All wasn't lost. "Do you know where he lives?" Stevie asked.

"I could tell you how to get there, but I don't know his address," she said. "Wait a sec."

She reached below the counter and pulled out a phone book. She opened it, ran her finger down a page, and said, "Here it is: fourteen Brill's Lane. It's no more than ten minutes from here if you're driving."

"Could a cabdriver find it?"

"Oh sure, I imagine so," she said.

Stevie wrote the address in his notebook, thanked her again, and walked back down the steps and out the door of the courthouse. It was a crisp fall day, and Stevie couldn't help but think it would be a comfortable night for baseball in Washington. He pulled out his phone and dialed Kelleher.

"Where have you *been?*" Kelleher asked when he picked up.

"Sorry, I had to turn the phone off in the courthouse."

"Oh yeah, that figures. So, what have you got?"

Stevie filled him in on what he had learned. Kelleher didn't interrupt him except to say "Whaa?" when Stevie told him it had been a one-car accident and "Hmm" when he brought up Donald Walsh's beating him to the file by a couple of hours. When he had finished, Kelleher said, "Well, you've got a lot to do, and so do I."

"What do you mean?"

"Well, first, like you said, you need to go talk to Officer Hatley. There are a lot of unanswered questions in that report."

"You mean like no sobriety test?"

"Exactly," Kelleher said. "Guy runs his car into a tree—even if he did swerve for an animal—how fast was he going? No mention of whether he was drinking, no mention of checking the skid marks to determine his speed."

"I wonder," Stevie said, "if the drunk driver who killed Norbert's wife might have been Norbert himself."

"Might explain why he talks about feeling guilty," Kelleher said. "What you need to find out from Hatley is why Doyle wasn't given a sobriety test, and why he didn't try to find out how fast he was going. You slam your car into a tree hard enough to kill someone on the spot, you were going *fast*."

Stevie felt his stomach getting queasy—perhaps because he hadn't eaten for almost seven hours; perhaps because the story was taking a scary turn.

"I don't think this cop is going to be too happy to hear questions like that," Stevie said.

"You're right," Kelleher said. "But if he's retired, he may be more willing to talk. You go find him while I see if anyone in baseball has heard the name Donald Walsh."

"You think the guy is in baseball?"

"No idea, but it's a logical place to start. The name doesn't ring a bell as anyone I know in journalism, but I'll check around on that too."

"Okay. I'll call you back after I find Hatley."

"Good. Be careful with him. Cops sometimes have mean tempers, especially if you're questioning the quality of their police work."

"Great," Stevie said. "I wish Susan Carol was here to charm him."

"So do I," Kelleher said. "But you'll be fine. Act fourteen and dumb."

"I *am* fourteen and dumb," Stevie said.

"Nah, just fourteen and in new territory. You can do it."

Stevie hung up and pulled Miles Hoy's card out of his pocket and was about to dial his number when he realized his head was pounding and his stomach really was growling. He looked down the block and saw a McDonald's. He put the phone back in his pocket. He knew he had to see officer James T. Hatley. But he didn't have to do it on an empty stomach.

Miles Hoy was delighted to hear Stevie's voice. When Stevie asked him if he knew where 14 Brill's Lane was, Hoy laughed. "Sure I do. Jim Hatley's place? I'll be right over to get you."

It was shortly after one o'clock and Stevie was still finishing his vanilla milk shake when Hoy pulled up. He knew Hoy was going to ask why he wanted to see Hatley, so he was prepared when he asked the question: "The ladies at the courthouse thought he might have known my grandfather."

That answer seemed to satisfy Hoy, which was a relief

to Stevie. Ten minutes after Hoy had picked Stevie up, he turned the cab onto a dirt road with a battered sign that said Brill's Lane.

"Easy to find," Hoy said. "It's the only house on the road. There it is up there."

He pointed to his right at what looked like an old farmhouse.

"What's Officer Hatley like?" Stevie said, suddenly realizing he should have asked Hoy if he knew him before they were almost on top of his house.

"First, don't call him Officer," Hoy said. "He retired a sergeant. Beyond that, he's like any cop—or ex-cop. He likes to hunt and fish, and he's a no-nonsense guy. Not exactly a barrel of laughs."

"Married?" Stevie asked.

"Was," Hoy said. "His wife apparently left him. I think he might have had some kind of drinking problem years ago. That was before I got to town. They had kids, but they're grown. He lives alone."

They pulled into a dusty driveway with a pickup truck sitting in front of the garage.

"You're in luck," Hoy said. "He's home. You want me to wait?"

Part of Stevie *did* want him to wait, but he figured he was going to need some time with Sergeant Hatley.

"Can you come back in about half an hour?" he asked.

"Sure, kid." He waved off the twenty-dollar bill Stevie had taken out. "I'll just run you a tab, it'll be easier that way."

Stevie got out of the cab and watched with some regret

as Miles Hoy backed down the driveway and headed off. But he squared his shoulders and walked up to the front door. There was a screen door, and as he approached, he could see someone standing in the doorway. He could also hear barking—loud barking.

"Mac, be quiet," Stevie heard the man say.

He didn't open the door when Stevie walked up.

"Can I help you?" he asked in a tone Stevie did not think sounded very friendly.

Just looking at retired sergeant James T. Hatley was intimidating. He was huge, at least six foot three, Stevie thought. His head was shaved and he had a mustache and a goatee. He was probably in his midfifties, and he wasn't smiling. The barking dog stood next to him. Stevie was a cat person, so he didn't know breeds, but this one was big and looked mean.

"Sergeant Hatley, I'm sorry to bother you—" Stevie began.

"Then why are you?" Hatley interrupted.

"I just need maybe five minutes of your time to ask a couple questions—"

"About what?" Hatley said.

"About Norbert Doyle and—"

"I've got nothing to say to you about Norbert Doyle or about the accident," Hatley said. "It's all in the report. There's nothing more to say."

How did he know I wanted to ask about the accident? Stevie's mind was screaming.

"Yes, Sergeant, I *did* read the report—"

"You've got fifteen seconds to get off my property," Hatley said. "You should have told your cab to stay. Now you're gonna have to walk."

"Hang on, hang on," Stevie said. "Hang on for just a minute."

"Ten seconds," Hatley said.

"Just one question," Stevie said, pleading. "Why didn't you give Doyle a sobriety test?"

"Time's up," Hatley said. "I'll give you a five-second head start on Mac because you're a kid. The guy said someone might show up, but he didn't say there would be kids involved."

The guy? Stevie's mind raced. Walsh! It had to be Walsh.

"Please," Stevie said, almost pleading. "Let me explain why this is important."

Hatley pushed the screen door toward Stevie and said, "Okay, Mac—go!"

Stevie didn't wait any longer. He turned and ran as fast as he could, keenly aware of the big dog right behind him. His backpack slapped against his back, and he knew the dog was going to run him down any second. He tried to lengthen his stride and felt himself trip. He went sprawling in the dirt and covered his head instinctively, waiting for the dog to attack.

"Mac, stop!" he heard from somewhere in the distance.

The barking and growling stopped. Stevie looked back and saw the dog no more than a step from him, standing stock-still. He couldn't see Hatley, but he could hear him.

"Get up and walk off my property," he said. "Say one word, take a single step in my direction, and I won't stop the dog."

Stevie was aware of a sharp pain in his shoulder, and he knew he had cut himself in several places, including his mouth because he could taste the blood.

"Get up *now*!" Hatley said. "I don't care if you broke your leg. Get up and get moving."

Slowly Stevie stood up, his shoulder throbbing, blood oozing from several scrapes. He looked back long enough to see Hatley standing in the yard, halfway between where Stevie was and the front door. He resettled his backpack on his back and started walking.

If only he could walk all the way home.

14: CLOSING THE LOOP

STEVIE WALKED TO THE END OF BRILL'S LANE before he even glanced over his shoulder. Seeing no one, he stopped and took his backpack off so he could check to make sure his computer hadn't been damaged when he fell.

It appeared to be fine, as was his phone. He then dialed Miles Hoy. "That didn't take long," Hoy said. "Hatley any help?"

"Not exactly," Stevie said, not interested in explaining but knowing Hoy would ask him about his bloody lip and the state of his clothes. His shoulder was throbbing, but the pain wasn't that bad. "Can you come pick me up at the end of Brill's Lane?"

"Give me ten or fifteen minutes. I came back downtown to eat. I forgot to get lunch."

Stevie didn't argue. He hung up, found a grassy spot near the road to sit, and dialed Kelleher. When he told him what had happened, Kelleher's first response was, "Oh jeez, your dad's going to kill me. I told him you couldn't possibly get into trouble."

"You wouldn't think that dealing with a retired policeman would be dangerous work," Stevie said. "What do we do now?"

For the first time since he'd met him, Stevie sensed that Bobby Kelleher was unsure what to do next. The silence on the other end of the phone was deafening.

"Bobby?"

"I'm thinking," Kelleher said. "Part of me says you should catch the next train home, come to the ballpark, and get your shoulder looked at by a doctor. Then we should sit Susan Carol down and tell her the time for keeping secrets has passed."

Stevie liked that idea. But he didn't think it was the right thing to do. He was already in Lynchburg. They knew now that Norbert Doyle had lied about his wife's death. But they didn't have enough facts to write a story yet or even to confront Doyle.

"I think I should stay awhile longer," Stevie said. "I think I should try to find the babysitter and see if she knows anything. It must've been Walsh who warned Sergeant Hatley someone might be coming, right? But maybe he figured that'd be enough. Maybe he hasn't found Erin James yet."

Again Kelleher didn't answer right away. "Okay," he

said finally. "Start with the phone book. There's obviously a good chance she doesn't live there anymore, but it's worth a shot while you're there. I'm still trying to find out who the hell Walsh is. He told that cop some kind of giant lie about you or, more likely, paid him off to not talk to you. So he's not another reporter."

"He could be a tabloid guy."

"Yeah, you're right. That's possible. I'm heading for the ballpark now. Maybe I'll find out more there."

"Okay, I'll call you back if I have any luck."

Stevie heard Kelleher sigh. "Do me one favor," he finally said.

"What's that?"

"Be careful."

"Bobby, I *am* being careful," Stevie said.

"I know. Be carefuller."

"That's not a word."

"For you I need to make up words. Call me back within the hour one way or the other."

He hung up just as Stevie saw Miles Hoy's cab come into view. He stood up and waved even though he was the only person on the road. He glanced at his watch and saw it was a little after two. He still had time to find Erin James— he hoped—and make that 4:45 train.

Hoy braked to a halt and Stevie climbed into the back-seat. Hoy turned and stared at him. "What in the world happened to you?"

"The guy's got a big dog," Stevie said. "I fell running from him."

158 ·

"He sicced his dog on you? That's crazy! What could you possibly have said to get him that upset?"

"I didn't get to say much of anything," Stevie said honestly.

"Wow," Hoy said. "So are you going to head home now?"

"Not just yet," Stevie answered. "There's one more person I need to find."

"I hope whoever it is doesn't have a dog," Hoy said.

Stevie laughed, which made his head hurt a little bit.

"I don't suppose you know Erin James?" Stevie asked. "She lived here about a dozen years ago. . . ."

"Still lives here," Hoy said. "She teaches my son history at the high school. She's also the girls' basketball coach. I would think we'll find her at practice right now."

"Really?" Stevie asked. He was a little surprised to find that Erin James was still in Lynchburg, stunned that Miles Hoy not only knew her but apparently knew just where she was at that moment. "Can you take me there right now?"

"I can," he said. "But we're going to stop somewhere so you can at least clean up. You're a mess."

Stevie didn't argue. Hoy stopped at a Wal-Mart, and Stevie bought a new shirt to replace the filthy, bloodied one he had been wearing and cleaned up as best he could in the bathroom.

"Good as new," he reported to Hoy, who had waited for him outside.

"Then you weren't very good new," Hoy laughed. "Come on, let's roll. It's almost three o'clock."

Hoy parked in back of Lynchburg High School and

walked Stevie into the gym. The boys' basketball team was on the court practicing.

"They switch off every day," Hoy said. "Today the boys must be first. That means Erin will be in her office. Come on."

They walked through the gym and up a flight of steps to a hallway that had several offices in it. Stevie followed Hoy until he stopped in an open doorway.

"Erin?" he said, poking his head inside the door. "I've got someone here who would like to talk to you for a minute. He's a friend of mine, and I'd appreciate it if you'd try to help him out."

Stevie heard a voice from inside the office. "Sure, Miles, send him in. I've got a few minutes before practice."

"I'll wait for you in the gym," Hoy said, patting Stevie on the back.

Stevie wasn't exactly sure why Miles Hoy had decided to take him under his wing, but he was grateful that he had.

Erin James was seated behind a desk and writing on note cards when he walked in. "Today's practice plan," she said, looking up at Stevie. She had short brown hair and piercing blue eyes.

"Ms. James, my name is Steve Thomas," he said shyly.

"Erin," she said, standing up and coming around the desk to shake hands.

Stevie almost gasped when she stood. Erin James was, without question, the tallest woman he had ever met. At five eleven, Susan Carol was extremely tall. Erin James was at least three inches taller. She smiled down at him, her hand out, and said, "What can I do for you, Steve?"

Stevie managed to find his voice. "I—I wanted to ask you about the night Analise Doyle died," he finally managed to say.

Erin James frowned down at him for a moment, then walked back behind her desk, indicating that Stevie should sit in the chair opposite. He was grateful that they were both now sitting.

"Why don't you tell me *why* you want to know about that night," she said.

Stevie nodded. He explained to her who he was and walked her through everything that had happened since he'd met Norbert Doyle—leaving out only the part about Susan Carol's Faneuil Hall meeting with David Doyle. He wasn't sure if he should be giving her so much information. Kelleher probably would have counseled him to say "I'm a reporter working on a possible story" and leave it at that. But something told Stevie that telling her everything was the best way to get her to trust him. Or maybe he was just dazzled by her. He couldn't be completely sure.

When he had finished, she leaned back in her chair for a moment.

"That's quite a story," she said. "I watched Norbert pitch the other night. I hadn't thought of him in a long time. And I couldn't help but wonder how long it would take the media to dig into his past and come back here. Turns out it was just two days. . . ."

Stevie wasn't sure what to say next. He wondered how Erin James felt about her old summertime employer.

"I always wondered," she finally said after a long pause, "if the truth would ever come out."

"What *is* the truth?" Stevie asked.

She put up a hand. "I don't *know* what the truth is. If Norbert Doyle told you his wife was killed by a drunk driver, I suspect he was talking about himself. But I'm no more sure about that than you are."

"What *do* you know? What do you remember about that night?"

She sat and looked out the window for a moment. "Do you want me to talk for the record?" she said. Stevie had taken out his notebook after they sat down.

"I don't know how to answer that," Stevie said. "Right now I'm looking more for information than quotes. We could go on background if you'd be more comfortable."

"I've heard the term. But tell me exactly what that means, will you?"

"It means you won't be quoted, but I can use the information in a story if I need it."

She nodded. "Okay. I think that works for me."

She paused again. Stevie wondered if it was okay to take notes when you were talking on background.

When she started to talk, he completely forgot about taking notes.

"I had finished my freshman year at Virginia Tech," she said. "As you might have guessed, I was a basketball player. . . ."

Stevie knew he should keep his mouth shut, but he couldn't resist. "How tall are you?" he asked.

"Six three," she said. "I was six three when I was fourteen. Believe me, it wasn't fun."

Stevie decided to shut up. Her height was not part of the story.

"Anyway," she continued. "The baseball team put out the word in the community that some of the players and their wives were looking for babysitters, and the Doyles hired me to sit for their twins right after I got back from school in early June. I was working as a camp counselor during the daytime and I liked making the extra money at night.

"They were very nice people. Most of the time I would sit when Mr. Doyle was pitching and Mrs. Doyle wanted to go to the game. But this was an off night and they were going out to dinner.

"I put the twins down just after sunset, about eight-thirty," she said. "It was a perfect night. Not even that hot. I sat on the back porch reading.

"They had said they wouldn't be that late—maybe ten-thirty or eleven. By midnight I was beginning to wonder what had happened. There were no cell phones then, so I couldn't try to call them. I tried the restaurant, but they had already left. I started work at my day job at seven, so I was getting a little concerned. About midnight I called my parents. They said they'd come over and stay with the kids so I could go home to sleep. They got there just before Officer Molloy showed up."

"Officer Molloy?" Stevie said. He hadn't heard that name before. "The report on the accident was written by—"

"Officer Hatley," she said. "That's what I heard later on. Nothing stays secret in a small town for very long. This is where the story has always been a little bit murky to me."

He waited, hoping they had arrived at the place where she might clear some things up for him.

"Officer Molloy told us there'd been an accident, that the Doyles' car had hit a tree. I remember my mom saying, 'Oh God, Joe, are they okay?' My parents knew Joe Molloy—*know* Joe Molloy—pretty well. Anyway, I remember he shook his head and said, 'He is. She's not. I'm afraid she's dead.'

"I sort of freaked out right then. I'd never known anyone who died except my grandmother."

She paused a moment. "I know I'm dragging this out, but I'm getting to the part that may be important to you."

Stevie just nodded.

"When I calmed down a little, Officer Molloy was describing the scene to my parents, and it sounded pretty terrible. He said the car was totaled. He said Norbert was incoherent, trying to get up to get to Analise. He said he left the scene to come tell us what was going on after Sergeant Hatley got there."

Stevie was rocked. There had been no mention in the report that another officer had been at the scene or, perhaps more importantly, that another officer had been there *before* Hatley.

"The police report doesn't mention Officer Molloy at all," he said.

"I've never seen it, but I guess I'm not totally surprised," she said. "My dad asked Joe Molloy why he had left the scene if he was the first one there. He said that Jim and Norbert were close friends and that Jim had wanted to stay with Norbert and handle the situation.

"I remember thinking that sounded reasonable, nice even, but also maybe a little suspicious. My dad said, 'Joe, was the pitcher drinking?'

"And Joe just said, 'That's a fair question. I'm sure Jim will check that out.'"

"Did you know there's no mention in the report of any kind of Breathalyzer being taken or any sobriety check at all?" Stevie said.

"Well," she said, "there was nothing in any of the papers or the TV reports about Mr. Doyle drinking. My dad wondered if maybe Jim Hatley had taken care of his friend the baseball player. I thought maybe they'd checked and found out he *wasn't* drinking. . . ." She paused. "So the report says he was never tested? That doesn't sound right."

"It doesn't say anything about a sobriety check. Just that he swerved to avoid an animal."

"He didn't pitch again that season," she said. "I remember that. They said it was the cracked ribs and his collarbone. But I remember the initial doctor's report said he'd be out two to three weeks, and there were six weeks left in the season."

She let that hang there without going on. Stevie's mind

raced. He looked at his watch. Almost three-thirty. "I know you have to go to practice," he said. "But one last question. Is Joe Molloy still around here?"

She smiled. "I thought you'd ask me that," she said. "He's the deputy chief of police now. He's probably at the station. Miles can help you find him, I'm sure."

"Thank you," he said.

She stood up and Stevie felt a little bit dizzy looking up at her again. "I liked the Doyles, they were always very nice to me. The kids were cute and smart. Watching him pitch the other night, I felt happy for him. But I've always wondered what really happened that night. Maybe you'll find out."

"Maybe," Stevie said. "I hope so."

"Come on," she said. "I'll take you back to Miles."

15: THE GOOD COP

WHEN THEY WALKED BACK TO THE CAB and Stevie asked if he could go next to the police station, Miles Hoy asked the question Stevie'd been waiting for: "When are you going to tell me what you're *really* looking for here?"

Stevie nodded. "You're entitled," he said, and on their way to the police station, he filled him in. Hoy listened and said little.

"I wasn't here back then," Hoy said after a pause. "I was still working in Atlanta."

"What brought you here?" Stevie asked.

"My grandparents owned a house here and they left it to me. I'd always liked Lynchburg—it's a nice, small town.

People are friendly—even Jim Hatley, most days. I drive the cab and I also do some part-time coaching at the junior high school. Keeps me busy enough."

Stevie asked him if he knew Joe Molloy.

"Everyone knows Joe Molloy," he said. "He'll be chief when Bob Lawson retires in a few years. Good man. I think you'll like him."

The police station, as it turned out, was behind the courthouse, just across a parking lot from the back door. It was just before four o'clock when they pulled up. Hoy volunteered to come inside and try to smooth the way for him—Stevie gratefully accepted the offer.

They walked into the small one-level building and found a burly cop with a mustache sitting behind the desk. "What's up, Miles?" he asked in a friendly tone. Stevie doubted he would have been greeted quite so warmly on his own.

"Young man here needs a minute with Chief Molloy," Hoy said. "Is he around?"

The desk cop, whose name tag said J. G. Brendle, looked at Stevie as if waiting for him to explain. When Stevie stayed quiet, he just shrugged. "He's here," he said, picking up the phone. "Let me see if he's busy. Why don't you guys have a seat."

Brendle put the phone down a minute later and said: "Miles, you're in luck. He'll be right out."

A few seconds later a door swung open and a tall man with blond hair and an easy smile walked over to them.

"Miles, what have you brought me today?" he asked, hand out as he approached Hoy.

"Someone who has some interesting questions for you, I think," Hoy answered.

Molloy turned to Stevie. "Joe Molloy," he said.

"Steve Thomas," Stevie said, shaking the proffered hand. "I work for the *Washington Herald*."

Molloy snapped his fingers. "*Kidsports*," he said. "You and that girl were on that show last year, weren't you?" he said.

Stevie nodded. "Didn't last very long," he said.

"Too bad, my kids really liked you. Come on back and you can tell me what you need."

Stevie looked at Hoy to see if he was going to come with him. "I'll wait here," Hoy said.

"You sure?" Stevie said.

"Oh yeah," Hoy said. "You're the reporter, I'm just the driver."

Joe Molloy led Stevie through a maze of hallways until they reached the back of the building. They passed a door marked Chief Lawson, turned one more corner, and walked into a comfortable office that belonged to Molloy.

"Have a seat," Molloy said. "Can I get you something to drink?"

Stevie was, he suddenly realized, very thirsty.

"Is a Coke too much trouble?" he asked.

"Be right back," Molloy said. He disappeared from the office and returned thirty seconds later carrying two Cokes.

He sat across from Stevie and said, "So, what can I do for a hotshot young sportswriter?"

Stevie figured he was going to have to go through the whole story one more time. "Well, I've been covering the World Series for the *Herald*," he began.

Molloy suddenly smacked himself on the forehead. "Oh God," he said. "Norbert Doyle. That's why you're here, isn't it?"

Stevie nodded.

Joe Molloy stood up and closed the door to his office. He sat down, took a long sip from his Coke, and said: "Why don't you tell me what you know. We'll go from there."

As he had done with Erin James, Stevie went through the entire tale, adding what she had told him about Molloy's visit to the Doyles' house that night. When he had finished, Molloy sat with his arms folded for a moment before standing up and walking to the window that looked out on a parking lot.

"You've covered a lot of ground today. I'm sorry about Jim Hatley. That sounds more like him in his drinking days—can't think what got into him. Maybe this Walsh guy gave him some money and told him not to talk to you. He took it a step further."

"It's okay," Stevie said. "I'm okay."

Molloy walked back to his chair and sat down again. He was having trouble staying still. "Look, I'm not sure what's going on here. You and I have to have an agreement," he said. "I'll tell you what I know, but for now you can't quote me. I'm not saying I won't go on the record ever, I just need to think the whole thing through first."

Stevie thought he understood. "So for now we're on background?" he asked.

Molloy nodded.

Stevie agreed, just as he had done with Erin James.

Molloy took a deep breath. "It was only twelve years ago, but a lot has changed. In those days we worked alone on patrol, nowadays everyone has a partner. I got a call saying someone had plowed into a tree on Route 260, and I was nearest to the site. I got there pretty quickly—under five minutes—and could see right away that it wasn't good.

"Norbert Doyle, who I didn't recognize because I didn't really follow the baseball team, was sitting next to the car. He was cradling his wife in his arms. I was pretty certain she was gone, but I put out an EMS call."

"According to the police report, Hatley put out the EMS call," Stevie said.

"I know that," Molloy said. "I know everything that's in the report."

He stood up again and walked back to the window. "After I called for the ambulance, I went back over to Doyle, who was kind of rocking back and forth. His eyes were blank and he kept saying over and over, 'I killed her, I killed her, oh my God, I've killed her.'" He paused again. "I was about to ask him how much he'd had to drink—I could smell liquor on his breath—when Hatley showed up." Molloy paused, and Stevie was tempted to prompt him but held back.

"He said something like, 'I've got this, Joe,' and that he needed me to go to the house and let the babysitter know what'd happened.

"I said, 'You know this guy?' And he said that it was Norbert and that he wanted to handle the case because they were friends. I didn't argue, I actually thought that was legit. He gave me the address for Doyle's house, and I left just as the EMS unit was arriving."

"So when did you know something was wrong with Hatley's report?"

"Well, my first clue was that he didn't ask me for a description of the scene when I arrived. That would have been SOP in a situation like that."

"What's SOP?" Stevie asked.

"Sorry. Standard operating procedure. When I came to work the next day, I asked Jim when he needed my report on the scene. He just looked at me and said, 'Report's written Joe.' And then added very pointedly, 'It's over. Understand?' I *didn't* really understand until I read the report."

"He covered up that his friend had been drinking."

"Well, he didn't exactly *un*cover it. One-car fatal accident on a dry road, even if you don't smell liquor on the driver's breath, you Breathalyze, or in this case, since he needed to be treated at the hospital, you run a blood test. It's routine. So it was odd that he didn't. But since he didn't, there's no proof now either way."

"Didn't anyone ever question it?"

Molloy shook his head. "This is a small town," he said. "The baseball team has been here a long time, and people tend to like the players. And the whole thing was tragic. Doyle's wife was dead, and he was left with two-year-old twins to raise on his own. . . ."

"So no one was going to say anything about him driving drunk, because he'd suffered enough?"

"I think it was more a question of what would be *gained* by having those kids be without their father too."

"But if he was responsible for their mother's death . . ." Stevie sighed. "One last question: You said Hatley and Doyle were friends. Do you know how they knew each other?"

Molloy nodded. "I didn't then, I do now," he said. "They both hung out at the same bar—King's Tavern. They were drinking buddies, you might say."

Of course they were, Stevie thought.

"If I get to the point where I'm going to write something, I'll call you to see if you're willing to go on the record," Stevie said.

"Okay," Molloy said. "But I don't see how you'll prove it unless Doyle has decided to come clean."

Stevie knew he was right. He was pretty sure he now knew what had happened on the night Analise Doyle died, but he was just as sure he didn't have enough to write about it even if both Molloy and Erin James went on the record. They were both just speculating. And you couldn't accuse people of drunk driving, what was probably some kind of vehicular manslaughter, *and* a police cover-up based on speculation.

He wondered if all this was what David had told Susan Carol.

The craziest part, though, was that it was Doyle—or Doyle's guilt—that had started Stevie down this confusing road in the first place.

He filled Miles Hoy in on the way back to the train station, finishing by telling him he was pretty convinced he didn't have a story.

"Would you do me a favor and keep me informed?" Hoy asked. "My e-mail address is on the bottom of the card I gave you."

They pulled up to the station. "How much do I owe you for all this?" Stevie asked.

Hoy put up his hand. "You know what, it's been a really interesting day, and I was really happy to help you out a little," he said. "When you're rich and famous, remember me, that's all I ask."

"Come on," Stevie said. "The paper's going to pay for it."

"In that case, it's a thousand dollars," Hoy said, causing Stevie's mouth to drop for an instant, until he realized he was kidding.

"Take the money and buy that girl a nice dinner," Hoy said. "Charge *that* to the paper. They owe you."

They shook hands and Hoy drove off as Stevie headed into the station. Stevie realized he was becoming so jaded that he couldn't help but wonder if Hoy had an agenda—maybe Walsh or someone had been paying *him* to keep an eye on him all day. He hoped not.

He had just missed the 4:45, so he was stuck waiting for the 7:25. He grabbed some pizza in the station and called Kelleher. When he pulled his phone out, he realized he'd turned it off when he went into Molloy's office and forgotten to turn it back on. There were six messages—three from Kelleher—waiting for him.

"Where've you been?" Kelleher asked. "I've been worried."

"I'm fine," Stevie said. "I'm waiting on the seven-twenty-five train."

"Good. Before you fill me in, let me fill *you* in. I found out who Donald Walsh is—get this, he works for David Felkoff."

"WHAT?"

"Yeah. For the first time in my life, I'm actually looking forward to talking to that SOB."

Stevie caught Kelleher up on what had happened with Erin James and Joe Molloy.

"You're right," Kelleher said. "We can't write anything based on what you've got now, but I think at some point we need to try to talk to Doyle about it. We can also make another run at Susan Carol. It may be that the story she got from David was different, and if she thinks either she or

David was lied to, she might decide to fill in some of the blanks."

"We'd still need to talk to Doyle, though, right?"

"Absolutely. You can't accuse a man of being responsible for his wife's death without giving him a chance to tell his side of it.

"Look, when you get in, take a cab to the ballpark. The game will still be going on, and even if it's not, we'll all still be here working. We can talk more tonight."

Stevie hung up and finished his pizza. He boarded the train an hour later and put his head back to think about the day. He wondered exactly what he was doing—or trying to do. He had started writing about sports because he loved sports. Going to the Final Four and the Super Bowl and the World Series had been amazing, even if he was becoming a bit jaded.

He certainly had *not* started writing in order to be chased by a giant dog or threatened by a drunken ex-cop. And beyond that, he couldn't escape one nagging thought: *why* was he chasing this story? Was it, in fact, a story? Doyle and his family had been through a tragic experience that still clearly affected them to this day. Doyle hadn't been as forthcoming as he might have been about the facts, but maybe he was entitled to that. It happened twelve years ago and was still painful. Who could blame him for not saying more?

Stevie sighed, wondering where it would all lead next. He closed his eyes and listened to the train as it chugged through the night. The next thing he knew, he heard the conductor's voice: "Washington, DC, in five minutes!"

He looked at his watch: 10:50. Maybe he would catch the end of the game. After all, that *had* been the reason he'd made the trip to Washington in the first place.

16: "CALL ME"

THE CABDRIVER, who was a little surprised when Stevie asked to go to the ballpark, had the game on the radio. It was the bottom of the seventh inning when Stevie got into the cab, the top of the eighth when he got out at the corner of South Capitol Street and Potomac Avenue. The Red Sox were leading, 4–3.

His press credential got him into the ballpark easily enough, and as instructed by Kelleher, he rode the elevator up to the sixth floor rather than heading for the auxiliary press box.

"Doug Doughty is in the writing room watching on TV," Kelleher told him when he arrived. "The wireless works better back there for some reason, and he's got to file his whole story as soon as the game's over. You can sit with me."

That sounded good to Stevie, but the Nationals press box was so high up the players looked tiny. Kelleher had mentioned to him that Stan Kasten, the Nationals' president, had told him the only reason it wasn't higher was because it was already at the top of the stadium. Doughty probably had a better view on TV.

The game had been back and forth all night, but as soon as Stevie settled in to watch, Big Papi slammed a three-run homer and blew it open. Stevie noticed more than a few cheers when Ortiz hit the home run. Clearly, a fair number of Red Sox fans had gotten their hands on tickets—even in Washington.

Stevie kept glancing at the TV monitor next to his seat during the ninth, which seemed to go on forever because Jonathan Papelbon, the Red Sox's closer, insisted on walking two hitters just to make things interesting. Every time Papelbon threw a ball, the cameras shot to Terry Francona, who, almost on cue, would spit sunflower seeds.

"How many of those does he put in his mouth a night?" Stevie said, pointing to Francona on the TV screen.

"What's the number just below infinity?" Kelleher answered, laughing. "It's a lot healthier than the old days when they all chewed tobacco."

"Now, *that* sounds gross," Stevie said.

"Used to be you weren't considered a major leaguer until you chewed," Kelleher said. "Rookies used to get sick trying to learn how to chew the stuff without swallowing. Now, thank God, they've banned it. Some guys still sneak up the runway to chew, but most go with the sunflower seeds or gum."

Papelbon finally struck out Adam Dunn with two on and two out to end the game and give his team a 7–3 win and a 2–1 lead in the series. The Nationals fans left quietly and quickly; the Red Sox fans lingered. Stevie heard one voice from the nearby upper deck bellowing: "It ends here on Sunday! No trip back to Boston!"

Stevie had been given the night off from writing, but he volunteered to go into the Red Sox clubhouse to shag some quotes for Kelleher, who was writing his column on what it meant for Washington to host a World Series game for the first time in seventy-six years. He wanted a couple of quotes from Red Sox players on the crowd, the stadium, and if they could relate to Washington's wait after being part of a franchise that had gone eighty-six years between world titles themselves before their breakthrough in 2004.

Stevie had just finished talking to Jason Varitek, who had said all the right things about the ballpark and the fans and seemed to really mean them. He was walking across the clubhouse to see if he might get close enough to David Ortiz to get a line or two from him when he saw Susan Carol. She was crossing in the other direction.

"Hey," he said awkwardly. "How goes it?"

"Fine," she said. "How was your day?"

"Interesting," he said.

"I'll bet," she answered, and kept walking.

Stevie started to turn around and follow her, then

thought better of it. He really didn't know what *he* thought of the day himself, and Kelleher was on deadline. He waited for the Ortiz crowd to thin—which didn't take as long as usual, since Mike Lowell had hit two home runs himself—and asked Ortiz what he thought of the ballpark and the crowd.

"Very polite," he said, drawing a laugh. "No, I mean it. Compared to Yankee Stadium, this was like a home game. I mean, we had a lot of our own fans here. You could certainly hear them when I hit the home run. Still, I don't understand why they build a stadium in downtown Washington and you can't see any of the monuments."

Someone pointed out to him that you could see the Capitol building from the upper deck.

"I'm not sitting up there, am I?" Ortiz said.

That, Stevie knew, would be plenty for Kelleher. He snapped his notebook shut and headed into the hallway. He was about to make the right turn to the elevator when he saw a familiar figure standing—alone—a few yards from the Nationals clubhouse. It was Morra Doyle. Her face brightened and she waved.

"Hey, Steve," she said.

"Hi, Morra," he said, returning the wave. He half turned to go when he noticed that she was walking rapidly in his direction.

"Have you got a minute?" she asked as she walked up.

"Actually, not really," Stevie said. "I've got to get some quotes upstairs to someone who's on a tight deadline."

"I understand," she said. She reached into her purse,

fished around, and pulled out a piece of paper. "Can I borrow your pen?"

He handed it to her. She wrote a phone number on the piece of paper. "Look, I know you know about David talking to Susan Carol," she said. "I'd really like to talk to you sometime tomorrow. Will you call me? That's my cell."

Stevie had a feeling he was being set up—though he wasn't sure how, or even why—but he nodded. "Sure, I'll call you," he said.

"Great," she said. She looked around as if to make sure no one was watching her. "This isn't a setup, honest," she said. She turned and walked back down the hallway.

So, Stevie thought, she can read minds. If nothing else, the Doyle family was always full of surprises.

Stevie filled Kelleher in on his meeting with Morra Doyle in the car on the way home. He and Tamara had come in separate cars because Kelleher had wanted to get to the ballpark very early.

"My guess is that Susan Carol told David about you going to Lynchburg, and Morra wants to find out what you learned," Kelleher said. "She's the logical one to pump you."

"Why?" Stevie asked.

"Come on, Stevie. She's a pretty fourteen-year-old girl, and you're a fourteen-year-old boy. How would you have reacted if David had come up to you tonight?"

"Probably would have punched him."

"I rest my case."

Stevie asked Kelleher if he had talked to David Felkoff about his henchman, Donald Walsh, turning up in Lynchburg. "Not yet," Kelleher said. "I'm not ready to tip my hand just yet."

Stevie sat quietly for a couple of minutes, trying to turn the whole thing over in his mind. He wondered what Morra had meant when she said this wasn't a setup. He asked Kelleher what he thought.

"Well, you were bound to be suspicious," he said. "She's trying to make sure you're curious enough to call."

"What if I hadn't run into her?" he asked.

"I think you would have gotten a phone call."

He supposed it made sense. But something else was bothering him about the whole thing. They were riding in silence along the George Washington Parkway. Kelleher started to turn on the radio. Stevie grabbed his hand and said, "Hang on a second."

Kelleher left the radio alone.

"You know what makes no sense at all in all this?" Stevie said. "The whole David meeting with Susan Carol thing. What was that about? It wasn't as if any of us were looking for this story or asking questions about it. We sat there at breakfast and bought the whole Disney-movie scenario. Why would David tell Susan Carol something off the record when she had absolutely no idea there was anything to tell? Morra's different because she probably knows that I *do* know something, and she's trying to do damage control. I get that. But the David part I don't get at all."

It was now Kelleher's turn to be silent for a moment.

"Good point," he said finally. "The only thing I can think of is that he somehow saw telling Susan Carol the story as an excuse to see her alone."

"You mean put the moves on her by telling her that his dad killed his mom?"

"I'm not sure I would phrase it quite that way, but yes. Look, we don't even know for sure what David and Morra know about that night. Maybe David wants sympathy from Susan Carol, or maybe there's *still* something we don't know. In fact, I think there's a very good chance we haven't got the whole story yet. Stuff like this is rarely black and white, good guys and bad guys. It's a lot grayer than that. So it's hard to know what David was doing until we know what he thinks happened that night. And really, just wanting to spend time with Susan Carol isn't the craziest thing I've heard so far."

Stevie laughed. "I know it sounds awful," he said, "but if that's what it is, you have to give the guy props for coming up with a unique way to try to impress a girl."

They pulled into the driveway. Tamara's car was already in the garage. She always wrote, Stevie had noticed, a little bit faster than Kelleher. He had no idea what Susan Carol had written about, since they hadn't really spoken for twenty-four hours. Tamara and Susan Carol were sitting at the kitchen table when they walked in.

"You are really slowing down in your old age," Tamara said as Kelleher put down his computer bag and Stevie dropped his backpack off his shoulders.

"I try to write in English," Kelleher answered his wife, walking over to give her a kiss.

Tamara looked at Stevie. "So, young sleuth, you want to tell us about your day?"

Stevie looked at Kelleher. Technically, Tamara and Susan Carol were their competition, since they worked for the *Post*, but that didn't really matter. This, however, felt different.

"I think we need to talk first," Kelleher said. He had poured himself a Coke and sat down across from Susan Carol. Stevie was standing at the counter, his mouth feeling dry, but not, he suspected, because he was thirsty.

"What do we need to talk about?" Susan Carol asked, no doubt sensing that she was not going to like it.

"Well, to be honest, Susan Carol, we need to know if we can trust you," Kelleher said. "I respect that you want to keep the promise you made to David—whether it was made to him as a source or a friend—even though it's a big pain for us to deal with. What worries me is the idea that you're telling David what *we* know."

"WHAT?!"

"Morra wants to meet with Stevie to discuss what David told you."

"WHAT?!"

"Yeah, that's right," Stevie put in. "Maybe she wants to tell me how her dad killed her mom and the cops covered it up for him."

"Quiet, Stevie," Kelleher said sharply. He wasn't sure if

he was shutting him up because he was revealing too much or because he didn't like the tone of voice he was speaking to Susan Carol in. Probably both, he figured.

"The story's not that simple, Stevie," Susan Carol said. "There's more to it than that."

Tamara kept looking from Bobby to Stevie to Susan Carol, as if trying to figure out what in the world they were talking about. Now, though, she put her arm around Susan Carol's shoulders and said softly, "Then you should tell us the rest. Off the record doesn't mean you can't talk to other people about what you know as long as you *know* they won't print it based on what you tell them. If Stevie and Bobby are going in the wrong direction, you need to give them some guidance."

"I can't," Susan Carol said. "It wasn't just off the record, it was a secret."

Stevie threw his arms up in disgust. "What is this, first grade? Doesn't it bother you that this guy basically got away with murder?"

"He did not!" Susan Carol said angrily. "He's lived with the guilt for twelve years, and he'll live with it the rest of his life. You just want to hate him because you think I like David."

"Do you?" Stevie asked.

She didn't answer, but the red in her cheeks was enough answer for Stevie.

"Okay, hang on," Kelleher said. "Let's try to be reasonable here. Susan Carol, if we tell you what Stevie found out today, do you *promise* to keep it a secret from David?"

"That seems fair," Tamara said.

Susan Carol nodded. "Okay," she said.

"And if you think we've got something wrong, you need to give us some clue so we don't go in a direction that's unfair to the Doyles," Kelleher said. "We aren't even sure there's a story here. We need *all* the facts."

She nodded again.

Kelleher looked at Stevie. "Go ahead," he said.

Stevie went through the entire day.

When he was finished, Tamara shook her head and said, "Wow." The three of them waited Susan Carol out, staying quiet.

"All I can tell you," she finally said, "is that you have most of the facts but not the story—you're spinning it in a way that isn't the truth."

"Or maybe someone spun the story for you in a way that was designed to get your sympathy—is that possible?" Kelleher said gently.

"I really don't know for sure, do I?" Susan Carol said. "And neither do you guys. The only person who knows for sure is Norbert, so you'll have to get it from him. But I don't think you will. It's his story and he's got a right to decide whether he wants to go public with it or not."

"That's true," Kelleher said. "Unless the story he and David Felkoff are pitching to Hollywood and New York publishers is the fantasy he pitched to you and Stevie in Boston. He definitely has a right to his privacy, but he doesn't have a right to lie to the public and try to make a fortune from that lie."

"You don't get it, do you?" Susan Carol said, her eyes filling with tears. She got up and ran from the room. Stevie couldn't help but notice that this was getting to be a nightly occurrence.

Tamara stood up. "I'll talk to her," she said.

"Good idea," Kelleher said. "I've never seen her like this."

"Try to remember she's fourteen, Bobby," Tamara said.

"So's Stevie," Kelleher said. "He may not like it that she likes David, but he's not bursting into tears and running from the room every ten minutes."

For the first time since he had met them, Stevie sensed tension between Tamara and Bobby.

"Cool it, Bobby," Tamara said. "She's our friend, not a ballplayer or a coach or an agent."

She turned on her heel and followed Susan Carol out of the room.

"Well," Kelleher said. "That went well, didn't it?"

No, it certainly hadn't gone well. But Stevie actually felt a little better. Kelleher had answered the question that he had been trying to answer on the train ride back: what was the story they were chasing? Now he knew: the story was about an athlete living a lie—no, more than that, selling a lie.

17: MEETING WITH MORRA

THE BEST NEWS OF THE LONG DAY for Stevie was that he was so tired when he went upstairs to bed he had no trouble sleeping. He tossed and turned briefly, wondering if he and Susan Carol would ever be friends again, but fell sound asleep soon after.

He hadn't set an alarm and no one came to wake him, but he was still up by seven-thirty. He went downstairs and, to his surprise, found Susan Carol sitting by herself drinking coffee and reading the newspaper.

"Mind if I have some of your coffee?" he asked.

"Of course not," she said.

He poured himself some coffee and sat down across from her. She had the *Herald*'s Sports section in front of her, so he picked up the *Post*'s.

"What'd Tamara write about?" he asked, hoping to make conversation.

"Stan Kasten," she answered. "She wrote about what it means to him to get this team into the World Series after starting from scratch the way he did back in Atlanta."

"Good idea," he said.

She sipped and read, so he sipped and read. He wasn't really reading, though. He kept trying to read Mearns's column but couldn't seem to get past the paragraph where she described how Kasten, when the Nats were struggling, had handed out cards that said "Stan Kasten—Village Idiot" on them.

"Look, Stevie, I need to tell you something," Susan Carol finally said, pushing the paper away. "I know Morra told you your meeting isn't a setup, that she just wants to talk. She's lying. It *is* a setup."

"How? I mean, how do you know?"

She shrugged. "David sent me a text last night."

"You guys communicating pretty regularly?"

"Yes," she said, looking him right in the eye.

He decided to steer the conversation in another direction. "What do you mean it's a setup?"

"They know you were in Lynchburg yesterday."

"How?!"

"I don't know, he didn't say. But the fact that they know and they *care* makes me wonder if something isn't rotten in Denmark."

"Denmark?"

She gave him the old "You are too stupid to live" look,

but there was a hint of a smile on her face. "I forgot you only read Sports sections. It's a line from *Hamlet*. It means something is suspicious."

Of course it was a line from *Hamlet*.

"Sorry," he said. And then, perhaps because she had almost smiled, he added, "And I'm sorry I've been acting like a jealous dope."

This time she gave him the real Smile. "Thanks for saying that," she said. "I haven't exactly been easy to deal with the last couple of days either. Look, I'm honestly not sure what's going on here. The story David told me in Boston was pretty convincing—and very sad. But based on what you learned yesterday, and the fact that they *must* be snooping around themselves, it makes me wonder if it's the truth."

"It's possible that David doesn't even know the truth," Stevie said, surprising himself by taking a position favorable to David.

"Yes, that's true," she said. "But somewhere along the line the grown-ups—Norbert, Felkoff, *someone*—has involved David and Morra in all this. It wouldn't shock me if the twins know about Felkoff sending Walsh down there."

"Did you tell David how much I know?" he asked.

"*No!*" she answered, flashing anger again. "I didn't tell him anything. All he knows is that you were in Lynchburg and that you and Bobby are looking into the accident."

"Which makes them nervous because their father has been lying about what happened."

She sighed. "Like I said, I'm not sure if he's lying or not.

Unfortunately, I made a promise, and even though I regret that promise right now, I'm not going to break it. But Morra is probably going to try to get you off the story today, and, well, I want to be sure you don't let her do it."

"You think she's going to dazzle me with her beauty?"

She almost smiled. "Funnily enough, I don't think you dazzle that easily. She'll bat her eyes at you a lot and she'll probably cry too. But more important, she'll try to get you to agree to hear the whole story off the record. You can't fall into that trap."

"Is that what happened to you in Boston?" he asked.

"Sort of," she said.

Stevie stayed quiet. He wasn't really sure whether he wanted her to elaborate or not.

She sighed. "Look, he called me after you and I left the hotel. He wanted to know if I was doing anything that afternoon. I wasn't, so I agreed to meet him at Faneuil Hall. It started very innocently, me just kind of babbling about how amazing his father's story was becoming, especially with him starting in the World Series."

"And?"

"He was talking about how proud he was of his dad, how much he'd overcome, more than anyone knew. That's when he told me the whole story—I mean everything— and swore me to secrecy."

"Do you think he was trying to make sure you didn't pursue the story?"

"No," she said, looking him in the eye. "I think he was trying to make me feel sympathetic toward him."

"So he was trying to put the moves on you, basically."

"Basically."

Stevie's stomach was twisted in a knot. The next question was obvious, but he wasn't sure if he really wanted to hear the answer. He took a deep breath and asked anyway.

"Did it work?"

She looked out the window for a second, which scared him, then back at him. "Almost," she said. "When we went for a walk on the Freedom Trail, he tried to hold my hand and I let him. Then, at the end, he tried to kiss me."

She stopped, leaving Stevie in a cold sweat. "I'm not going to tell you I wasn't tempted, Stevie. He's handsome and he's smart and I *did* feel for him after he told me the story. So in that sense his plan worked. But I stopped him and told him I had a boyfriend."

Stevie felt his heart start to pump again. He felt an adrenaline rush. "Has he tried again?" he asked.

"No," she said. "But I've made a point of not being alone with him since then."

"Really?" Stevie said. He felt overwhelmingly grateful for this news.

For the first time in what felt like weeks, she gave him the Smile. "Remember what I said? I have a boyfriend. If he still wants to be my boyfriend."

She gave him the Smile again. That was all the encouragement he needed.

He stood up, walked to where she was sitting, leaned down, and kissed her. He was about to put his arm around her when he heard Tamara's voice behind him.

"Well, isn't this a sight for sore eyes," she said.

Stevie jumped back, embarrassed but fully aware that he had a silly grin on his face.

Tamara was smiling but was too polite to say anything more. "I guess I need to make more coffee," she said, looking at the empty pot and the half-empty mugs on the table.

"Sorry," Susan Carol said. "I should have made more."

"No worries," Tamara said. "I think your time was well-spent."

She was still grinning. So was Susan Carol. Suddenly, Stevie's day was looking up.

Kelleher showed up in the kitchen a few minutes after his wife. Susan Carol volunteered to make eggs for everyone, and they spent a while discussing that night's pitching matchup—Boston's Jon Lester against Washington's Jordan Zimmerman—while they ate.

"Lester is a great story himself," Kelleher said. "Cancer survivor. Came back to pitch the clinching game in the 2007 World Series and then pitched a no-hitter last year."

"And his story's the real deal," Stevie said, feeling emboldened after his conversation with Susan Carol.

"As far as we know," Tamara said.

Stevie showered after breakfast, called his parents to tell them everything had gone fine in Lynchburg—he was grateful his dad answered and didn't ask for details the way his mom would have—and then called Morra Doyle's cell phone number shortly after nine o'clock. She answered on the first ring.

"I was afraid you might not call," she said.

She had, he noticed, just a hint of a Southern accent. It wasn't as pronounced as Susan Carol's, but it was there.

"Of course I'd call," he said. "Why wouldn't I?"

She didn't respond to the question. "Is there any way we can meet for lunch?" she asked. "We're staying downtown at the Renaissance Hotel on Ninth Street."

"I can find out where that is, I'm sure," he said. "I'm staying out in Maryland. Is there anyplace to eat nearby?"

"We ate at a place called Clyde's the other day," she said. "It was very good. It's right near the Verizon Center."

Stevie knew the Verizon Center was the downtown arena where Washington's NBA and NHL teams played.

"I'm sure I can find it. Why don't I meet you there at noon?"

"Great!" she said, sounding a little bit, Stevie thought, as if they'd just made a prom date. "I'll see you then."

Stevie told Kelleher about the conversation. "Clyde's is easy," he said. "It's a few blocks from my office. I need to go in for a couple hours today anyway. I'll drop you off, and then you can walk over there and meet me when you're finished."

"When do we talk to Doyle or Felkoff?" Stevie asked.

"Easy there," Kelleher said. "Let's see what Miss Morra has to say first."

Stevie killed the rest of the morning reading the papers—easier to do when he wasn't a nervous wreck—and, grudgingly, trying to finish *The Great Gatsby*. Susan Carol reminded him one more time about not being charmed by Morra before he and Kelleher left.

"If she comes on to you, remember to tell her you have a girlfriend," she said, smiling. She leaned down and gave him a quick kiss as he was going out the door, causing Stevie to climb into the car with what he knew was a goofy grin.

"So all is well in paradise again?" Kelleher said.

"Yup," Stevie said. "He came on to her, but she told him she had a boyfriend."

"You see?" Kelleher said. "You should never underestimate Susan Carol."

"I should know that by now, shouldn't I?" Stevie said.

The trip downtown passed quickly. Traffic on a Saturday morning was light. As Kelleher pulled up to the restaurant, they could see Morra Doyle waiting outside. The day was warm, and she was wearing a light blue sundress and high-heeled sandals.

"Whoa," Kelleher said. "She's come to play. You be careful, now."

Stevie smiled. "I'm fine," he said, although he had to admit, if he didn't know he was being set up *and* if he didn't have a girlfriend, he would be pretty fired up about a lunch date with Morra Doyle.

"Call me when you're done," Kelleher said as Stevie got out. "I'll tell you how to get to my office."

Stevie slammed the door just as someone behind

Kelleher honked at him to get moving. Morra Doyle was waiting with a big smile on her face.

"Who was that?" she asked.

"Bobby Kelleher," Stevie said, remembering that Morra had never met him. "He works for—"

"The *Washington Herald*," she said. "I've been reading his columns *after* I read your stories."

Stevie was almost tempted to laugh. He wondered if pretty girls went to some school to learn how to make teenage boys do their bidding, or if it was just genetic. They walked inside and a moment later they were escorted up a flight of steps into a massive dining room. Clyde's had to be the biggest restaurant Stevie had ever been in.

"Nice place," Stevie said as they settled into a booth.

"They serve everything here," Morra said with a smile. "Since I don't know what you like, I figured this was a good choice."

They ordered, then small-talked about the game the night before and the importance of the Nationals evening the series that night.

"Manny Acta told Dad he might pitch game six or he might pitch game seven, depending on the circumstances," she said. "Of course, we have to make sure we get to a game six or a game seven first."

"Wow, game seven of the World Series, that would be amazing," he said. "Could make for a real Hollywood ending."

He said it intentionally, hoping to draw a response. If

he caught her off guard, she didn't show it, just smiled again without saying anything. She took a couple more bites of her crab cake and put her fork down.

"So, you probably think I asked you to lunch so I could talk to you about your trip to Lynchburg yesterday," she said.

He had to give her credit for coming right to the point when she thought the time was right. "It did cross my mind," he said. "How'd you know I was there?"

"You have to understand something about my dad and David and me. There are no secrets. His new agent told Dad that the first thing any publisher or movie studio will want is to be sure that the story they're buying is the real deal—especially these days. That's why he sent his assistant—"

"You mean Walsh?"

"Yes, him—to Lynchburg. Dad didn't know what was in the police report. I don't think he really wanted to know. But Mr. Felkoff said we *needed* to know."

"But how did he know I was going to Lynchburg too? The cop I went to see—"

"Hatley."

"Right. He said that Walsh told him I'd be coming."

"Susan Carol told David you were going."

Stevie was tempted to call her a liar, but she put up a hand as if anticipating what he was about to say. "She didn't do it to give anything away. She asked David if there was anything you might find that he hadn't told her."

"What did David say?"

"That he didn't know. Because he didn't."

"I know what you found out down there now," she continued. "That there was only one car involved in the accident that killed my mother."

Clearly, Walsh had carried that information back to the Doyles and Felkoff. Since she had to know he'd looked at the report too, he shrugged and said, "That's what the police report said." He stopped there, not willing to tell her anything more.

"Except it's not true," she said. "There *was* another car."

"But—"

"I *know* what the report says," she said, smiling to remind him, he guessed, that they were still friends. "But there was another policeman at the scene first, before Officer Hatley. I'll bet you didn't know that."

Interesting that she would bring up Joe Molloy, he thought, but he decided to play along and see where she was going.

"What are you talking about?" he said.

"His name is Joseph Molloy," she said. "He's a big shot down there now, I think a deputy chief or something."

"And?"

"Dad told him about the other car before Officer Hatley got there. Molloy called him a liar, with my mother lying there either dead or dying."

"Why would Molloy do that?" Stevie asked. "And why didn't Hatley mention the other car in the report?"

She was nodding as if to say he was asking the right questions. "Molloy hated my father," she said. "He and my dad pitched on the same team in Sumter, South Carolina, four years before the accident. Sumter is where my parents met."

This didn't jibe at all with what Molloy had said about not being a baseball fan. Stevie was tempted to take out a notebook to write all this down but resisted. He wanted her to keep talking. If she was lying about Molloy, it would be easy enough to check out.

"Go on," he said.

"Joe Molloy was dating my mom when she and my dad met. She dropped Molloy to go out with my dad. No big deal, she just liked him better."

Stevie sat back in the booth. He was beginning to wonder if *anyone* involved in this story was telling the truth.

"My father did *not* cause the accident," she continued. "A pickup truck going way too fast swerved into his lane, and he yanked the wheel to avoid hitting him.

"When Hatley showed up, Molloy was screaming that Dad had killed Mom and that he was sure he was drunk. When Dad told Hatley there was another car involved, Molloy kept insisting he was lying. So then Hatley pulled rank and told Molloy he was going to take over the investigation."

"But if Molloy was convinced your dad was drunk, why didn't he accuse Hatley of a cover-up after he wrote the report?"

"I don't know, and neither does Dad. All he knows is Hatley told him not to worry about it, that he'd taken care of it."

"You realize," he said, "if it comes out that Hatley

covered up for your dad, the movie and the book are probably out the window."

"He *didn't* cover up!" she said, raising her voice for the first time. "My dad's not a liar. If he said there were two cars, there were two cars. Molloy is the liar."

"Then why didn't Hatley mention the second car in his report?" Stevie said. "Is he a liar too?"

"No. I mean, I don't know exactly." Stevie thought her eyes were glistening just a bit. "I didn't even know what was in the report until yesterday, remember?"

Stevie nodded and decided to let the silence be his next question.

She leaned toward him and smiled again, eyes still glistening.

"Can I tell you something completely off the record?" This was happening just as Kelleher and Susan Carol had predicted it would.

"Actually, I'd prefer you didn't," Stevie said. "I can't take a chance that you'll tell me something I already know, or might find out later, and then won't be able to use because I agreed to let you tell me off the record."

For the first time since they had sat down, the look on her face betrayed a hint of anger. "You mean after all I've told you, you might still write a story?"

"Honestly, I don't know," Stevie said. "But I can't put myself in a position where I *can't* write the story."

"But I told you what happened," she said. "You can easily check what I told you about Molloy and Dad playing in Sumter. I'm *not* lying about any of that."

"I'm not saying you're lying about anything," he said. "But you don't have all the answers either: your dad says two cars were involved; the police report only mentions one car. Was your dad drinking? One cop—who you say hated your father—insists yes. The other cop—your dad's friend—says nothing about it in the report. And the fact remains that the version of the story your dad has told you may not be the way it happened at all.

"But what really bothers me is that David Felkoff, apparently with your dad's approval, sent Walsh to Lynchburg to check the report and then sent him to tell—and I assume *pay*—Sergeant Hatley to keep quiet about it all. That doesn't exactly make your dad out to be innocent."

"But I *told* you why Felkoff wanted to do it. He wanted to be sure no questions would come up later about Mom's death." Her tone had changed from flirtatious to angry. "He didn't know what was in the report either. Walsh was sent there to make sure the report jibed with what had happened."

"Well, if your dad's buddy Hatley wrote it, why *wouldn't* it jibe? But it *doesn't* jibe, does it?"

He realized he was cross-examining her and that wasn't the best way to get someone to talk to you. But there were *so* many holes in her story.

"Don't you understand?" she said, her voice rising. "Dad didn't do anything wrong that night, but the truth is not what publishers and Hollywood producers want to hear. The truth ruins the story."

He leaned across the table. The tears in her eyes were, Stevie guessed, real.

"Morra," he said softly, hoping to convince her he was still her friend, even though it was probably way too late for that. "Did your dad and Felkoff send you here today to try to get me off the story?"

"*No!*" she said. "They don't even know I'm here!"

For some reason he was instantly convinced she was telling the truth—at least about this. Still not raising his voice, he said, "Morra, I know you don't want to hear this, but the truth *is* the story. It's the only story. And if your dad is lying on any level, it's going to come out."

WHACK!

Stevie felt his face sting and burn all at once and realized, since he hadn't seen it coming, that she had just slapped him. He wondered if they taught that at pretty-girl school too.

"Turns out David was right," she said, standing up. "He said I'd be wasting my time trying to convince you there was no story to write, that you were so insanely jealous of him you'd want to get Dad no matter what."

"But this wasn't a setup, right?" he said, gritting his teeth a little because he was in pain. She was stronger than she looked.

And she looked as if she might hit him again—but she didn't. Instead she just said, "I thought journalists were supposed to be the good guys—not people who ruin people's lives."

She turned on her heel and stormed away from the table and out of the restaurant. Stevie looked around and saw people staring at him. The waiter hustled over to the table.

"Is everything okay, sir?" he asked. "Do you need some ice or something?"

Stevie figured his cheek was probably bright red, judging by the burning he was feeling. "No ice," he said. "Just the check would be good."

He sat back in the booth again. Covering the World Series was becoming less and less fun by the minute.

18: TO TELL THE TRUTH?

STEVIE LEFT THE RESTAURANT QUICKLY, checking to make sure Morra wasn't outside waiting for him. Seeing no one familiar, he called Kelleher.

"How'd it go?" he asked.

"It's too complicated for the phone," Stevie said. "I need directions."

Thankfully, the directions were pretty simple. Down three blocks to E Street and then up six blocks to the *Herald*'s offices.

The guard at the door called Kelleher to come down and get him. When Bobby saw Stevie's cheek, his jaw dropped.

"What happened to you?" he said. "No, wait, tell me when we get upstairs. Clearly, it's a long story."

For all the writing he'd done, Stevie had never been in

the newsroom of a major newspaper before, and he was awed by how big it was. Since it was Saturday, the massive room was fairly empty.

Kelleher led Stevie through the newsroom to the sports section. A number of writers and editors were sitting at their desks, some working on computers, others reading the newspaper. Several were seated around a television set watching a college football game.

"Navy–Notre Dame," Kelleher said. "Navy is trying to start another streak."

"Streak?" Stevie said. He thought he remembered that Navy had broken a forty-three game losing streak to Notre Dame a few years earlier. His dad had called it one of the great upsets in the history of football.

"Yeah," Kelleher said. "Navy beat them one in a row, then the Irish won last year."

"Hey, Matt, how's Coach Rockne doing?"

"It's seven to seven in the second quarter," Matt answered. "Coach Rockne just went for a fourth and nine and got stopped."

"Coach Rockne?" Stevie asked.

"Yeah, we call Charlie Weis Coach Rockne because he thinks he's so smart, he might as well be Knute Rockne. Not so much the last two years when he was ten and fifteen."

He introduced Stevie to Matt Rennie, who was the deputy sports editor.

"You've done great work," Rennie said, shaking Stevie's hand. "Especially considering you've had to put up with Bobby."

"I'd be *so* much better if I had some decent editing," Kelleher said.

"Don't hold your breath waiting for that to happen, pal," Rennie said with a smile before returning to the game.

As they walked back to the small glass office that said Bobby Kelleher on it, Kelleher said quietly: "Best editor we've got. By far."

"But you'd never tell him that, would you?"

"I'd sooner die."

They sat down in Kelleher's office.

"So, fill me in," Kelleher said.

Stevie did—starting with the slap and then working backward. Kelleher let out a low whistle. "You have quite an effect on young women, don't you?" Then he turned serious: "Clearly, she thought you'd be so charmed by her that you'd let her go off the record so she could take you off the story the way David did with Susan Carol."

"Susan Carol had no idea what he was going to tell her . . . ," Stevie said.

Kelleher put up a hand. "No need to defend Susan Carol," he said. "You know how I feel about her abilities as a reporter."

"What do we do now?" Stevie said.

"First thing is pretty easy," Kelleher said. "We check with the Braves to see if Joe Molloy played in Sumter."

He pulled out his cell phone and hit a few buttons. "Here it is," he said. "Bill Acree."

Without explaining who Bill Acree was, Bobby dialed. Stevie heard a voice on the other end of the phone say,

"I'm watching Georgia play Tennessee, why in the world are you calling me?"

Clearly, Bill Acree was a good friend of Kelleher's. "How close are you to halftime?" Kelleher asked, then nodded at the answer. "When you get there, I need you to check on whether someone played for you guys at Sumter in 1993 or even '92 or '94." He paused again before saying, "Joe Molloy." He thanked Acree, said, "Go, Dogs," and hung up the phone.

"Who's Bill Acree?"

"He's the Braves' traveling secretary," Kelleher said. "Old friend. Very smart guy. He'll check on Molloy at halftime and call me back. He said the name sounded familiar."

"So if Morra *is* telling the truth, what do we do next?"

Kelleher shook his head. "You're not going to like it."

Stevie looked at him. "You're kidding."

"Is there any choice? You have to go back and talk to Molloy again, and you might have to try to talk to Hatley again too."

"Oh joy," Stevie said.

"Don't panic. We'll get you some help."

Stevie let out a sigh of relief. He would definitely feel better going back to Lynchburg if he had a grown-up with him.

"Can the paper spare someone right now?" he said.

"Don't think so," Kelleher said. "But the *Post* might be able to spring a freelancer."

"Susan Carol?" Stevie said. "I doubt she'd want to go."

"I'll bet different," Kelleher said. "We'll tell her what

happened when we get to the ballpark. I think you guys can stay for the game tonight and then go down tomorrow morning. You still have the card for that cabdriver in Lynchburg? I'll bet he'll help you again. Just tell him this time you're going to pay him."

Stevie nodded. He suddenly felt very tired. He'd felt so good about mending fences with Susan Carol in the morning. He had thought he was back at the series for good. And he felt so comfortable and safe in the newsroom. Now he would be back on the train in the morning. If Susan Carol went too, it wouldn't be so bad. Jim Hatley probably wouldn't sic his dog on *her*.

The phone on Kelleher's desk rang.

"Halftime already?" Kelleher said. He pulled out a pen and began scribbling on a notepad in front of him. "Got it, thanks a million. I'll tell you the whole story very soon."

He hung up and looked at his notes. "Joseph Wilson Molloy. Signed out of high school by the Braves. Spent four years in the organization: one year of rookie ball in '92, a year at Sumter in '93 and two years in Greenville. Released at the end of the '95 season."

"So Molloy's a liar too."

"Apparently. Lying cops really piss me off. And this many lies usually means there's a serious story. You're going to have to go back, I'm afraid."

"This week just keeps getting better," Stevie said.

"Relax," Kelleher said. "You've got Susan Carol back on your side. And you guys are undefeated."

"We'll see," Stevie said. He wasn't sure if Susan Carol

was actually back on his side. And he was *really* sure that he was a long way from undefeated. His burning cheek confirmed that.

They made reservations on the 9:00 train, the first one available on a Sunday. Kelleher called Tamara to ask her to get to Nationals Park a little earlier than normal so the four of them could find a quiet place to talk. Kelleher and Stevie pulled into the press parking lot at four-thirty—four hours before game time.

"You're here early, Bobby," the parking attendant said as they pulled into the lot.

They walked up the sidewalk that commemorated historic moments in Washington baseball history. Stevie couldn't help but notice there weren't too many of them.

Once inside the ballpark, they rode the elevator to the sixth floor and found Tamara and Susan Carol waiting for them in what was the media dining area during the regular season.

Stevie noticed that Susan Carol was drinking another cup of coffee. "How many is that for you today?" he asked, pointing at the cup.

"Not enough," she answered. "These late-night games are killing me."

"Speaking of which, I could use some," Kelleher said, making his way to the small food-service area, where a large coffeepot sat in the corner. No one else was in the room except for a couple of Nationals employees who were getting set up for later.

"So," Kelleher said to Stevie, "tell the girls about your lunch."

Stevie did, and noticed Susan Carol wince when he got to the part about the slap. When he had finished, including Bobby's conversation with Bill Acree about Joe Molloy, Tamara shook her head in disbelief.

"There are just no truth tellers in this story, are there?" she said.

"There's only one thing we know for sure," Susan Carol said. "This ain't no kids' movie."

Stevie laughed. It was the Susan Carol he knew.

"So what do you think, Bobby? Another trip to Lynchburg?" Tamara said.

"Yes," Kelleher said. "But I don't think Stevie should go alone."

"I agree," Susan Carol said instantly. "I'll go with him."

Stevie was amazed. In under twenty-four hours she had gone from storming out of the kitchen never to speak to him again to helping him chase the story. Susan Carol read the look on his face.

"Look, we're way past anything David told me in Boston," she said. "There was no Joe Molloy in his story and no police report full of all sorts of contradictions and questions that weren't answered. There was just this horrible tragedy in which all four of them were victims. I still think it's sad and awful, but the story he told me is *not* the real story. And off the record only counts if your source is telling you the truth, isn't that right?"

"Absolutely right," Tamara said.

Susan Carol nodded. "In that case, I think two of us down there is better than one, especially if we have to go see that Hatley guy again."

"How well does your cabbie friend know Hatley?" Kelleher asked Stevie.

"I'm not sure. A little bit, anyway," he said.

"I think you should ask if he can call Hatley and see if he'll meet you someplace, so there's no issue about trespassing or dogs."

"What should we do about Molloy?" Stevie said. "Should we have Miles call him too?"

"Absolutely not," Kelleher said. "If he knows you're coming back, his antenna will go up that something's wrong. You need to just show up on his doorstep."

"Are we worried that we'll be followed or watched?" Susan Carol said. "After Stevie's lunch with Morra, they're bound to be worried that we're going to keep going after the story."

"Glad you brought that up," Kelleher said. "I think we need to throw some misdirection at them."

"How?" Susan Carol asked.

"You still in touch with David?"

"Yes," she said. "He's been texting me, I think trying to figure out what you and Stevie have been up to."

"Good. Send him a text saying something like, 'Bobby

and Stevie have decided not to pursue this until after the series is over—if then.'"

"You think he'll buy that?" Stevie asked.

"Not sure," Kelleher said. "But it's worth a try."

"Let's hope," Stevie said.

"Okay then," Kelleher said, standing up. "Let's do something different for a few hours: let's concentrate on baseball."

Game four was playing out a lot like game two in Boston. The visiting team—in this case, the Red Sox—scored a run early, and then the game settled into a pitcher's duel. The Red Sox and Jon Lester were still leading 1–0 heading to the bottom of the eighth. Terry Francona was spitting sunflower seeds faster and faster as the game went on. He brought in Hideki Okajima in relief after Lester had squirmed out of a men-on-second-and-third-with-one-out jam in the seventh to keep the lead and the shutout intact.

The crowd was on its feet as Cristian Guzman came to the plate to lead off the eighth inning. The fans knew that the Nats *needed* to score now against Okajima, since their chances of getting to the usually unhittable Jonathan Papelbon in the ninth weren't very good.

Guzman struck out. So did Ronnie Belliard. The crowd got very quiet, especially when Okajima threw two quick strikes to Ryan Zimmerman, who was just one for fourteen in the series as he came up to bat. Okajima threw an outside fastball, and Zimmerman, lunging for it, hit a ground ball right at Mike Lowell, Boston's sure-handed third baseman. Lowell took a step to his left, went down to get the ball, and then suddenly jerked his head back as the ball hit on the edge of the infield grass and took a wicked hop right into the side of his face.

The ball rolled away while Okajima scrambled to pick it up and hold Zimmerman at first. Lowell lay on the ground as the Red Sox trainer and Francona rushed out to see if he was okay.

"He's bleeding from the mouth," said George Solomon, who had binoculars with him. "He got nailed."

"Tony Kubek, 1960," Mark Maske said.

Stevie knew a fair bit about baseball, but he had no idea what Maske was talking about. Naturally, Susan Carol did.

"Game seven in Pittsburgh," she said. "Yankees had the lead in, I think, the eighth inning. Routine ground ball to Kubek at shortstop, and it took a bad hop and hit him right in the Adam's apple. Opened the door for a Pirates rally, and they won the game on Mazeroski's home run in the ninth."

Stevie was no longer amazed when Susan Carol knew things like this. His only surprise, really, was that she hadn't been the one to bring it up.

Lowell was being helped off the field, and the towel held to his mouth was turning red quickly. The Nationals fans gave him a round of applause as he disappeared into the dugout.

Okajima was given a couple of warm-up tosses because of the delay before Aaron Boone stepped in. "Well, what-dya know," Barry Svrluga said. "It's Aaron Bleepin' Boone at the plate in a key situation against the Red Sox."

"Can't happen again," Solomon said. "It's too good a story."

Whether Okajima remembered 2003—or even knew about it—was hard to say. But he worked Boone carefully, falling behind two balls and no strikes on breaking pitches.

"He would be wise," Svrluga said, "to not give in and throw him a fastball. Aaron Boone can hit a fastball."

"I'll bet he's taking here," Solomon said. "A walk puts Zimmerman in scoring position."

Okajima looked in to catcher Jason Varitek for a sign. Stevie glanced over to the on-deck circle to remind himself who would come up next if Boone walked. Adam Dunn, the Nationals' best power hitter, stood there.

Okajima came to his set position, checked Zimmerman at first, and threw. Boone wasn't taking. His bat whipped through the strike zone, and Stevie heard the distinct *crack* of bat meeting ball. The ball jumped off the bat, climbing high into the night air, headed in the direction of the left-field bleachers. Everyone in the park—including Stevie and those around him in the auxiliary press box—stood, watching the ball as Jason Bay circled back in the direction of the left-field fence.

He got there, paused for a split second, and then leaped. His glove went up over the wall, and he came down looking in the glove for the ball. Stevie thought he saw him smile weakly. His glove was empty. The ball had fallen just beyond his reach, just over the wall.

Aaron Bleepin' Boone had done it to the Red Sox again!

The ballpark exploded with sound as Boone followed Zimmerman around the bases. The entire Nationals dugout came out to greet him even though the game wasn't over.

"Nice call on Boone not doing it again," Svrluga said to Solomon.

"Hey, it was the old jinx technique," Solomon said. "Say it won't happen so it will."

Apparently, there was nothing that could jinx Aaron Bleepin' Boone, especially against the Red Sox in October.

Okajima struck out Dunn on three pitches, but the damage was done.

Joel Hanrahan came on to pitch for the Nationals in the ninth. And even though he walked both Ortiz and Bay with two outs, he got J.D. Drew to ground out to—who else?—Aaron Bleepin' Boone to end the game.

The series was tied at two games each. Judging by the reactions of the Nats and the fans, you might have thought it was over.

Stevie's cell phone was ringing as he watched the celebration.

"I'm obviously doing Boone," he heard Kelleher shout over the noise. "You go to the Sox clubhouse and see if Lowell is up to talking. Either way, ask anyone in there if they remember Tony Kubek. He was the guy—"

"I know, 1960," Stevie said. "Got it."

He followed Susan Carol and the other writers out, relieved—for this one night—that Kelleher wanted him to go to the losing clubhouse. He had no interest in seeing Norbert Doyle celebrating with tonight's winners. Not yet, anyway.

19: THE BAD COP

AS IT TURNED OUT, Mike Lowell did speak to the press, although he did so while holding an ice pack to his face, which was already swelling and had turned several different colors. He *had* heard of Tony Kubek.

"The good news is that this wasn't game seven," he said. "We still only have to win two more games, and the last two are in Boston. I'll take those odds."

He insisted he would play the next night even if he had to have some stitches taken in his lip, which appeared likely.

The only other person in the Boston locker room Stevie could find who had heard of Tony Kubek was Terry Francona. "My dad was playing in those days," he said. "I watched a lot of games. I remember Tony working for NBC

218 •

in the late sixties and early seventies. Whenever someone hit a bad-hop grounder, the other announcer would say, 'Hey, Tony, does that remind you of the '60 series?'"

Standing in the middle of the clubhouse, Ortiz said he thought Jason Bay was going to catch Boone's home run. He shook his head. "Dude always seems to get us."

Stevie had gotten about three steps outside the club-house door when he heard a voice calling his name. He looked up to see Morra Doyle. He might have turned and run, but she was smiling.

She rushed up to him, threw her arms around him, and said, "David told me that you and Mr. Kelleher aren't going to pursue the story. Thank you!" Before Stevie could say anything, she gave him a firm kiss on the lips, which, if nothing else, was a good deal more pleasant than getting slapped.

"Don't thank me," he said. "Bobby has the final word on all this."

He liked the answer because he hadn't really lied. Clearly, Susan Carol had carried off her part in the mis-direction perfectly.

"Doesn't matter," she said. "You're doing the right thing. I'll see you tomorrow night."

She turned and walked down the hall, leaving Stevie just a bit dizzy.

"That was a touching scene," a voice said behind him. He turned and saw Susan Carol, who had just come from the Nationals clubhouse and had apparently seen the kiss.

"Well, I guess I have you to thank for it," he said, giving

her *his* best smile. "She's thrilled that we're backing off the story."

"Good," Susan Carol said. "Let's hope that means we won't be bothered tomorrow in Lynchburg."

They walked down the hall in the direction of the elevators.

"Pretty girl," Susan Carol said while they waited.

"Don't even go there, Scarlett," Stevie said. "My loyalty has never been at issue this week."

She moved closer to him so she could speak softly and said, "Neither was mine, really. I hope you know that."

He said nothing, and she slid her arm through his as they pushed onto the elevator to go back up to the press box and write. It had been, Stevie thought, quite a day.

Stevie called Miles Hoy on the way to the train station the next morning and was relieved when he answered right away. He explained that he needed to talk to Joe Molloy again and that he was coming back to town with a friend.

"Let me find out if he's working or at home today," Miles said. "I'll pick you and your friend up at the train station."

"I'd rather he didn't know we were coming," Stevie said.

"Gotcha," Miles said. "I'll handle it."

Stevie told him what time the train got in—12:40— and he said he'd call back if there was any sort of problem.

As soon as they got on the train, Susan Carol started to

work on a paper for school. Stevie grabbed the Sports section of the *Post*. Stevie always enjoyed comparing Tom Boswell's columns in the *Post* with Kelleher's. Boswell saw wonder and beauty in everything that took place on a baseball field; Kelleher was skeptical about the teenage choral group that sang the national anthem.

The trip passed fairly quickly. Stevie finished off the two Sports sections and then quickly fell asleep—again—while trying to wrestle *The Great Gatsby* to the ground.

Stevie noticed a chill in the air and an overcast sky when they got off the train. "Wonder what it will be like for the game tonight," he said as they walked through the small station.

"Supposed to be cold and maybe rainy," Susan Carol said. "Great football weather."

"Well, when you play the World Series the last week in October, that's bound to happen."

Miles Hoy was waiting with his cab as promised. Stevie introduced him to Susan Carol.

"Wow, a budding Erin James," he said, shaking hands with Susan Carol.

"What's that mean?" Susan Carol said as they slid into the backseat of the cab.

"She's very tall," Stevie said. "I guess I didn't get a chance to tell you that."

"How tall?"

"She said six three."

Susan Carol winced. "Ooh God, I hope I'm not that tall. Five eleven is plenty for me."

"Me too," Stevie said, and saw the Smile—which made him smile.

Hoy jumped behind the wheel. "So, here's the deal," he said. "Our timing should be perfect. Joe's on call today, but he's not at the station. He and his family go to church in the morning and then out to brunch. But they should be home by now."

"You didn't tell him we were coming, did you?" Stevie asked.

"Absolutely not," Hoy said. "One of the guys who works for me driving one of my other cabs lives down the street from Joe. He gave me the info."

"Miles, you should have been a reporter," Susan Carol said in her best Scarlett O'Hara voice.

Stevie saw Miles smile in the rearview mirror.

It started to rain en route to the Molloy house. "I hope this isn't a harbinger," Susan Carol said.

"I think you and I working together again is a harbinger of *good* things," Stevie said.

"Why, Stevie, you *do* say the sweetest thangs."

"Stop it, Scarlett," he said, a wide grin on his face.

They pulled up to a brick two-story house at the far end of a quiet cul-de-sac.

"Do we have a plan here?" Stevie asked as they pulled up.

"Do we ever have a plan?" Susan Carol answered.

She had a point.

"I'll be right here," Miles Hoy said.

They jumped out and hustled up to the front porch to get out of the rain.

"Ready?" Susan Carol said.

Stevie nodded. She rang the doorbell. They waited. Several seconds went by. Stevie heard a dog bark. Oh please, he thought, not another dog. Finally the door was opened by an attractive woman of about forty wearing what was no doubt her Sunday go-to-church dress.

"Hi," she said. "May I help you?"

"Mrs. Molloy?" Stevie said, just to be sure.

"Yes?" she said.

Susan Carol, as usual, took over from there. "Mrs. Molloy, my name is Susan Carol Anderson, and this is Steve Thomas. We're reporters covering—"

"*Kidsports!*" Mrs. Molloy said. "I recognize you both! Hey, come in. The kids will be thrilled to meet you!"

Stevie had been uncertain what kind of reception they might get at the Molloys', but a hero's welcome was not on the list he had made in his head.

"Well, we really don't want to bother you . . . ," Susan Carol said.

"No, no, please come in, it's starting to rain hard out there."

She ushered them into the front hallway. "Joe, Joey, Denise, come out here, we've got surprise visitors," she called toward the back of the house.

Joe Molloy, still wearing a white shirt and tie, and two neatly dressed kids, maybe eleven and nine, Stevie guessed, appeared in the hall.

"Steve?" Joe Molloy said. "Is that you? What brings you back here?"

Before Stevie could attempt an answer, his wife was introducing her two kids. "This is Joey, he's a seventh grader," she said. "And Denise is in fifth. They both used to love your show."

Stevie and Susan Carol thanked them for watching and shook hands with both of them. "Hey, kids, why don't you go find some paper and pens so you can get autographs," Joe Molloy said. That seemed a bit much to Stevie, but the kids both scrambled off to find paper and pens.

"So what brings the two of you back to Lynchburg on a rainy Sunday afternoon?" Molloy asked.

"We're really sorry to just show up like this, Chief, but we need some more help on the story you talked to Steve about on Friday," Susan Carol said. She had been in full Scarlett mode since Mrs. Molloy opened the door.

Molloy shrugged. "Sure. I'm not sure what else I could tell you, but I'll try."

The kids came back with pens and paper. Stevie and Susan Carol both signed, writing the kids' names and "Best wishes."

Susan Carol looked around. "Is there someplace quiet we can talk?" she said. "Given the subject matter . . ."

Molloy nodded. "I understand. Follow me." He turned to his wife, who had come back after the kids had retreated to the family room. "Nance, we'll be on the back porch. Give us a few minutes, okay?"

"Of course," she said. "Anyone thirsty?"

"We're fine," Susan Carol said. "Thanks, though."

They followed Molloy to the back porch, which was

screened in. It was chilly but dry, and they sat on comfortable chairs. Stevie was very glad he'd worn a sweater and a rain jacket.

"Little bit cold," Molloy said. "But private. So, what exactly can I do for you kids?"

Susan Carol looked at Stevie. Since he had talked to Molloy on Friday, it was really up to him to start. Stevie took a deep breath.

"Chief, after we talked Friday, I went back to Washington," he said, "and as you can imagine, we're doing research on everyone involved in this story—"

"And you found out that I played with Doyle in Sumter," Molloy said. "I knew I should have brought that up when we talked."

"Why didn't you?" Susan Carol asked, her tone soft and nonaccusatory.

Molloy shook his head as if to say he didn't know. "Good question," he said finally. "I assume we're under the same ground rules as Friday?"

Stevie shook his head. "Not telling the truth changes things a little," he said. "We need the truth now, and we need to be able to use the information you give us. We'll check with you first if we need to quote you specifically on something, though."

Kelleher had briefed him on how to handle this. "Rules of protecting sources are fairly basic," he said. "As long as they tell you the truth, you protect them. You catch them in a lie, all bets are off."

Molloy leaned forward for a moment, and Stevie

wondered if perhaps he'd been too rough and they were going to get thrown out of the house.

"That's not unfair," he said finally.

Susan Carol reached into the purse she was carrying and pulled out a tape recorder. "So we get it right," she said. "Okay?"

"Okay," Molloy said as she turned the tape on and put it down in front of where he was sitting.

"After you left, Steve, I almost tried to call you because it occurred to me that you'd have to talk to Norbert eventually, and when you mentioned my name, the fact that we played together in Sumter was bound to come up," he said, his voice calm and measured.

"Actually, we haven't spoken to him yet," Stevie said.

"Then who—"

"Doesn't really matter," Stevie said. "But it does raise some issues. You told me you didn't follow baseball, didn't even know who Norbert Doyle was. That kind of goes beyond forgetting to mention you were teammates."

"You're right," Molloy said. "And I suppose whoever told you we were teammates also told you that Analise and I dated before she and Norbert met."

"That did come up," Susan Carol said. "The version of the story we heard was that you wanted to nail Norbert Doyle for Analise's death, and that Jim Hatley wouldn't let you do it."

He shook his head. "It wasn't nearly that simple," he said. "Whoever gave you that version is leaving a lot of facts out."

"Why don't you fill us in," Stevie said.

Molloy sighed and looked at the tape recorder. It seemed to Stevie as if he was making a decision.

"Okay," he said finally. "I *was* upset with Norbert—obviously. Everyone in town knew he was a drinker. But I didn't try to nail him. I didn't really want the truth about that night to come out either."

"What is the truth?" Susan Carol said quietly.

"The truth is that he didn't belong behind the wheel that night, and I knew it."

"You mean because you smelled alcohol on his breath at the scene?"

"No, I knew it *before* the accident."

"How?"

"I got a call from the manager at the restaurant where Norbert and Analise were having dinner. He said they'd had a fight and that Norbert had had a lot to drink. I told him to keep them there and that I would come and drive them home.

"I got there about two minutes too late."

"And this manager will confirm your story?" Stevie asked.

Molloy shook his head. "I don't know. His name was Tom Barton. He left town years ago. I have no idea where he is now."

"Is there anyone who can confirm the story?" Susan Carol put in.

Molloy smiled sadly. "Jim Hatley. But I don't think he's likely to talk to you two anytime soon. There might still be a record of the restaurant's call in about a drunk patron, I don't know."

Stevie and Susan Carol looked at each other. "So the part about you being first on the scene . . . ," Stevie said.

"Is true," Molloy said. "I was closest to the scene because I was still at the restaurant when the call came in.

"I was probably as much of a wreck when Jim showed up as Doyle was. That's why he sent me away to go tell the babysitter. Jim showed me the report the next day and said to me, 'He's going to have to live with the guilt the rest of his life.' I felt pretty guilty myself, so I said I'd go along on one condition."

"What was that?" Susan Carol asked.

"That he get Norbert into rehab. He agreed."

"So what was the purpose of your lies on Friday?" Stevie asked. "Why embroider the story for me?"

Molloy sighed again. "I was being both stupid and selfish, I guess. Stupid to think the truth wouldn't come out. Selfish because I want to be chief. And if it becomes public knowledge that Jim and I knew Norbert was drunk and that we let it slide, and then basically falsified the report, I'm done. They can't touch Jim—he's retired. I might not get fired, but I'll never be chief now. I probably don't deserve to be chief."

He stopped and looked away, clearly upset.

Stevie looked at Susan Carol, who gave a tiny shake of her head to indicate he shouldn't ask another question right at that moment. Molloy broke the silence.

"If Norbert had not been an alcoholic, Analise would

be alive today. If the restaurant manager had kept them there longer, or if I'd gotten there . . ." Molloy paused again and sighed. "Look, I give him credit because I think he's stayed sober since rehab. He *did* go out and turn his life around after that night. But it doesn't change what happened."

This was the first Stevie had heard of Norbert's going to rehab. If Susan Carol was surprised, she didn't show it.

"But why do *you* feel guilty?" Susan Carol said. "You got there as fast as you could. You helped get the guy into rehab. Yes, you let him off the hook on the accident, but your intentions, it seems to me, were good."

"Well. *Did* I get there as fast as I could? I didn't turn the siren on and speed to the restaurant. It didn't seem that urgent. It's hard not to think of all the ways you might have done it differently when someone ends up dead. . . ."

Molloy shook his head again. "That's not even the point, though, really. We all knew Norbert Doyle did a lot of drinking and driving. We should have stopped him *before* someone died."

The tape clicked, indicating it needed to be flipped over. Susan Carol leaned forward and turned it off.

"I think we're done," she said. "For now. We'll be back in touch before we write, and we may call if we have follow-up questions. I'm sorry to have to dredge all this up again."

They walked in silence to the door and shook hands briefly and said goodbye. The rain was still pelting down as Molloy closed the door behind them. Miles Hoy's cab was at the curb waiting for them. They sprinted for the car, dove in through the back door, and were surprised to see someone sitting in the front seat next to Miles.

"Miles?" Susan Carol said before the man swung around so that Stevie could see his face.

"Oh my God!" Stevie yelled.

"Don't panic, kid, everything's going to be fine," Jim Hatley said. "Miles, my house please. The fare is on me."

20: JIM HATLEY

MILES HOY PULLED AWAY from the curb and had driven to the corner before Stevie recovered from his shock and found his voice again.

"Miles, what's this about?" he said. "Are you in on this too?"

Hatley laughed. "Miles isn't in on anything," he said. "Nancy Molloy called me and said you kids were talking to Joe. She's scared because Joe's scared. She asked me if I would talk to you because she's afraid you won't believe Joe."

"Why wouldn't we believe him?" Susan Carol asked.

"Because he lied to you on Friday," Hatley said. "He called me that night to ask me why I ran you off. Then he told me he panicked and lied to you."

"So you two are friends?" Stevie asked, becoming more incredulous by the minute.

"No, not at all," Hatley said. "But he told me you snooping around could be trouble for Norbert Doyle. And *he* was my friend, once upon a time."

"So what did happen that night?" Stevie said. "What's the truth?"

Hatley held a hand up. "Let's wait until we get to my house. You can run a tape recorder once we get there."

"So you'll talk to us on the record?" Stevie said.

"I will *only* talk to you on the record."

They drove in silence through the rain until they came to Brill's Lane, which Stevie recognized immediately. His stomach churned a little bit at the memory of the great dog chase. Hoy pulled into the driveway.

"You stay here, Miles," Hatley said.

"I think maybe I should come in," Miles said.

"I understand," Hatley said. "But you stay here. The kids will be fine."

Stevie wasn't so sure he wanted to take Hatley at his word, but the look on his face made it clear that Miles wasn't going to be welcome inside.

"It's all right, Miles, we'll be okay," Stevie said.

"Don't worry," Hatley said, climbing out of the cab. "Remember, I came looking for them, not the other way around. This won't take long. You can probably make it back to Washington for the game tonight."

He got out and started walking into the house. Stevie

looked at Susan Carol. They could easily get away right now. "Should I take off?" Miles said.

"No," Susan Carol said. "We need to talk to him anyway. Let's go, Stevie."

They both followed Hatley up his front steps and into the house, which was apparently unlocked. He led them into a large living room with a high ceiling and a large fireplace. Hatley gestured for them to sit, then tossed a couple of logs into the fireplace and knelt to light them.

"You kids want anything to drink?" he said once the fire was started, acting as if they were old friends who had dropped by for a Sunday visit.

"Thanks, we're fine," Susan Carol said.

"Actually, I'd like a Coke if you have one," Stevie said. He was thirsty and he wanted a moment alone with Susan Carol.

"Be right back," Hatley said.

He walked off, presumably to the kitchen.

"Why do I feel like this is another setup?" Stevie hissed at Susan Carol.

"Stay calm," she said. "He clearly wants to talk, so we'll let him talk. Maybe we'll even believe him. . . ."

Hatley walked back in carrying an ice-filled glass of Coke and a coffee mug. He looked at Susan Carol. "You sure I can't get you something?"

Susan Carol shook her head. Hatley sat down in a chair next to the couch. He turned to Stevie. "First, I want to apologize to you for Friday," he said. "I got carried away.

Watching Norbert pitch the other night—I was so happy for him after everything he'd been through. And then this guy Walsh came by telling me there'd be reporters down here snooping around, trying to ruin it for him. And not two hours later there you were. I overreacted."

The man sipping coffee in front of a fire on a rainy Sunday afternoon was considerably different than the snarling jerk who had confronted Stevie two days earlier.

It suddenly occurred to Stevie that he hadn't seen or heard the dog who'd chased him. "Where's your dog?" he asked, even though it was an irrelevant question.

"Out in the barn," Hatley said. "I didn't want to scare you to death again."

This was all too weird. Two days ago Hatley sics his crazy dog on him. Then he shows up out of nowhere and half kidnaps them, and *now* he's mister sensitive? Susan Carol was clearly thinking the same thing.

"Okay, Sergeant Hatley," she said. "Why don't you tell us your version of what happened that night?"

"It will be my pleasure," Hatley said. "Where's your tape recorder?"

The back part of Hatley's story wasn't all that different than what they already knew—or thought they knew—except for one key thing: Hatley had been friends with Norbert Doyle and they did hang out at the same bar, but they were not (according to Hatley) drinking buddies.

"If you do any research on cops, a lot of us drink too

much," Hatley said. "But it wasn't like that with me and Norbert. I went into King's Tavern after work to *eat*. The food there was good, and it was the only place in town where the kitchen stayed open late.

"I'm fifteen years older than Norbert. He was a kid when he was here—twenty-four, twenty-five? I was closer to forty. It was a happy time in my life. My marriage was good, and my kids were teenagers. I already had fifteen years in on the force and wanted to get to twenty-five so I could have enough money to build a house like this, hunt and fish, and maybe do some part-time work teaching. I have a degree in animal pharmacology from Virginia Tech, and I teach part-time over at Radford University."

He paused, picked up his coffee mug, and smiled.

"I'm betting Joe left that out of his story."

Stevie and Susan Carol both nodded. He had.

Hatley went on to say that Doyle was one of several ballplayers who had come into King's—same reason as the cops: good food and a kitchen that stayed open late.

"Norbert, sober, was a good guy," he said. "Good sense of humor, very self-deprecating, especially after he didn't pitch well. But he drank a *lot*. It got to the point where I was driving him home a lot of the time. That was when he'd talk about his marriage."

"What about his marriage?"

"It was falling apart. He said he and Analise were fighting all the time. He was convinced she was cheating on him when he was on the road. That's kind of a ballplayer's ultimate nightmare, you know. The travel schedule is hard on any marriage, especially when you're kicking around the minor leagues. And drinking makes you paranoid."

"Paranoid?" they both said.

"Yes, paranoid," Hatley said. "Norbert thought there was something going on between Analise and Joe Molloy."

"And you're saying there wasn't?"

Hatley shook his head. "Like I told you, Joe and I were never friends. He was always a pretty boy who played a lot of politics in the department. That's how he got to where he is right now. But he loves his wife. I can't know for sure, but I don't believe there was anything going on.

"Sober, Norbert knew Analise would never cheat on him. Drunk, he wasn't so rational."

Stevie and Susan Carol looked at one another. The story kept getting more complicated by the minute.

"Just so I'm clear on this," Susan Carol said. "You aren't trying to say that the accident *wasn't* an accident, are you?"

Hatley shook his head. "No, I'm not saying that. What I'm trying to tell you is the reason Joe went along with the way I wrote the report."

Stevie started to say that they already knew why, but Susan Carol shot him a look that clearly said, "Keep quiet."

"Joe knew that Norbert shouldn't have been driving that night," Hatley said. "He got a phone call from the restaurant where Norbert and Analise were having dinner."

"He told us that," Susan Carol said. "He got there too late."

"No, he didn't," Hatley said. "He never went. He called me and said, 'Your pal's drunk again, go drive him home so he doesn't hurt Analise.' I was the one who got there too late."

"Why didn't he go himself?"

"I guess he thought Norbert Doyle was my problem, not his."

Stevie's mind was swimming upstream. At that moment he was completely convinced that Hatley was telling the truth. Molloy had lied once, why not a second time? The good cop was turning out to be the bad cop, and the bad cop was turning out to be the good cop.

"Does Norbert know this?"

"I don't know. . . . Norbert was a mess after the accident, as you can imagine. I may have told him, I don't remember, but he wasn't in any state to take it in one way or the other. He only ever blamed himself."

"Molloy told us the reason he went along with your report was because you agreed to get Norbert to go to rehab."

Hatley laughed. "He told you that? Wow, that's good. I told Norbert he was going to rehab in the hospital that night. You can ask him that if you want. Joe went along with the report because he knew if he had responded to the call from the restaurant himself, instead of calling me, the Doyles wouldn't have been in the car that night. He was saving his own skin."

"Does Mrs. Molloy know all this?" Susan Carol asked.

"No, I'm sure not," Hatley said. "And I'll be very sorry when she finds out her husband hasn't been honest with her all these years."

"Have you talked to Norbert this week?" Stevie asked.

He shook his head. "No. We keep in touch sporadically, mostly by e-mail now. He updates me on the kids, things like that. I wrote to him to congratulate him after game two but didn't hear back, which certainly isn't surprising. Then that guy Walsh showed up on my doorstep saying that if I talked to anyone in the media, it could cost Norbert millions."

"You just talked to us," Stevie said.

"I know," Hatley said. "But the ship sailed on this staying secret days ago. I mean, what are the chances I could convince you this has nothing to do with baseball and that you shouldn't write about it? About zero, I'd guess. So if it's going to come out, it should come out the way it really happened."

"Norbert hasn't told the truth about what happened," Susan Carol said. "That makes it a story."

"Maybe. But maybe you can understand why he wouldn't want it splashed over the headlines. Norbert was a good guy going through a very bad time: he was killing his career and his marriage with his drinking. He's carried the guilt for Analise's death around for twelve years, and I don't think he's had a drink since that night. That may not be the squeaky-clean, feel-good story people are looking for, but it's not a bad story of redemption, if you ask me."

There was something to that, for sure. Susan Carol stood up. "Can we get a phone number for you?" she said. "I'm sure we'll want to get back in touch before anyone writes anything."

He pointed at her notebook, which she handed him,

and wrote down a phone number. "There's my e-mail too," he said, handing the notebook back. He led them to the door. "I'm sorry again about Friday," he said. "I overreacted. All I really want is what's best for Norbert and those kids."

They shook hands at the door and then sprinted back through the rain to the cab.

"You guys okay?" Miles Hoy asked when they climbed back inside.

"We're fine," Susan Carol said. "Just completely, absolutely, and totally confused."

Stevie called Kelleher from the cab to tell him they had spoken to both Molloy and Hatley.

"That's good work," Kelleher said. "What'd you figure out?"

"It's complicated," Stevie said. "The next train back is at four-thirty. Why don't I call you from the train? I'll fill you in then."

On the way to the train station, they told Miles Hoy about Hatley's version of events.

"I never heard about him teaching over at Radford," Hoy said. "But that doesn't mean it isn't true. Easy enough to check, I guess."

"Miles, can we possibly ask you one more favor?" Susan Carol said.

"Name it," he said.

"I know you weren't here back then, but you must know some of the cops who have been on the force long enough to remember what it was like at King's Tavern back then. We don't have time to hang around here and try to track them down, but maybe . . ."

"I can do that," Miles said. "In fact, I think I can do better than that. I know the guy who's owned the place since it opened. Mickey DeSoto. Nicest guy you'll ever meet. I think he'd remember those days."

Stevie looked at his watch. "Is King's open today?" he said.

"Absolutely," Hoy said. "They serve a brunch and then dinner on Sunday."

"Do you think Mr. DeSoto would be there now?"

"I'd think so. . . ."

"We've got an hour and fifteen minutes until the train," Stevie said. "How about we swing by there?"

He looked at Susan Carol, who nodded. "Great idea," she said. "Maybe we can get a better sense of who—if *anyone*—is telling the truth."

21: CONFRONTATION

KING'S TAVERN LOOKED NOTHING like Stevie had pictured it. He'd imagined a dark place with tattered furniture and a bartender named Joe.

Instead it was brightly lit, with comfortable-looking booths and tables with white tablecloths on them. The bartender was definitely not named Joe. Her name tag said Amber, and she reminded Stevie a little bit of Tamara Mearns.

"Hey, Amber, is Mickey around?" Miles asked as the three of them approached the bar.

"In his office," she said, pointing in the direction of a hallway. "You want me to bring you something to drink back there?"

The place was pretty full, considering that it was midafternoon. Stevie noticed TV screens placed strategically around the bar area, with a different NFL game being shown on each screen.

"No thanks, hon, I'm fine," Miles said, waving at Amber and leading Stevie and Susan Carol down the hall.

"Are you the mayor of Lynchburg or something?" Susan Carol asked. "Does everyone know you?"

"Something like that," Miles said with a smile. He knocked on a door that was marked Big Boss and pushed it open just as they heard "Come on in" from the other side.

The office wasn't very big, or maybe it was but it appeared small when Mickey DeSoto stood up from behind the desk, hit a remote to turn off the TV, and came around to greet his visitors. He was, by Stevie's estimate, at least six foot five, and although he wasn't fat, he was just plain *big*—big shoulders, long arms, big all over. He had a shock of white hair and an easy smile.

"Hey, Miles, what's up!" he said enthusiastically. Seeing Stevie and Susan Carol, he stopped short and pointed. "I know you kids. Why do I know you kids?"

"*Kidsports*," Miles said.

"That's it!" DeSoto said. "Hey, grab chairs. What in the world brings you two to Lynchburg and my little establishment? Are you hungry?"

Actually, Stevie was starving. "We're kind of in a rush, Mr. DeSoto," Susan Carol said as they sat down. "We're trying to catch the four-thirty train to Washington."

"That's in an hour!" DeSoto roared. "Tell me what you want and I'll get the kitchen cranking. We'll have you fed and out of here with time to spare, won't we, Miles?"

"Take him up on it," Miles said. "The food's good."

Stevie ordered a hamburger and French fries and, coaxed by DeSoto, a vanilla milk shake. Susan Carol asked for lemonade and a Cobb salad—which made DeSoto wince noticeably.

"Come on, girl, we need to put some meat on your bones," DeSoto said. "Best steaks in town. It's on me. Give it a shot."

She thanked him but said no, and he raced off to put in the order.

"We need to get cracking here," Susan Carol said to Miles.

"If we're out of here at four-fifteen, even four-twenty, you'll make the train," Miles said. "Station's five minutes away."

DeSoto came back in and sat again. "So, much as I wish it were true, you didn't come to see me because you've heard how good our food is. What can I do for you?"

They had decided before coming inside that the best way to get a straight answer about Hatley and Doyle was to just ask about what he remembered about the two of them from twelve years ago without going through the whole story again.

"Mr. DeSoto—" Susan Carol began.

"Mickey, please," he interrupted.

"Okay, Mickey. I'm sure you know what a great story Norbert Doyle has become during this World Series. We're wondering what you remember about him from his days in Lynchburg."

The big smile vanished from Mickey DeSoto's face. "Is this to be quoted?" he asked.

"No, it's not," she said. "We're just trying to confirm some things. . . ."

"Like the fact that he drank?" DeSoto said. "Look, the guy straightened his life out. He went to rehab. He's raised those kids. Why revisit all this now?"

"We understand what you're saying," Stevie said. "But there are conflicting stories."

"About what?" DeSoto said.

Stevie looked at Susan Carol. She squared her shoulders. "How about if we ask it this way: what, if anything, can you tell us about Norbert's relationship with Officer Jim Hatley?"

The smile returned. "His relationship with Jim? Hell, he probably wouldn't be alive if not for Jim Hatley. The number of nights Jim drove him home from here when he was drunk are almost countless. I remember one night the two of us couldn't even stand him up. I had to throw the poor guy over my shoulder to get him to the car. How Jim got him inside his house, I have no idea."

"So Jim didn't drink with him then?" Stevie asked.

DeSoto laughed again just as the door opened and Amber came in carrying a tray full of food and drinks. She cleared space on a table next to DeSoto's desk and set up the food. She put down a plate with a healthy-looking steak on it for Miles.

"Amber, I didn't ask for anything," Miles said.

"I know," she said, smiling at him. "But I know what you like."

She walked out, leaving Miles looking a little bit red-faced. Stevie was curious but knew this wasn't the time to ask Miles any personal questions.

"You were saying about Jim Hatley," Susan Carol said, taking a sip from her lemonade.

"Jim never drank in here after work—never," DeSoto said. "He came for the food and the company. That summer he just more or less adopted Norbert because the kid needed help. He was the one who got him to go to rehab after the accident."

"What do you know about Joe Molloy's relationship with Analise Doyle?" Susan Carol asked, switching subjects on a dime.

DeSoto shrugged. "Not much. I know that he had dated her before she ended up with Norbert, but to be honest, I don't remember if I found that out before she died or—"

He stopped in midsentence and smacked himself in the forehead. "I can't believe I forgot about that," he said, almost to himself.

"Forgot about what?" Susan Carol said.

"The night of the accident, Joe Molloy was in here."

"Afterward?" Susan Carol said.

"No. Before. He came in for dinner and sat at the bar. I remember asking him if he had the night off, because he was having a glass of wine with his dinner. I was surprised when he said he had the graveyard shift, because it wasn't like Joe to drink at all, much less drink before he went on duty."

"Did he drink a lot that night?" Stevie asked.

"I don't know," DeSoto said. "I wasn't working the bar, I just stopped to talk for a minute. He might have only had the one glass of wine. Even that surprised me. Like I said, he was never a drinker—still isn't, in all the years I've known him."

This was an interesting twist to the story—or maybe not. Maybe it was another meaningless scrap of information. But what was truly important was that DeSoto had confirmed Jim Hatley's version of his relationship with Doyle. They finished their food and thanked him for his time.

"What kind of story do you plan to write?" he asked as they stood to leave.

"Honestly? We have no idea," Susan Carol said. "There's one more person to talk to, and if he won't tie up the loose ends, then they can't be tied."

"Joe Molloy?" DeSoto said.

Susan Carol shook her head. "Norbert Doyle," she said. She reached across the desk to shake his hand. "Thanks very much for the meal. And the conversation." She turned to Stevie. "We need to go catch that train."

Miles Hoy tried hard to turn down the hundred-dollar bill Kelleher had given Stevie that morning to pass on to him.

"I'm not allowed back in Washington if I'm still carrying this money," Stevie said. "You've more than earned it."

"I'll take it on one condition," Miles said. "You invite me to Philly for a game next year and Susan Carol comes up for the game too."

"Done," they both said. Hugs were exchanged and they made the train with about a minute to spare.

As soon as they were settled, Stevie called Kelleher, who was headed to the ballpark. "What's the weather like back there?" Stevie asked.

"Lousy," he said. "It's drizzling right now and cold. They say the rain will clear off but the temperature will probably be in the forties for the game."

Stevie groaned at the thought. He walked Kelleher step by step through their afternoon. When he was finished, Kelleher sighed.

"Let's assume that Hatley's version is the truth," he said. "That would mean Molloy has now lied twice. Is there more that we don't know? That he's not telling us?"

Stevie thought. "Well, if he knows that going straight to the restaurant rather than just calling Hatley might have been the difference . . ."

"Then he's got a lot to feel guilty about," Kelleher said. "It's bad police work, and really bad human work. It probably would hurt his career. And it could hurt his reputation even more, especially with Norbert Doyle being a national hero right now."

"Why wouldn't he just tell us about it off the record?" Stevie said.

"With his wife maybe listening around a corner?" Kelle-her said. "I doubt he's ever told her or anyone else the truth, if that's what the truth is. Plus, you guys told him he couldn't go off the record today, right?"

"True," Stevie said. "So, what do we do now?"

"We wait until tomorrow and find a way to talk to Nor-bert Doyle. Whether *he'll* tell the truth is a completely different question."

Stevie hung up and filled Susan Carol in on what Kelle-her had said. Which reminded him of something.

"The thing you knew that you didn't want to tell me last night," he said. "It was rehab, right?"

She nodded. "Yes. Now that three different people told you about it today, I'm off the hook. I never broke my word to David, and you've got the story anyway."

"I'm not so sure what we've got," he said.

"We're close," she said. "I think Bobby's right. There is a missing piece to the puzzle. Molloy is still lying for some reason, and Doyle or Felkoff or both didn't want us talking to Hatley because he might tell us the truth."

"But the part Molloy seems to be lying about makes him look bad, not Doyle," Stevie said. "Molloy and Hatley both agreed that Norbert shouldn't have been driving and probably caused the accident because he was drunk."

Susan Carol nodded. "You're right. The big difference is that in the Molloy version he's the hero because he forced Doyle to go to rehab. In the Hatley version he and Norbert decided that on the night of the accident."

"Seems to me we're splitting hairs here—especially in

terms of what the public outside of Lynchburg, Virginia, cares about."

"Good point," she said.

Stevie reopened *The Great Gatsby*, hoping to get some serious reading done before they got back to Washington. It wasn't a very long book if he could just focus for a while. Susan Carol was working on her computer, finishing her paper, writing along as if it were a ball game sidebar. He decided to try to finish his book before the train pulled back into Union Station.

Twenty minutes later he closed the book after having read about two pages. He couldn't stop thinking about Doyle and Molloy and Hatley and Analise and David and Morra. He must have dropped off, because Susan Carol roused him as the bright lights of the station came into view.

"Come on, Sleeping Beauty," she said. "With luck, we'll be at the park in time for first pitch."

They actually walked in during the national anthem, drawing comments from their seatmates about how nice it was of them to show up.

"Believe it or not, we had to catch up on our schoolwork today," Susan Carol said as they sat down. "We're only moonlighting here, you know." In her case, at least, there was some truth in what she was saying.

Game five, unfortunately, was a lot like game one, except that the weather was miserable. Even wearing a sweater and a rain jacket, Stevie found himself shivering as the temperature kept dropping.

The Red Sox jumped ahead 3–0 in the first inning when Jason Bay hit a three-run home run, and the Nationals simply couldn't touch Josh Beckett's pitching. He left after seven innings with a 5–0 lead even though he had thrown only eighty-two pitches.

"Why would they take him out after he's only thrown eighty-two pitches?" Stevie asked.

"So they can bring him back if they need him to pitch an inning or two of relief in game seven," Barry Svrluga said. "Smart move by Francona, unless the bullpen blows up."

It didn't. Okajima walked Ryan Zimmerman and Adam Dunn to start the bottom of the eighth and stir the crowd slightly. John Farrell, the Red Sox pitching coach, trotted to the mound.

"What does he say to a Japanese-speaking pitcher in this situation?" Stevie asked.

"I think 'Throw strikes, damn it' is a universal in any language," Svrluga said.

"I've always wondered what they say on the mound," Susan Carol said.

"Well, it's not like *Bull Durham*," Svrluga said. "They don't talk about getting candlesticks for a wedding gift or gloves being jinxed. In this situation it's basic: 'You've got a five-run lead, let them hit the ball.' Sometimes the pitching coach will come out because he sees something technically wrong. Other times it's to talk about how to pitch to a specific hitter."

"And sometimes," Mark Maske put in, "it's just to give the guy a rest or to stall so the bullpen can get ready."

There was no one warming in the Red Sox bullpen at that moment, and Farrell appeared to be talking animatedly to Okajima, who kept nodding his head. Stevie decided Svrluga was right: "Throw strikes, damn it" was a universal.

Whatever Farrell said worked. Okajima found the plate as soon as he left the mound and got the next three hitters in order. The Red Sox went down one-two-three in the ninth, but it didn't matter. Jonathan Papelbon was lights-out in the bottom of the inning, ending the game with a three-pitch strikeout of Aaron Bleepin' Boone.

This time Kelleher wanted Stevie in the Nationals clubhouse to get the hitters to talk about why Beckett—who was now 10-2 lifetime in postseason and 4-1 in the World Series—was so unhittable in October.

"If you see Doyle, just keep moving," Kelleher said. "We don't want to talk to him until tomorrow in Boston at the earliest."

Stevie kept an eye out for Doyle as he moved around the quiet clubhouse. He had talked to a few players but then wandered over to Boone's locker, since he had made the last out and was always good for a smart one-liner or explanation of what had happened.

Just as he arrived, a TV crew from Boston pushed in close to Boone and a guy with a blow-dried TV haircut stuck a mike in Boone's face and said, "After that strikeout in the ninth, Aaron, do you feel as if the Red Sox evened the score with you in this World Series?"

Stevie couldn't help himself, he laughed out loud. Boone looked right at him and winked. Then, with a straight face, he said: "Oh yeah, I would definitely call it even. I was thinking, even though the bases were empty, If I could just hit a six-run home run right here, I could win the game just like last night."

The TV guy didn't even flinch a little. "So it's all even now, then?" he said.

"Actually, they're up three to two," Boone said.

Stevie had enough for his sidebar. As he started for the door, he noticed someone moving to block his path.

Norbert Doyle.

He tried to keep moving, but Doyle got right in front of him.

"Norbert, hi," Stevie said, trying to sound friendly and casual.

Doyle ignored the greeting. "Why are you doing this?" he said, standing very close to Stevie. "Do you understand what's at stake here? Do you know what happens if you write your damn story?"

"The truth comes out?" Stevie said, glancing around in the hope that no one would notice the conversation.

"The truth?" Doyle said, his voice rising. "You don't know the truth. You aren't even close to it."

"How do you know what we're close to?" Stevie asked, then regretted it because he really didn't want an argument.

"I know," Doyle said. He moved even closer to Stevie. "Let me tell you something, you write anything that hurts my kids, and I'll come after you."

He wasn't shouting, but his voice was raised in an angry sort of whisper, and Stevie noticed a TV light shining in his face. Then another. Uh-oh. Player confronting kid reporter after World Series game. YouTube, here I come, he thought. Not to mention every local broadcast and maybe national too.

"Let's talk about this tomorrow," he said to Doyle. "Alone." He looked around and said quietly, "Off camera."

Doyle noticed the cameras too.

"Fine," he said. "But this isn't over."

He walked back in the direction of his locker. Stevie tried to get to the door as fast as he could, but two TV cameras and a radio microphone blocked his path.

"What was that about?" one of the TV guys asked, a mike shoved in his face.

Stevie knew he had to come off very calm or he would make things worse. "Nothing important," he said. "I have to get going, I'm on deadline."

"But he was angry at you?" the guy persisted.

"Lots of people get angry at me," Stevie said. "My English teacher is going to be *really* angry with me when I get back to school. I'm sorry, I have to go now."

He bolted for the door before anyone could ask him another question.

He could feel his heart pumping from adrenaline. He walked as quickly as he could, head down, in the direction of the press box elevator.

He was stopped by the sound of a familiar voice. "Did my father talk to you?"

He looked up and saw Morra Doyle and felt his face burning.

"Only for a minute," he said. "I think we're going to talk tomorrow. I gotta run, Morra, I'm right on deadline."

"That's fine," she said as he moved past her. "You may get some phone calls later."

"Phone calls?"

"I think I may have to tell people how I had to fend you off at lunch when you tried to come on to me."

He stopped and turned around. "Whaa?"

She gave him a sweet smile. "Do you think people won't believe me?" she said. "See you in Boston."

She turned and walked down the hall, leaving Stevie standing there wishing he had never heard the name Doyle.

22: BACK TO BOSTON

STEVIE DIDN'T SAY ANYTHING about what had happened downstairs until everyone had written and filed their stories and they were on their way home in Kelleher's car.

"So, now they're resorting to blackmail," Tamara said when Stevie had finished.

"But it can't work," Susan Carol said. "No one will believe a story like that."

"As a matter of fact, there are people who *will* believe it," Kelleher said. "But being accused of getting a little forward on a date isn't that big a deal on today's gossip meter. Stevie, you're going to have to suck it up and just tell your side if it comes to that and not worry about what people think."

"Great," Stevie said. "My parents will be so proud."

"Mine too, if it comes to that," Susan Carol said.

Tamara's cell phone rang. She looked at the number for a second and then answered.

"What's up, Chico?" she said.

Stevie knew that Chico Harlan was the *Post*'s Nationals beat writer. Tamara listened for a minute, rolled her eyes, and said, "Hang on a sec."

Holding her hand over the phone, she said, "According to Chico, several people went to talk to Doyle after the clubhouse incident. He said he had been telling you to stay away from his daughter, to stop calling her all the time."

"That didn't take long," Stevie said.

"They can't not write it," Tamara said. "It'll just be a note, but he wants to know if Stevie has any comment."

Stevie looked at Kelleher, who looked at him in the rearview mirror. "Tell him that Stevie says, 'This isn't worthy of comment.'"

Tamara put the phone back to her ear and said, "Chico, Stevie says, 'This isn't worthy of comment—for the moment.'"

After she hung up, Kelleher said, "That's a better answer. Lets people know there will be some kind of response coming."

Stevie felt a little bit better, but not much.

He called his parents the next day and filled them in. His dad had read a note in the *Philadelphia Inquirer* similar to Harlan's except that it said he couldn't be reached for comment.

"Maybe you should come home instead of going to Boston," Bill Thomas said to his son. "It wouldn't be awful if you got back to school a couple days sooner, you know."

About the only thing Stevie was dreading more than Boston was going back to school. "No thanks, Dad, I'm going to go to Boston," he said.

His dad didn't argue. "Tell Bobby I expect him to keep an eye on you around the clock the rest of the way," he said.

"I'll tell him," Stevie said, intending to do nothing of the sort.

The flight back to Boston went smoothly, but when Stevie turned his phone back on in the airport, there were thirty-four messages for him. People had gotten his number and were looking for a follow-up on his brief no-comment to Harlan. Kelleher rolled his eyes when Stevie told him.

"You can answer all of them at once when we get to the ballpark tomorrow," he said. "Nothing before that. The clubhouses will be closed when we get there, and they'll all probably come at you when you walk onto the field. You'll deal with it then."

"What am I going to say?" Stevie asked.

"I'm not sure yet," Kelleher admitted.

The four of them were sitting in Tamara and Bobby's room back at the Marriott Long Wharf, which had a wonderful view of Boston Harbor. Stevie found it hard to believe it was only six days ago that they had sat in this same hotel getting ready for the series to begin.

"The bigger question is, how do we nail down this

story?" Susan Carol said. "We can't write it without talking to Doyle, can we?"

"No, we can't," Kelleher said. "In fact, until we talk to Doyle, I'm not even sure there *is* a story."

"What do you mean?" Stevie asked.

Kelleher shrugged. "I can understand why the cops didn't go after him, and I'm not sure we should go after him either. His wife died—he has to live with that forever. If he admits he was drinking and tells us that the movie of his life isn't going to make up a second car or make him out to be innocent . . ."

"*If* there's a movie," Tamara put in.

"Right," Kelleher said. "If he admits it, I'm not sure we write it."

"What if he keeps lying?"

"Then we have two cops on the record saying he was drinking that night. Maybe then we have to write it, I don't know. But first we have to talk to him."

Tamara said, "May be easier said than done. Doyle may have wanted to confront Stevie last night, but I'm sure Felkoff will advise him *not* to talk to us about the night of the accident. Too much to lose, not a lot to gain. Felkoff—jerk that he is—should be smart enough to know there's no story unless we talk to him again."

"Felkoff may be talking to Norbert about all this, but he's probably not talking to David and Morra much," Susan Carol said. "What if I talked to David again?"

"Have you two still been talking?" Tamara asked, an instant before Stevie could ask the same question.

"No," she said. "Not since Saturday. He sent me a text yesterday saying he knew I had gone with Stevie to Lynchburg and that he was very disappointed in me. I wrote back that I had *not* broken my word to him. That's the last I've heard from him."

"So, what do you propose?" Bobby said.

"I could ask for a meeting. Just the two of us. Try to make him understand we aren't out to get his dad or him or Morra, but we need to talk, we need to know the truth."

"I don't think that's going to work," Bobby said. "With all due respect to your ability to charm people, Susan Carol, even if he thinks it's a good idea, Felkoff won't."

"So, what do we do then?" Susan Carol asked.

Stevie had been quiet throughout the conversation. Now he sat up straight. "How about if we bluff them?" he said.

"What do you mean?" Bobby said.

"What if we sit down and write the story—everything we know. *Then* Susan Carol calls David and asks for a meeting with him and Morra. We present the story to them and say it's going in the paper on Thursday and that his dad has until Wednesday to tell us his side."

Stevie looked at Tamara.

"It might work," she said.

"We still have to try to call Doyle first," Kelleher said. "Just straight-out say we need to talk to him."

"What if he says no or doesn't respond?" Stevie asked.

"Then maybe we go with your plan," Kelleher said.

"Do you think Doyle and Felkoff would know it's a bluff?" Stevie said.

"I don't think they can afford to take the chance, do you?" Tamara said.

Kelleher nodded. "You might be right."

He picked up the phone, called the Ritz-Carlton, and left a message for Doyle. He looked at Susan Carol. "In the meantime," he said, "why don't you give David a call."

She took out her phone and began punching buttons. Even though he completely believed her when she said nothing had happened that day on the Freedom Trail, Stevie was very relieved to see that David Doyle was not on Susan Carol's speed dial.

Not surprisingly, Susan Carol got his voice mail. She left a message telling David, "It's very important that you call me about the story Stevie and I are writing right now."

"That should get a response," she said.

Only it didn't. The afternoon passed with no answer from either Norbert Doyle or David Doyle. Kelleher called John Dever to ask him to please pass a message to Doyle. An hour later Dever called him back. "Norbert says he's got no interest in talking to you guys," Dever said. "I'm sorry, I did try."

Shortly before they left for dinner, Susan Carol sent David a text saying the same thing as the phone message. They ate at a very crowded, very loud—but very good—restaurant called Grill 23.

There were lots of baseball people in the restaurant—

writers, TV people, and folks who worked for Major League Baseball.

Stevie saw Phyllis Merhige and Rich Levin, the two PR people whom Bobby and Tamara were friendly with, walking toward the table. Right behind them was a familiar figure: Bud Selig, the commissioner of baseball.

"You all know the commissioner, don't you?" Merhige asked as they walked up.

"No, we've never met," Kelleher said, clearly joking as he stood up to shake hands.

"Tamara, *when* are you going to explain how you ended up with this one?" Selig said, moving on to give Mearns a kiss.

"He promised he could get me into baseball games," Tamara said.

"And this must be young Mr. Thomas and young Miss Anderson," Selig said as both Stevie and Susan Carol stood to shake his hand.

"I guess the good news for us is that you two are covering the World Series and no one has been kidnapped or blackmailed or covered up a drug test," Selig said with a smile.

"As far as you know, Commissioner," Kelleher said.

"Don't even joke about that, Bobby," Selig said.

He waved his goodbyes and followed Levin to the front door.

Merhige lingered for a moment. "Everything okay?" she said, mostly to Kelleher but clearly to the whole table.

"Everything's going to be fine, Phyllis," Kelleher said.

"I hope so," Phyllis said. "If you need me . . ."

"Thanks, Phyllis, we know," Kelleher said.

She followed Selig and Levin to the door.

"You like Selig?" Susan Carol asked.

"I like him a lot," Kelleher said. "I don't always agree with him—in fact, I disagree with him often. But I definitely like him."

They decided to walk back to the hotel. It was a brisk night, but it wasn't windy and it wasn't that far. They were about halfway back when Susan Carol's phone began playing the Duke fight song. She pulled it out of her pocket, looked at the number, and said, "It's him."

They all knew who "him" was without asking.

"David, I didn't think you were ever going to call me," she said, picking up, not in a Scarlett voice but in a pleasant one. After Doyle had talked for a few seconds, she responded.

"I think you probably have a good idea what's in the story," she said. "But you should see it so you understand exactly what's at stake."

She listened for another moment. "As long as we give your dad the chance to answer our questions, we've done our job. Bobby Kelleher tried to contact him today, and he said he wouldn't talk to us. If he won't meet with us alone, then we'll try to talk in the clubhouse tomorrow night. And if he ducks that, we'll try one more time. But if all we get is 'No comment,' we've still done all we need to do."

She pulled the phone away from her ear suddenly and Stevie could hear shouting coming from the other end.

"How about one o'clock tomorrow in Faneuil Hall?" she said. "We'll get pizza and meet you in the dining area."

"Crowded is what we want, David," she said in response to his next comment.

She listened one more time. "Of course I'm bringing Stevie. You should bring Morra. Maybe she can apologize for those lies your dad was telling about Stevie last night."

She looked at the phone and smiled. "He hung up."

"You think they'll show?" Stevie said.

"They'll show," Susan Carol said. "The question is, will they take our bait?"

"Well, as of this moment we have no bait," Kelleher said. "You guys need to get to bed so you can get an early start on writing this 'story.'"

Stevie and Susan Carol agreed to meet for breakfast at eight o'clock so they would have plenty of time to work on the story before the one o'clock meeting. Stevie picked at his French toast while staring out at the harbor. It was a crisp, gorgeous New England fall day.

"I think I could live here," he said to Susan Carol.

"Come back in January and tell me if you still feel that way," she said.

He knew she was right, although Philadelphia wasn't exactly Fort Lauderdale that time of year either.

They went to her room after breakfast and by eleven o'clock had a story they were ready to show Kelleher and Mearns. It was long—way long, close to three thousand words—but it seemed impossible to Stevie to explain everything without writing that long. Since they didn't have a printer available, Kelleher sat with their laptop, with Tamara reading over his shoulder.

"Well?" Susan Carol said when they were done.

"To be honest, you haven't got it," Tamara said. "This would never get in the paper because it's completely unclear if Doyle is anything more than someone who made a horrible mistake and paid a huge price for it. It's also not clear if Molloy is the bad guy or if no one is the bad guy. You can't say for sure whether or not the accident happened because he was drinking. It seems clear there was some kind of police cover-up, but not what they were covering up or why."

"All of which doesn't matter right now," Kelleher said. "Tamara's right, of course, but we aren't selling this to editors or lawyers, we're selling it to Morra and David. If they believe we're prepared to print this, they might convince their dad to talk to you before it goes in the paper."

"In fact," Mearns said, "you should add a sentence saying he refused to comment, to show them that's how it will look if he doesn't talk."

Kelleher and Mearns made a few more changes: they wanted to pump up the notion that Doyle had lied on some level when he told Stevie the week before that his wife had been killed by a drunk driver.

Then Kelleher also added:

If there is one thing clear in the police report, it is that only one driver was involved in the accident that killed Analise Doyle. If, as Doyle said a week ago, she was killed by a drunk driver, was he saying that *he* was the drunk driver responsible for his wife's death?

And while Doyle has said he missed the rest of that season due to injuries suffered in the accident, two police officers said this week that he went directly to an alcohol rehabilitation clinic after the accident.

Doyle refused comment when asked for further details this week.

Mearns shook her head reading that. "You *know* that wouldn't make it past a lawyer in a million years," she said.

"Yes," Kelleher said. "I know. But I doubt that the Doyle kids do. Felkoff might advise Doyle that it's libel, but we've got both Hatley and Molloy on the record, so it's not so cut-and-dried."

Stevie and Susan Carol went downstairs to the hotel's business center to print out some copies of the story. They gave copies to Kelleher and Mearns and left the hotel at about twelve-thirty, wanting time to eat and be ready before the Doyles arrived. Stevie was both nervous and hungry. He was also wishing they were just taking a walk on this beautiful fall day.

"It's such a nice day, I'd even go for a walk on the Freedom Trail with you."

"You know, you *might* actually enjoy it," Susan Carol said. "Wouldn't you at least like to see the church where Paul Revere told them, 'One if by land, and two if by sea'?"

"I think I'd rather go see Harvard Stadium," he said. "Oldest in the country, you know."

She groaned. They ordered their pizza and walked to the dining area. Stevie was considering going back for a third slice when he saw David and Morra approach. Neither was carrying any kind of food. Clearly, they were here strictly for business.

"Make this fast," David said by way of a greeting.

"Nice to see you too," Stevie said, going very quickly from nervous to annoyed.

"Have you got the story?" Morra asked.

Susan Carol reached into her purse and pulled out two copies of the story.

David's and Morra's eyes narrowed as they read. At one point David said, "How can you say my dad had no comment when you haven't asked him about any of this?"

"Bobby Kelleher left him a message yesterday *and* called John Dever, who said he wouldn't talk to us," Susan Carol said. "Obviously, if he talks to us, we'll change that. We can change anything. Right now these are the facts as we know them."

"This is *so* unfair!" Morra screamed.

"Then tell your dad to talk to us so we can make it fair,"

Stevie said. "*He* started all of this by saying a drunk driver killed your mom."

"You're nothing but a self-righteous asshole, Thomas!" David Doyle said, leaning close to Stevie so he wasn't heard by everyone around them. He appeared to be about eleven feet tall at that moment, but Stevie wasn't going to back down.

Stevie said, "You're just pissed because you've tried every dirty trick to keep us from getting this story, and we got it anyway."

"No you *didn't*. You've got nothing!" David said, shoving Stevie so hard that he tumbled backward and fell into someone at the next table.

"*Hey!*" Stevie heard the person shout. Jumping up, Stevie ran straight at David, and the two of them went flying, landing on the ground with Stevie on top. Doyle was stronger than he was, and he could feel him rolling over to get on top of him. That would not be good. He pulled a hand free and swung a fist at David, catching him on the side of the head. He felt a stinging sensation in his hand and then heard loud voices saying, "Break this up, break this up!"

A security guard was pulling David away, and another was pulling Stevie to his feet. David struggled briefly, but the beefy guard was holding on tight. Stevie didn't struggle. He was relieved someone had intervened. The fight, he suspected, would not have gone well for him if it had continued.

"You want to fight, you take it someplace else," the security guard holding David said. "You got that?"

David didn't answer. "Hey, kid, you got that?" the guard repeated. "Start in again and we'll call the cops and let them deal with you. Understand?"

Stevie nodded that he understood.

"Yeah, yeah, fine," David said.

The two guards let the boys go, then stood there to make sure no one lunged for anyone.

Stevie pointed a finger at both Doyles. "The story runs Thursday," he said, aware that people were still watching and listening. "One way or the other."

He turned to Susan Carol. "Let's go," he said.

"This isn't over, Thomas," he heard David shout as he turned to walk away. "I promise you it's not over."

Stevie knew that David Doyle was right. This was far from over.

23: THE MEETING

STEVIE WONDERED HOW SUSAN CAROL WOULD FEEL about his fight with David, and if she had noticed that when the security guards showed up, he was about to lose. Her concern didn't seem to be about the outcome of the fight so much as the fact that there had been a fight.

"Are you okay?" she kept asking. "You know how badly you could have been hurt fighting with someone that size? What is it with you boys that you have to start fights?"

"I'm fine," he said. "My hand's a little sore from punching him, but I'm okay."

She paused—they were crossing the street in front of the hotel now—and gave him the Smile. "Stevie, you were very brave to go after that bully," she said. "You were also very stupid to stoop to his level."

He started to respond but was just smart enough not to.

They went straight to Bobby and Tamara's room to report what had happened. Kelleher was smiling when he opened the door. "So, you're giving up journalism for boxing, I hear?" he said as he ushered the two of them into the room.

"How did you hear anything?" Stevie asked.

"Sit down and I'll tell you. But first tell me if you're hurt. You don't look any the worse for wear."

Stevie held up his left hand, which was still throbbing a bit. "I could probably use some ice for this," he said.

Tamara jumped up. "I'll go get some. Bobby, you fill them in on the call."

"Call?" they both said.

Kelleher nodded. "Felkoff. I just hung up with him. I'm guessing David and Morra called him or their dad right after you all went in separate directions. He said he's going to read the story and get back to us on whether there will be any comment from Doyle. He also said, 'If it's the bunch of lies that David and Morra say it is, I'll get a court order to stop you.'"

"What'd you say to that?" Susan Carol asked.

"I suggested in the kindest terms possible that they deal with the facts in the story rather than making threats about it. We won't be the only ones chasing this down—he might as well deal with us."

Tamara returned with the ice and wrapped it in a towel for Stevie.

"So, let's get to the good stuff," Kelleher said. "Tell us about the fight. Felkoff claimed you jumped David."

"Oh, that is *such* a lie," Susan Carol said indignantly.

"I figured as much," Kelleher said. "Did you hurt him when you punched him, Stevie?"

Stevie shook his head. "I doubt it. I caught him on the side of the head, and he's got a pretty hard head."

In a cab to the stadium, they actually talked about baseball and the chances of there even being a game seven for Norbert Doyle to pitch in. For that to happen the Nationals would need a winning performance from Shairon Martis against Daisuke Matsuzaka tonight.

"I just have this feeling," Stevie said as they pulled up to the ballpark, "that this thing is going seven."

"Me too," Susan Carol said. "Stevie and I don't do routine endings very often."

"You got that right," Kelleher said with a nod.

Even though this was only the third time Stevie had been through the Fenway press gate and walked down the hallway to the field entrance, he felt as if he'd been doing it all his life. He felt almost calm as they walked past the Red Sox clubhouse. The series could end tonight if the Red Sox won. Even if it went seven games, he would be back home in school no later than Friday. That thought made him less calm: he still hadn't finished *The Great Gatsby*.

As soon as they walked onto the field, he heard some-one call his name: "Steve, hey, Steve Thomas."

He turned and saw a coterie of media heading in his di-rection. Right! He'd almost forgotten that he was news af-ter Doyle's accusations.

Kelleher held up a hand to stop them. "Okay, fellas, we know why you want to talk to Steve," he said. "Why don't you tell everyone who wants to talk to him to meet us over by the Red Sox dugout in five minutes."

Phyllis Merhige was standing a few feet away. "Jeez, Bobby, you guys want to use the interview room?"

"*No,*" Kelleher said, not noticing the smile on her face that told Stevie she was joking. "The less time this takes, the better."

"What do I say?" Stevie said as they walked in the di-rection of the dugout.

"Very simple," Kelleher said. "You tell them that all their questions will be answered when you finish the story you've been working on, and that the Doyles don't always get their facts straight. Do *not* call them liars, we don't want to be that strong just yet."

"And when they ask follow-up questions?"

"Just say, 'Read my story.' That's your mantra."

"Why don't I come too," Susan Carol said. She had walked up behind them while they were talking.

"Fine with me," Stevie said. "I could use the support."

A group of cameras and microphones were waiting for them.

It was Tyler Kepner, the *New York Times* Yankees beat

writer, who asked the first question. "Look, Steve, we don't want to make this a big deal," he said. "But the guy who may pitch a potential seventh game in the World Series pretty much confronted you in the clubhouse the other night, then said you were pursuing his daughter. What can you tell us?"

Before Stevie could give his Kelleher-coached answer, Susan Carol jumped in. "Here's what I can tell you," she said. "If Steve was pursuing Morra Doyle, the first person he'd have to answer to would be me—because *I'm* his girlfriend."

"So there's no chance he made phone calls without you knowing?" someone said.

This time Stevie jumped in. "Be serious," he said. "If you looked like me, and you were dating Susan Carol, would *you* be calling another girl?"

That got a laugh.

"Why is Doyle making this claim, then?" Kepner asked.

That was when Stevie went into his routine about the story he was working on and the Doyles having trouble getting all their facts straight. Several people tried to get him to break down, pointing out that if what the Doyles said was true, Stevie probably shouldn't be allowed to continue covering the series.

"That's right," Susan Carol said, jumping in. "But the *Herald*'s still got him here—another good reason to doubt the Doyles' claims."

Kelleher showed up at that point to ask if there were any more questions. There were none. "Thanks, Susan

Carol," Stevie said as the crowd began to break up. "You bailed me out. . . ."

"Again," she said. "I have to go find Tamara. I'll see you in a couple minutes."

Stevie and Kelleher were walking in the direction of the exit to head upstairs when Kelleher's cell phone rang.

"Felkoff," he said, looking at the number.

"I was about to give up on you," he said, picking up.

"Fine," he said in response to whatever Felkoff had said. "We'll be there in five minutes." He snapped the phone shut.

"He says Stan Kasten gave him use of his box for the next thirty minutes," Kelleher said. "Let's go."

They took an elevator up to the luxury suite level. Stan Kasten, the Nationals' president, was waiting for them as they got off. "These are the guys I told you about," he said to the guard at the door. "They're with me."

"Stan," Kelleher said with a smile, "tell me you're not in cahoots with Felkoff."

"I'm *not*," Kasten said, clearly not as amused by Kelleher's gibe as Kelleher. "But he represents my game-seven pitcher—if there is a game seven—and he's all over me saying you guys are about to drop a bomb on us. I told him he could use our box to talk, so you can have some privacy."

"Did he tell you what it's about?" Kelleher said.

"No. And I don't want to know unless you really are going to drop something big on us. Then I expect a phone call from you, giving me fair warning."

"You got it, Stan," Kelleher said.

They had reached the box marked Washington Nationals Ownership.

"He's waiting," Kasten said. "You've put me in a terrible position."

"Why?" Kelleher said.

"I think I may be rooting for Felkoff on this one," he said. "The thought makes me just a little bit sick."

He headed down the hall.

"Ready?" Kelleher asked.

"Never more ready in my life," Stevie said.

Kelleher pushed the door open. David Felkoff, printout of their story in hand, was waiting for them.

There were no niceties or phony handshakes when they walked in. Felkoff started right in on them.

"This story isn't even close to true," he said. "You print this, you'll have libel suits coming at you from about ten different directions."

"Really?" Kelleher said. "Doyle told Stevie his wife was killed by a drunk driver. Stevie got the police report, talked to the police officers involved *and* the Doyles' babysitter to piece together the truth, and this is what he got. How are you going to prove malice, which you'd need to do in this case since Doyle's a public figure?"

Felkoff stared at the two of them for a moment. "So you're willing to put your paper's reputation on the line based on the reporting of a fourteen-year-old?" he said. "I'm betting Wyn Watkins won't be quite so confident about that when I call him in the morning."

Wyn Watkins was the executive editor of the *Herald*. He had almost pulled the story Stevie and Susan Carol had written accusing the owner of the California Dreams of covering up steroid use by his players on the eve of the Super Bowl. But he hadn't, and the story had been proven completely true.

"Go ahead and make the call," Kelleher said. "Watkins has put his faith in Stevie on a page-one story before, and it paid off. I doubt you'll have much luck, but please, be my guest and call him."

Felkoff was red in the face. "How can you print this *now*? He may be pitching game seven of the World Series tomorrow night. You expect him to talk to you on the day he pitches game seven? Are you crazy?"

"He could have talked to us on the off day or today," Stevie said, jumping in. "Instead he spent the time spreading lies about me and refusing our calls. So don't blame us if the timing doesn't suit you guys."

"Was I talking to you, kid?" Felkoff said.

"You better talk to him," Kelleher said. "It's his story."

Felkoff paced around in a circle for a few seconds. Stevie started to say something else, but Kelleher put a restraining hand on his shoulder.

"Okay," Felkoff said. "Here's the deal. You come to my Boston office at eleven o'clock tomorrow morning and I'll have Norbert there."

Kelleher shook his head. "No way we're doing this on your terms or in your office. There's a small park on the back side of the Marriott Long Wharf. It's never very crowded. You guys meet us there at nine o'clock in the morning."

"Nine o'clock?" Felkoff said. "You know Norbert won't be in bed until one a.m. tonight. Why so early?"

"Because none of the writers will be in bed before two," Kelleher said. "We want to be sure no one wanders by on their way out for breakfast. At nine o'clock it will be just us and a few out-of-work joggers. He can take a nap after the meeting."

Felkoff stared at both of them with a kind of pure hatred Stevie couldn't remember ever seeing before.

"All right, nine o'clock," he said finally. "You better be quick."

"If Doyle answers our questions, and tells the truth, it won't take long at all," Kelleher said. "We'll see you then."

They turned to walk out the door. "Hey, kid," Felkoff said.

Stevie turned back. "The name's Steve."

"Yeah, whatever. Just one question: how do you sleep at night?"

Stevie looked at Felkoff, searching for an answer for a moment. Then it came to him. "On my side, occasionally on my stomach."

Kelleher laughed out loud. And the two of them walked out the door.

•   •   •

The rest of the night was incident-free. And the game seemed pretty average too. Neither Martis for the Nationals nor Matsuzaka for the Red Sox pitched very well. It was 3–3 after five innings, but then Matsuzaka lost the plate in the sixth. With one out he walked Cristian Guzman, hit Elijah Dukes with a pitch, and then walked Ryan Zimmerman. After the pitching coach paid a visit to the mound, presumably to suggest in both English and Japanese that Dice-K throw strikes, Adam Dunn came to the plate for the Nationals.

Matsuzaka threw ball one. Then catcher Jason Varitek trotted out to the mound.

"Now they're just stalling," Barry Svrluga said. "They didn't have the bullpen up soon enough, and they're not ready."

"Shouldn't they get a lefty in here to face Dunn?" Stevie asked.

"They should get someone in who can throw a strike," Mark Maske said.

"Sometimes you just have to take a sack," George Solomon put in, causing everyone to stare at him as if *he* were speaking Japanese.

Matsuzaka threw ball two and the crowd grew restless, beseeching Matsuzaka to find the plate.

"Is he swinging here?" Susan Carol asked.

"If the ball's anywhere near the plate, he's swinging," Svrluga said. "Dunn knows he *has* to come in with a fastball. This is his chance to break the game open."

Matsuzaka checked the runners—who were all dancing

around, trying to distract him even though they had no place to go—and threw again. Svrluga had called it. The pitch was a fastball straight down Broadway, and Dunn crushed it. The ball rose high into the night and easily cleared the wall in right-center field, landing in the Red Sox bullpen.

Except for a small coterie of Nationals fans, the ballpark was absolutely silent as Adam Dunn trotted around the bases. Terry Francona came to the mound to get Matsuzaka, causing Susan Carol to shake her head and say, "Talk about shutting the barn door too late."

Even with a 7–3 lead the Nationals weren't home free. Martis gave up a run in the sixth. Then the Red Sox scored single runs off the Nationals bullpen in the seventh and eighth. With men on first and second, and just one out in the eighth, Manny Acta brought in his closer, Joel Hanrahan.

"He's got no choice," Maske commented. "He can't trust anyone else at this point."

Hanrahan struck out Youkilis and got Pedroia to pop out to end the inning, and the Nationals clung to their 7–6 lead. Wanting to be sure the lead *stayed* at one, Francona brought in closer Jonathan Papelbon to pitch the ninth, and he held the Nats right there.

"This won't be easy," Stevie said, looking at his scorecard as Hanrahan warmed up. "Ortiz, Bay, and Lowell."

Ortiz proved him right, crushing a 2-0 Hanrahan fastball into the gap for a double to start off the ninth inning. Hanrahan then walked Bay. Out to the mound came

Manny Acta. Stevie hadn't even glanced at the bullpen, since the Nationals already had their closer in the game.

"Wow, look at this," Svrluga said when Acta waved his arm in the direction of the bullpen. "This takes some guts."

Out of the pen came John Lannan—the Nationals' number one starting pitcher. "He hasn't pitched in relief all year," Susan Carol said, her media guide already open.

"It's the World Series," Maske said. "Those two runners score and the season is over. This is what they call all hands on deck."

Lannan came in throwing strikes. He was quickly ahead of Lowell with no balls and two strikes. His next pitch was a darting slider that Lowell tried to pull to left field. Instead he hit the ball right at Guzman, who flipped to second baseman Ronnie Belliard for a force at second base. Belliard's relay to first easily beat the slow-footed Lowell. The crowd, which had been on its feet as Lowell came up, sat down. The tying run was on third, but now there were two men out.

"Manny *is* magic," Susan Carol said.

"Not yet," Svrluga said. "Lannan still has to get Drew."

And he did. Drew hit a long fly ball to dead center field. If he had pulled the ball to right field, it might have been a series-winning home run over the Green Monster. Instead Dukes, the center fielder, drifted back and made the catch, and just like that, Manny Acta *was* magic and the series was tied at three games apiece.

Part of Stevie wished that the Red Sox had ended the series. But another part of him knew that a seventh game with Norbert Doyle pitching for the Nationals against knuckleballer Tim Wakefield pitching for the Red Sox was the way this series was probably supposed to end.

There were two questions left: who would win game seven, and what would be the big story the day after?

Stevie set the alarm for eight. They had decided that he and Susan Carol would go to the meeting with Kelleher and Tamara nearby if needed.

"Felkoff may not like you, Stevie, but he hates me," Kelleher said. "And I think Doyle will be less antagonistic to the two of you than to Tamara and me."

"Do you think we can ask all the right questions?" Susan Carol asked.

"I *know* you can ask all the right questions," Kelleher answered.

The four of them met for breakfast at eight-fifteen. If there was one thing Stevie would miss about Boston, it was eating breakfast looking out at Boston Harbor. Just before nine, he and Susan Carol walked out the back door of the hotel to the picturesque little park that separated the Marriott from the residential section of Boston's North End. They left Kelleher and Mearns just inside the door.

"We're on your speed dial, right?" Kelleher said to Susan Carol. "Any trouble at all, hit that button and we're there in about sixty seconds."

"Got it," Susan Carol said.

It was a brisk, breezy morning. It would be cold in the ballpark that night, but at the moment it was cool and, with sweaters on, quite comfortable.

Doyle and Felkoff were standing by a bench that looked out at the water—a slightly incongruous pair, with Felkoff in an expensive suit and Doyle in sweats and a baseball cap.

"Good morning," Susan Carol said as they walked up. The response was a curt nod from Felkoff and a halfhearted wave from Doyle.

"Maybe we should sit down," Stevie said.

"No need, we won't be here long," Felkoff said.

Even in sneakers Susan Carol was a couple of inches taller than Felkoff. She walked over to him, looked down, and said, "Mr. Felkoff, we need to ask our questions, and we need to tape-record Mr. Doyle's answers so we get this story exactly right. So the three of us are going to sit down on the bench and talk. What you do while we talk doesn't really matter; you're free to stand if you like."

Felkoff stared at her for a second, then snapped, "Now look, we can just call this off right now if you're going to cop an attitude—"

"It's okay, David," Doyle said, finally speaking up. "Where do you want me to sit, Susan Carol?"

She pointed to a spot on the bench, and he sat. She sat next to him, with Stevie next to her. She produced a tape recorder and put it on the bench between them. Felkoff stood behind the bench, arms folded, looking extremely unhappy.

"If you're going to record, I'm going to record too," he said, pulling a tape recorder out of his suit pocket.

"That's fine," Susan Carol said.

Susan Carol looked at Stevie, who nodded that she should begin.

"We didn't want it to come to this," she said to Doyle.

"Then why has it?" Doyle said. "What did I do to deserve having the two of you digging into my past?"

"You weren't honest about your past," Stevie said, leaning around Susan Carol to make sure Doyle could look him in the eye. "If you had told the truth about the accident from the beginning, we wouldn't be sitting here today."

"And Disney, DreamWorks, and Universal might not be in a bidding war for his story either," Felkoff said angrily.

"I guess they won't be after tomorrow, will they?" Doyle said.

"I don't know," Susan Carol said. "Sometimes the truth makes a better story than a fantasy. I know you feel terribly guilty about what happened, I understand—"

"*No, you don't!*" Doyle shouted. "How can you know what it feels like to be responsible for the fact that the mother of your children died when they were two years old! Do you know how that feels!?"

No, they didn't.

Susan Carol took a deep breath. "I apologize. Bad choice of words."

Stevie stepped in now. "Would you tell us what happened that night? Can you help us to understand?"

For a moment Stevie thought Doyle wasn't going to answer. Finally he nodded and started to talk very slowly.

"We'd gone out to dinner," he said. "We needed to talk about . . . things. It was a long night, a difficult one. I don't think, to tell the truth, I could tell you how much I had to drink. At that point I had a pretty high capacity."

"Did the conversation end well?" Susan Carol asked. "I mean, did you resolve things?"

"I don't want to get into that," he said. "It has nothing to do with the accident."

"It might," Stevie said. "It might explain why the accident happened."

"The accident happened because I was an alcoholic," Doyle said flatly.

"Did it also happen," Susan Carol said, speaking very slowly, "because of Joe Molloy?"

He stiffened and gave them a funny look. "Why would you ask about Joe?"

"We heard that you suspected there was something between Joe and your wife. . . ."

"Oh—that."

"Is it true? Is that what you were arguing about at dinner?"

"No. I might have thought that once or twice, when I'd been drinking, but it wasn't true. We weren't talking about Joe." Doyle paused a moment and then let out a breath he'd been holding.

"Analise told me in April, right at the start of the

season, that she was giving me until her birthday—August twelfth—to get sober, even if it meant going to rehab and missing part of the season," he said. "That night at dinner she told me she was done, she was going to leave me. You'd think that'd be enough for me to set my glass down, but no. Instead I got drunker. It was a terrible night. Analise was drinking too—which was unusual for her."

He stopped, and Stevie wondered if he was going to keep telling the story, but after a bit he continued.

"When we were leaving, the manager tried to take the keys from me, but I wouldn't let him. He said he'd call someone to take us home. . . ."

Tears suddenly appeared in Doyle's eyes. He put his hand up to wipe them away, then buried his head in his shoulder.

"Come on, Norbert, let's go," Felkoff said, putting a hand on his shoulder. "Enough is enough."

"No!" Doyle said fiercely, pushing Felkoff's hand away. "I've had enough of slippery half-truths. . . ."

They gave him a while to compose himself, before Stevie prompted, "So, the restaurant manager said he'd call someone to drive you home. . . ."

"Yeah. Jim Hatley's always felt that if he'd gotten there sooner, he could have prevented the accident, but I don't know. I wouldn't give up my keys to the manager, and I might not have given them to Jim either."

"But it wasn't Jim the manager called," said Susan Carol. "It was Joe Molloy."

"Who told you *that?*" Doyle seemed genuinely surprised.

"He did. And Jim Hatley confirmed it. But Jim said that Joe called him instead of going to the restaurant himself."

Doyle was silent for a moment. "Huh," he said. "Well, there are parts to the story even I didn't know, I guess. But that would explain why Joe was there later."

"At the accident scene, you mean?" asked Stevie.

"No, before then."

Now Stevie was completely confused. But Doyle pressed on with his story.

"I insisted I was okay to drive home, which, believe it or not, I probably was. I knew how to drive slow and careful when I was drunk. I'd had a lot of experience."

"Only this time you weren't okay," Susan Carol said.

"I don't know," Doyle said. "I never got to find out."

"What do you mean?" Stevie said, struggling to keep up.

"We got about a mile down the road," he said. "I was driving carefully, but all of a sudden a police car came up behind me and pulled me over. I couldn't figure it out. I really thought I was driving fine."

"And?" Stevie said, hoping he didn't sound as impatient as he was.

"It was Joe Molloy," Doyle said. "He asked how much I'd had to drink. I told him not that much, and he asked if I'd take a sobriety test. I really didn't want to do that, but I bluffed and said, 'Sure, fine.' Then Molloy said, 'Tell you what, since we're old teammates, I'll cut you a break. Let Analise drive home, and I won't test you."

"Oh my God," Susan Carol said, the truth hitting her at the same instant it hit Stevie.

"I agreed," Doyle said, starting to sob. "Analise might not have been as drunk as me, but she'd probably never driven drunk in her life. We'd gone a couple miles when we came around that curve too fast and . . ."

His voice broke up and he buried his head in his hands.

"Feel pretty good about yourselves?" Felkoff said low in Stevie's ear.

"Shut up, Felkoff," Stevie said. "You're not helping."

Susan Carol had her arm on Doyle's back.

"So, Analise was driving when the accident happened?" she asked softly.

He looked up at her, tears rolling down his face. "Do you understand?" he said. "If I'd been driving, we probably would have gotten home okay. But I didn't want to take that sobriety test. A DUI would have got me suspended, heck, maybe released. It wasn't like I was pitching all that well. So she drove. And she lost control of the car."

"But the police report?"

"I asked Jim not to tell anyone Analise was driving. It was my fault, and I didn't want the blame to fall on anyone but me. I never even told Jim that Molloy pulled us over . . . I don't know if he knows. . . ."

"Do the *kids* know? Any of this?" Stevie asked.

Doyle shook his head. "No. When they were little, I

told them there was another car involved—it just seemed easier than the complicated truth. When they were older and figured out that I went to rehab right after the accident, well, I'm sure they put it together. I've told them some of my memories about the accident scene because they seemed to need to know, but I've never told them all that led up to it. And I certainly never told them Analise was driving. Now I guess they'll know everything."

"Not if they can't prove you said all this," Felkoff said. He reached down suddenly and swiped both tape recorders off the bench and began running. Stevie jumped off the bench and chased him. It wasn't hard to catch him—Felkoff was overweight and over forty. Stevie tackled him halfway across the minipark, and they rolled in the grass.

Stevie saw one tape recorder fly out of his hand. He twisted Felkoff's wrist and heard him scream in pain. Then Felkoff kicked him in the stomach, and it was Stevie's turn to yell in pain.

Then, all of a sudden, someone was pulling Felkoff off of him. Had Susan Carol been able to call Kelleher that quickly?

No. Stevie looked up and saw Felkoff struggling in Norbert Doyle's arms. "Stop it, David," Doyle said. "Look at yourself. It's not worth it. It's over."

He looked at Stevie, who was sitting up with a bad stomachache.

"Write the story," he said. "Twelve years of lying is enough."

Susan Carol was standing right behind him—with the tape recorder in her hand—and Stevie could see Kelleher and Mearns sprinting toward them.

Doyle pushed Felkoff out of his grasp, turned, and walked away.

24: GAME SEVEN

DAVID FELKOFF DUSTED OFF HIS SUIT, glared at everyone, then took off after Doyle without saying another word.

"What the hell happened?" Kelleher asked.

"Let's go back to your room and we'll tell you," Susan Carol said.

As they walked back, Kelleher couldn't help but tease Stevie about his inability to conduct an interview without getting into some sort of fight. "Let's see, you've been chased down by a dog, been slapped by a girl, wrestled with someone in Faneuil Hall, and tackled an agent," he said as they headed up the escalator to the lobby. "In all, a pretty good week."

"Can't wait to hear your parents' reaction when you tell them about it," Susan Carol put in.

"Oh sure, I'm going to tell them," Stevie said. "That way the next time I cover a sports event, I'll be thirty."

She put an arm around him for a moment and said, "Would it help if you tell them I'm proud of you?"

"Doubt it," he said, but he wrapped an arm around her too, and that did help.

They walked Tamara and Bobby through the entire meeting and played them the tape, in part to make sure it hadn't been damaged during Stevie's tussle with Felkoff. When they were finished, Kelleher looked at Mearns and said, "What do you think?"

"I think it's a pretty tragic story. And a tough call," Mearns said.

"You mean whether to write the story at all, don't you?" Susan Carol asked.

Kelleher stood up and walked to the window, gazing out at the harbor for a moment. Then he turned and faced them. "Look, you guys have done an amazing reporting job on this," he said. "Stevie, you've done everything but go to the hospital to ferret out the truth."

"Give me a little more time and I can probably oblige," Stevie said, forcing a smile. He wasn't sure where Kelleher was going, but he was pretty sure it wasn't going to make him happy.

"There are two questions you have to ask when you publish a story, especially a story like this one," Kelleher continued. "First: is it true? The answer there is easy. You've got the truth, you've got it from the main source, and you've got it on the record. The story won't even need to be lawyered. You've got Doyle on tape telling you what happened that night."

"And the second question?" said Susan Carol.

Kelleher sighed. "Is a lot more complicated. Is it *necessary*? Does the story serve a purpose?"

Stevie had been wondering about that one since his first trip to Lynchburg. But now that the hard-won truth was in their hands, he didn't want to give up on it.

"Of course it's necessary," he said. "Doyle lied about his past. If he's selling his story to Disney or DreamWorks and it isn't true . . ."

"Exactly right—we shouldn't let him do that," Kelleher said. "That's the reason the story was worth pursuing in the first place. But what if he's not? What if, after this morning, he tells Felkoff to buzz off. What if he decides to tell the truth: that he's a recovering alcoholic and that he's always felt responsible for Analise's death?"

"You mean leave out the rest?" Susan Carol said. "Leave out the fact that she was drinking that night too, and that she was driving because Molloy made her drive?"

"That's the part I wonder about," Kelleher said. "Did he lie? Yes. Did Hatley lie on the report? Yes. But why did they do it?"

"To protect the kids later on," Stevie said.

"To allow them to remember their mother in the best way possible," Susan Carol added.

Kelleher nodded. "That's not evil. This isn't a team owner covering up drug test results. It certainly isn't blackmailing a basketball player or faking a kidnapping."

"It's a lot easier when it's clear-cut," Stevie said.

"Good-versus-evil stories are pretty simple to write once you've got them," Susan Carol said.

"Right," Kelleher said. "Do either of you think Doyle is evil?"

"No," they both answered, Stevie with some extra vigor, remembering Doyle pulling Felkoff off of him.

Tamara had been quiet throughout the conversation, letting Kelleher lead Stevie and Susan Carol to what he clearly thought was the right decision.

"It's still not that simple, though, is it, Bobby?" she said. "Is it fair to hold things back from the public—to only tell part of the story?"

"That's a damn good point," Kelleher said. "You and I both know there are times reporters hold back things that are personal as long as they don't affect what the person does in public: a child with a serious health problem; a marriage in trouble before either person files for divorce; a mistake made years ago.

"You ask yourself the question: does the public *need* to know this? Sometimes the answer is yes. Sometimes no. There are tough calls to be made all the time. In this case I think the only reason the public would need to know this particular truth is if Doyle wrote a book or allowed a movie to be done on his life in which he lied about it."

"I don't think he's going to do that now," Stevie said.

"Me neither," Susan Carol put in. Tamara was nodding in agreement.

"So what do we do now?" Stevie asked.

"I think we need to tell him before the game tonight that you aren't writing the story, so it won't be on his mind. Tell him you assume the movie's off, and that if that's the case, you don't see any reason to tell the kids or anyone else what happened that night."

"What about Joe Molloy?" Stevie said. "All he's done is lie."

"Yeah, but Joe Molloy is not news," Kelleher said. "And I suspect he's lived with a lot of guilt for the past twelve years. And you can even make the case that he thought he was doing the right thing."

"So why didn't he just tell us the truth?" Susan Carol asked.

This time it was Stevie who answered. "He kind of did. . . . Remember, he said, 'I can't help but think of all the things I might have done differently that could have averted the accident'?"

"One more question," Susan Carol said. "What if we find out next week that Doyle has made a movie deal?"

Kelleher held up the tape. "You'll still have this in your back pocket," he said. "And then you'll use it."

On the way to the ballpark, Kelleher read over the letter that Stevie and Susan Carol had written to Doyle one more time. It basically came down to this: "If you don't sell a false story about yourself, we don't think there's any reason to tell this true story."

"But how do we get Doyle to read this before the game?" Stevie asked. "The clubhouses are closed."

"I've got that covered," Kelleher said.

Should have known, Stevie thought.

As soon as they arrived at the ballpark, they headed for the field. Kelleher made a beeline for his friend Phyllis Merhige, with Stevie and Susan Carol in tow.

"Hey, guys, what's up?" Merhige asked.

"Glad you asked," Kelleher said, pulling the envelope with the letter out of his pocket. "I need you to deliver this to Norbert Doyle for Stevie and Susan Carol."

Merhige looked at the three of them quizzically. "You'll all get to see him after the game, why do you need me to do it?" she asked.

"Because you need to do it right now," Kelleher said.

"*Now?!*" Phyllis shouted. "Bobby, the man is pitching game seven of the World Series in three hours and you want me to deliver a note to him *now*? Are you completely nuts?"

"Phyllis, how long have we known each other?" Kelleher asked.

"Too long," she responded.

"What do you think the chances are I'd ask you to do something like this if it wasn't vitally important *and* the best possible thing for the player involved?"

Merhige looked at him, then at Stevie and Susan Carol.

"I trust you two more than I trust him right now," she said, half kidding, Stevie guessed. "Is it really *that* important?"

They both nodded. "He'll thank you for getting it to him," Stevie said.

She took the envelope from Kelleher's hand.

"Oh, there's one more thing," he said.

"What?" she said, exasperated.

"You have to wait for an answer."

"An answer? What kind of answer?"

"He needs to write on the back of the note 'Agreed' or 'Do not agree.'"

"That's it?"

"Yup. That's it. Simple task. I will explain the whole thing to you over dinner the next time I'm in New York."

She gave him a look. "It better be an expensive dinner," she said.

"Smith & Wollensky," Kelleher said. "I'll have Murph set the whole night up."

Without another word she walked down the steps into the third-base dugout and disappeared.

"Wait a second," Stevie said. "What if the answer is 'Do not agree'?"

"Then you guys will have a lot of writing to do before the night is over," Kelleher said. "In fact, you'll probably have to write during the game."

Twenty minutes later Phyllis Merhige reappeared, envelope in hand.

"The fact that I didn't look at this is testimony to either what a good person I am or what a lousy PR person I am,"

Merhige said. "Whatever it is, though, you appear to have made his day."

"Did he thank you?" Stevie asked.

"He hugged me to within an inch of my life," she said.

She handed Kelleher the envelope. Kelleher leaned down and gave her a kiss. "Thank you, Phyllis," he said. "You're the best."

"Save the charm," she said. "You owe me Smith & Wollensky and a *great* bottle of wine."

Phyllis walked away. Kelleher handed Stevie and Susan Carol the envelope.

"You guys open it," he said.

Susan Carol pulled the note out and turned it over. Stevie could see that Doyle had written five words on the back, all of it in capital letters: "ABSOLUTELY AGREED. THANK YOU . . . FOREVER . . ."

They handed the note to Kelleher, who handed it to Tamara.

Susan Carol looked at Stevie and gave him the Smile. "I guess," she said, "we get to watch the game."

"All that work and we don't write a word," Stevie sighed.

"And I've never been more proud of you both," Kelleher said.

After all that had gone on, game seven was almost anti-climactic for the first six innings. Doyle walked Dustin Pedroia with one out in the first, and then David Ortiz promptly hit his next pitch into the right-field bullpen for a 2–0 Red Sox lead. The lead went to 3–0 in the third on back-to-back doubles by Mike Lowell and J.D. Drew.

But the Nationals answered with three runs of their own against Tim Wakefield in the fourth on a single by Ryan Zimmerman, a double by Adam Dunn, a triple that scored two runs by Elijah Dukes, and a sacrifice fly by Aaron Boone.

"That didn't take long," said George Solomon. "Sort of like going eighty yards in four plays."

"Sort of like quieting the crowd," Mark Maske pointed out.

Wakefield came out of the game after six innings with the score tied 3–3. Manny Acta continued with Doyle on the mound, even though the Red Sox seemed to be hitting line drives right at fielders in every inning.

There were men on second and third and two outs in the seventh when Ortiz hit a shot to the gap in right-center. The crowd stood as one, then sat again, deflated, when Dukes tracked the ball down.

"How much longer will Acta stick with him?" Stevie asked. Watching him pitch was nerve-wracking.

"What are his options?" Barry Svrluga asked. "He obviously doesn't trust his bullpen, even with all the other starters out there. Doyle's pitch count is only eighty-eight so far and it's a cool night."

"Freezing is more like it," Susan Carol said.

"Good pitching weather," Svrluga said. "I think if he gets in any trouble in the eighth, he brings in a starter—

298 ·

maybe Lannan again. I'd be surprised if Doyle's still out there for the ninth."

The crowd was now officially restless. This was not supposed to be a seven-game series to begin with, especially after the Red Sox had gone up 3–2 coming back to Boston. Twenty-three years earlier, in 1986, the Red Sox had led the Mets 3–2 after five games—except that year the last two games were in New York.

"People forget that even after Buckner's famous error in game six, the Red Sox led three to nothing in game seven," Susan Carol pointed out after Okajima had retired the Nats one-two-three in the eighth.

"Just like this game," Stevie said.

"Yes. Except in that game the Red Sox bullpen collapsed and the Mets won eight to five. That's not happening here."

The bottom of the eighth was remarkable because Doyle only threw five pitches. The Red Sox clearly seemed to think all his pitches were hittable, and since he hadn't walked anyone since the first inning, they were swinging at everything. Jason Bay popped up on the first pitch; Mike Lowell took a ball and a strike and then hit a fly ball just short of the Green Monster in left field; and J.D. Drew lined the first pitch right at Aaron Boone at first base.

"Ninety-three pitches," Svrluga said. "He might just come out to pitch the ninth."

"They're still hitting the ball hard," Stevie said.

"But not in the right places," Susan Carol said.

Francona went with the old baseball strategy of bringing

in your closer to pitch the top of the ninth in a tie game at home—the thinking being if he gets three outs, your team can win the game in the bottom of the ninth. Jonathan Papelbon could pitch at least two innings if the score stayed tied.

"He should be fresh," Maske said. "He only threw eleven pitches last night."

Stevie noticed both Lannan and Hanrahan warming in the bullpen as the ninth started. Clearly, they were the only two guys out there that Acta trusted.

Boone led off the ninth. Perhaps not wanting to give up *another* October home run to him with a game on the line, Papelbon walked him on four pitches. The crowd stirred nervously.

Wil Nieves was next. "He has to bunt," Susan Carol said.

"I'm not sure he *can* bunt," Svrluga said. "He's not the kind of guy you ask to bunt."

Acta asked Nieves to bunt. Sure enough, he fouled the first two pitches off, and everyone assumed he would be swinging away with two strikes on him. But on the third pitch he actually pushed a bunt down the first-base line. Surprised, Papelbon fielded it and threw to Kevin Youkilis for the first out.

"Amazing he got a bunt down," Maske said.

Next up was shortstop Cristian Guzman. Papelbon had no trouble with him, striking him out on a 97-mph fastball. Two men were out and Boone was still on second.

Up came leadoff hitter Austin Kearns, who had been

moved to that spot in July to try to snap him out of a slump. He had hit so well there that he had stayed. Kearns worked the count full with three balls and two strikes, then fouled off four straight pitches. Each time Papelbon stretched to try to get the last strike, every fan in the ballpark was on their feet trying to will him to get the last out. He kept throwing fastballs, and Kearns kept fouling them off.

"He throws a breaking pitch, Kearns might break his back trying to swing at it," Maske said.

"He won't," Svrluga said. "He won't see anything but a fastball."

He almost got the next fastball by him, but Kearns somehow hit it off his fists toward right field. Dustin Pedroia went back as right fielder J.D. Drew charged in. The ball landed smack in between them. Drew, who had been playing fairly deep to try to cut off an extra-base hit, charged the rolling ball as Boone flew around third base heading for home. Stevie felt himself hold his breath as Drew came up throwing.

The ball came in to Varitek on one bounce as Boone dove for the plate. The throw was just a tad off-line, and Varitek had to move up the first-base line, grab it, and then dive at Boone.

Boone slid wide to avoid the tag and groped for the plate with his left hand. Varitek swiped at him and held the ball up to show that it was in his hand. But John Hirschbeck, the home plate umpire, shook his head at Varitek and pointed to the spot on home plate where Boone's hand had swiped it just a split second before the tag. Hirschbeck gave the safe sign as the entire ballpark exploded in boos of disbelief.

Boone, *again* a villain in Boston, leaped to his feet and was pounded on the back by his teammates as he headed to the dugout. There were TV sets in the auxiliary press box, and Fox showed the play again several times. Each time it was clear Hirschbeck had the call right. Boone's hand brushed the plate an instant before the diving Varitek tagged him with the glove.

"They got it right," Susan Carol said above the din. "He was safe."

Most of the Red Sox and their fans clearly disagreed. Francona came out briefly to argue, but it wasn't going to do any good.

Ronnie Belliard popped to shortstop for the final out, but the Nationals had the lead 4–3.

"Three outs away," Susan Carol said. "I can't believe it."

"Here's something for you to really not believe," Stevie said, gesturing in the direction of the third-base dugout. Doyle had just popped out, heading for the mound to at least start the ninth.

"If they blow this lead now, Manny Acta will be crucified," Svrluga said. "Why wouldn't he go to Hanrahan here?"

"Because he's been up and down all year," Maske said. "The easy move is to bring him in. This takes some guts."

"One base runner and he's got to get the guy out of there, right?" Stevie said.

They all agreed. For a moment it looked as if there

might not be a base runner. Varitek, who had started so many key Boston rallies through the years, grounded meekly to shortstop. Jacoby Ellsbury worked the count to 2-2 but then hit an easy fly ball to Dukes in center field. Remarkably, the Red Sox were down to their last out.

"I can't believe this," Susan Carol said softly, as if afraid to raise her voice and change Doyle's luck.

"He's going to do it," Stevie said. "I can't believe it."

"Shhhhh!" Solomon said. "You'll jinx him."

For once, he appeared to know what he was talking about.

Shortstop Julio Lugo sliced a single to right field. Then Youkilis singled to right. The crowd came back to life. Nieves trotted to the mound to talk to Doyle.

"He's not stalling here," Svrluga said. "Hanrahan's got to be ready."

"I think he's reminding him that he wants to get this over with *now*," Maske said. "Pedroia's very good, but they've got Ortiz on deck."

Reminded or not, Doyle pitched carefully—too carefully—and walked Pedroia to load the bases.

"Uh-oh," Susan Carol said as Ortiz walked to the plate and Acta jogged to the mound. Hanrahan was ready in the bullpen. This had to be it. The entire infield surrounded Doyle and Acta, ready to give him a hero's send-off once Acta signaled for Hanrahan.

But the signal never came. Acta gave Doyle a pat on the back and jogged back to the dugout.

"Is he completely crazy?" Svrluga said.

Stevie could think of only one answer: apparently so.

Even at thirty-five, Ortiz was arguably the best clutch hitter in baseball, and he was smacking his hands together as he always did while walking to the plate. Fenway, almost silent after the first two outs, was now so loud there was no point in anyone trying to talk. In the Nats dugout Acta never moved. He had ridden Doyle this far, he would stay with him—do or die—for one more batter.

Ortiz stepped into the left-hand batter's box. With the bases loaded, the Nationals overshifted as almost every team did against Ortiz: Ryan Zimmerman moved from third to the shortstop's normal spot; Guzman moved to the first-base side of second; second baseman Belliard moved into shallow right field between first and second; and Aaron Boone, at first base, played deep and fairly close to the line.

Doyle quickly threw a strike on the outside corner. The next two pitches weren't close, and the count went to 2-1. Amazingly, the place got louder. Ortiz took a huge cut at the next pitch, a slider that appeared to hang a little. But he just missed getting solid wood on it, fouling it into the seats.

Now it was 2-2. Doyle tried to get Ortiz to chase a high fastball, but he held back. The count ran to 3-2. The tension was unbearable. Doyle had to throw a strike or walk in the tying run. Stevie felt as if he couldn't breathe.

With the bases loaded, Doyle was pitching from the full windup. He rocked, kicked his leg in the air, and threw. Ortiz timed the pitch perfectly. The ball screamed off his bat on a line, headed toward the right-field corner. As soon as

Stevie saw the ball come off the bat, his heart sank. Two runs would score easily by the time Kearns tracked the ball down, and then the series would be over.

But suddenly, seemingly from nowhere, Stevie saw Boone leap into the air, his arm stretching out as far as it could possibly go, lunging at the ball as it was going past him. Somehow, with his entire body parallel to the ground, he got his glove on it—the ball smacked off the top edge of his glove and popped into the air. Lying on the ground, Boone reached as far as he could with his bare hand and caught the ball no more than an inch from the ground.

For a split second nobody moved. Boone was lying on his stomach, holding the ball up for everyone to see, and umpire Tim McClelland was giving the out signal.

"OH MY GOD!" Susan Carol screamed.

They were all on their feet, looking in disbelief while the Nationals raced en masse from their dugout to engulf both Boone and Doyle.

"Aaron Bleepin' Boone again!" Stevie shouted. "He'll never get out of this place alive!"

But then an amazing thing happened. As the Nationals celebrated, the Red Sox, instead of just leaving the field, came out of the dugout themselves, led by Francona, to offer congratulations. As they did, the crowd, recovering from the shock of what it had just seen, responded. Slowly a wave of applause began, and after a few moments almost everyone in the ballpark was standing and clapping—for both teams.

Stevie felt chills run down his spine. He looked at

Susan Carol, who was crying. He thought he might cry too. It had never occurred to him in the last week that their story might have a happy ending. But now, remarkably, it did.

Soon after they had fought their way through the crowds to meet Kelleher and Mearns in the interview room, Major League Baseball announced that Norbert Doyle and Aaron Boone had been selected as co-MVPs of the World Series. Both Stevie and Susan Carol were assigned to write about Aaron Boone. "Doyle is everyone's lede, and Manny Acta leaving him in is the column," Kelleher said. "The other sidebar writers will get into what this means to Washington. Tamara and I both think you guys should do Boone."

That agreed, they awaited the arrival of the game's heroes. Manny Acta went first. Then came Boone, who joked about his "blazing speed on the base paths" and said, "I really do love Boston, it's a great city, but I guess I'll never live here."

Then, finally, came Doyle. He was asked all the questions you might expect about being surprised to still be in the game (yes); whether he thought Ortiz's ball was a hit (absolutely); and how amazed was he to be sitting there as the World Series co-MVP having never won a regular-season game in the major leagues (flabbergasted).

Finally, someone asked if he thought his story was likely to become a movie pretty soon.

"No," he said firmly. "It won't. I pitched two good games at the right time. End of story."

Stevie and Susan Carol walked into the hallway a few moments later. They hadn't gone four steps before they found themselves face to face with David and Morra Doyle, who had security people escorting them to see their dad in the interview room.

Stevie felt himself go tense preparing for a confrontation. Instead David walked up with his hand out.

"Dad texted us before the game that we owe you both an apology and thanks," he said. "He says you did a lot more reporting than any of us knew and decided in the end there was no story to write." He looked Stevie in the eye. "I'm sorry I acted like such a jerk yesterday."

"Apology accepted," Stevie said.

Everyone shook hands, which made Stevie feel like a grown-up. There were no hugs—which Stevie was grateful for. That would have been too awkward. The Doyles went down the hall to wait for their father to finish talking to the media.

Stevie and Susan Carol continued along the hallway, heading for the Nationals clubhouse to ask Boone some follow-up questions before they went upstairs to write.

"Well," Stevie said. "We did it again, I guess."

She put an arm around him for a moment. "You did most of it this time," she said.

"In the end we didn't do anything," he said.

"I know," she said. "But nothing was the right thing to

do. And there's nothing wrong with just writing a great story about a great World Series, is there?"

"No," Stevie said. "That is pretty cool, actually. Maybe I'm just a little spoiled."

"No doubt you are," she said. "But you did great work this week. I lost it for a while, but you never did."

"You *did* lose your cool for a little while." Stevie grinned.

She rolled her eyes. "So what exactly do I have to do to make this up to you?"

"That," Stevie said, "is a question I will be happy to think about for a while. Let me get back to you on it."

"I'm sure you will," she said, her face lighting up with the Smile. "I'm sure you will."

"The best writer of sports books in America today."*

More Sensational Sports Mysteries from NEW YORK TIMES Bestselling Author
John Feinstein!

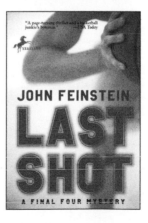

*The Boston Globe

626